I'm

我識出版社
17buy.com.tw

I'm

我識出版社
17buy.com.tw

I'm

我識出版社
17buy.com.tw

1
補教名師**王舒葳**教你
4天聽懂
老外說的英語

英語聽力權威
英國倫敦大學英語教學碩士
王舒葳老師
最暢銷代表作

■ 如果你也有以下困擾，這本聽力書絕對是你需要的：

1. 英語初學者，完全沒有聽力基礎。
2. 英語有一定程度，但對聽力學習有恐懼或障礙之學習者。
3. 英語有一定程度，但還是聽不懂外國客戶或友人說的英語之學習者。
4. 英語有一定程度，但聽不懂ICRT、HBO或CNN等外語頻道之學習者。
5. 英語有一定程度，去外國觀光旅遊聽不懂當地人說的英語、無法順利溝通之學習者。

■ 透過14天技巧講解與互動練習課程，保證教會你五大聽力技巧：

1. 瞭解老外的連音變化原則，正確解讀字義

　　老外口中的 "Tell her I miss her." 為什麼聽起來像 "Tele ri mi ser." ？不只是這句話，很多時候老外說的話會令我們摸不著頭腦，主要都是因為老外說話一說得快，便會產生所謂的「連音」現象。本書以深入淺出的方式讓你輕鬆學會「連音」規則。

2. 熟悉字與句子的重音位置，掌握關鍵音與關鍵字

　　字彙重音的重要性，會直接左右你聽話時的理解，就算是你熟悉不過的單字，重音一但放錯位置，仍會造成你完全無法聽懂這個字；而句子的重音則關係著說話者的表達重心所在，你會發現，事實上很多時候我們並不需要

聽懂每一個單字。

3. 分辨易混淆的母音與子音，減少句意的誤解

　　許多母音或子音發音相似的字彙，常常會造成我們分辨字義時的困難，而造成溝通上的誤解，因此「正音」是訓練聽力時很重要的基礎，本書整理出使用頻率高的範例，幫助讀者清楚掌握易混淆字彙的正確發音。

4. 習慣老外的節奏與語調，不需聽懂每一個單字也能瞭解意思

　　節奏和語調就像是話語的表情，除了表現出說話者的情緒之外，同一句話，用不同的節奏和語調說出來，有時會代表截然不同的意義與重點，非常有趣，只要熟練此技巧，不僅聽力技巧提升，也能幫助你說出更道地的英語。

5. 其它技巧：非重點字的弱化、語意單元與慣用語使用

　　其他我們需要知道的老外說話習慣，例如非重點字被說得又輕、又快的弱化現象，換氣與停頓的使用方式，以及學習老外「口語英語」的重要慣用語……等，帶領讀者真正進入外國人口語英語的邏輯與領域，跳脫我們以往只懂得用「眼睛」學英文的不好習慣。

U使用說明
sers' guide

1 14天聽力速成計劃

本書將聽力訓練課程分為14天兩週的速成計畫,第1~10天為聽力技巧的學習課程,第11~14天則為總練習與成果驗收。每天的課程主題都不同,我們會在一開始為讀者引導學習重點。

> **DAY 1** 辨別**發音相似**的母音
> Cap, cop, 還是cup?
> 01-1-01-8
>
> **> 學習重點**
>
> Cap, cop 還是 cup? 這三個字你說得對、分得清嗎?
> 可能從來沒有人告訴過你,想要輕鬆聽懂老外談英語,或要老外聽懂我們說什麼,第一件要做的事其實是正音。因為發音相似的英文母音,是造成我們說不對、也聽不懂老外說什麼的因素之一。如果我們能確實分辨這些發音的不同,並且自己也能說清楚,一定有助於聽力的改善喔!
> 本課我們要幫同學抓出容易混淆的母音,並多方向練習,幫助同學檢視自己的發音和辨音能力,進而打穩良好聽力的基礎喔!

2 互動練習與技巧分析

每天的主題課程底下再畫分成1~3個單元。請讀者依照本書指引進行互動練習或內文閱讀。

> **DAY 1** 辨別**發音相似**的母音
> Cap, cop, 還是cup?
> 01-1-01-8
>
> ## Lesson 1 > 聽聽看,說說看
>
> **> 舒葳老師說** 🎧 01-1
>
> 你是否能準確地聽出不同的母音呢?先來測測自己的辨音能力!
> 請聽MP3,並從A, B選項中選出正確的關鍵字:
>
> 1. A. work   B. walk
> 2. A. pan   B. pen
> 3. A. collar B. color
> 4. A. sheep   B. ship
> 5. A. cup   B. cop
> 6. A. cap   B. cape
>
> ● Answers
> 1.A 2.A 3.A 4.B 5.B 6.B

3 逐題詳細解說

在每回合的練習題之後,皆附詳細解說,逐題為你說明其中的「聽話」技巧與撇步。

> **> 詳細解說** 🎧 01-2
>
> 1. Why are you working in the dark?
>   你為什麼在黑暗中工作?
>
>   A. work 工作 (正確答案)
>   B. walk 散步
>
>   這裡他說的是 working,母音發 [ɝ],有捲舌。答案B的

4 14天聽力 速成MP3

全書標註MP3標誌處，即為可配合隨書附贈MP3學習的內容，請依照軌數指示聆聽MP3中外籍教師發音。

Lesson 2 ▶ 自然發音

▶ 舒葳老師說

英語的字母和音標有緊密的關連性，我們只要掌握一些原則，大半的字看就會念，會念得會拼。念得準了，也聽得懂了。下面我們就一起來看看發音和拼字間的關係。

英文用26個字母來組成單字，却用另一套注音符號（音標）來標注這些字母。以第一個字母 a 來說，它的讀音用音標來表示是 [e]。反過來我們也可以說，音標 [e] 的發音就如同字母 a。這樣的規則，對我們來說反而是學正確發音的好方法。26個字母中的五個母音 a、e、i、o、u 的讀音用音標標示，分別如下表： 🎧 01-3

5 補充與延伸 學習

從練習題的內容中，舒葳老師為讀者整理出更多相關及實用的會話句型，幫助你進一步熟悉老外的英語使用習慣，不僅在與外國人對話交談時更能得心應手，英文閱讀與寫作功力也跟著進步。

▶ 焦點句型用語

Why are you...? 你為什麼要…？
in the dark 在黑暗之中；在暗處

▶ 老外時常這麼說

Why are they sitting in the dark? 他們為什麼坐在暗處？
Why are you dancing in the dark? 你們為什麼在黑暗中跳舞？

▶ 延伸活用例句

I'm afraid of the dark. 我怕黑。
She couldn't see anything in the dark. 她在黑暗中什麼也看不見。
I was kept in the dark. 我（那時）被瞞在鼓裡。

6 舒葳老師經驗分享

學習什麼事物都一樣，很多時候你只是沒開竅；「舒葳老師說」、「舒葳老師小叮嚀」、「聽力小秘訣」點醒你英語聽力的制勝技巧。

▶ 舒葳老師小叮嚀

上面的練習你都做對了嗎？在日常生活中，我們聽不懂或聽錯老外的意思，常常是因為混淆了發音相似的字喔。因為很多字我們自己都念不正確，聽到時自然也就分辨不出，或誤以為是別的字。所以培養良好聽力的第一步便是把母音發得正確，自然也就聽得輕鬆囉！

要學就要學「老外」聽得懂的英語！！

　　有學習英語經驗的人都知道，「聽」和「說」一直是台灣人難以突破的一個障礙，不僅初學者對此抱持恐懼，就算是對於英語閱讀和寫作領域有一定程度的人，也常常不一定能夠對聽和說有把握，主要是因為我們普遍缺乏英語聽說環境與練習機會，另外就是，我們從老師和教材那裡學到的聽與說往往和外國人的實際口語有一段差距，所以造成可能聽得懂台灣人說的英語，而面對老外說的英語卻完全鴨子聽雷的窘況。

　　很多人會誤以為，自己聽不懂老外說話的主要原因，可能是自己背的單字還不夠多，或者對文法句型不夠熟悉，當然這些可能也是部分原因，但是很多時候都不是造成你聽不懂的關鍵，真正的關鍵在於——你不懂外國人說話的方式與習慣，所以有時會誤解對方的語意，或抓不到對方表達的重點。《補教名師王舒葳教你14天聽懂老外說的英語》本書為舊作《聽力王》的全新改版，並收錄更多更實用的「聽力」技巧，就是要幫助台灣學習者突破以往聽說學習的障礙，真正快速、有效的學會如何「聽懂」老外的英語。

舒葳老師14天要教會你的五大聽力技巧：
1. 瞭解老外的連音變化原則，正確解讀字義
2. 熟悉字與句子的重音位置，掌握關鍵音與關鍵字
3. 分辨易混淆的母音與子音，減少句意的誤解
4. 習慣老外的節奏與語調，不需聽懂每一個單字也能瞭解意思
5. 其它技巧：非重點字的弱化、語意單元與慣用語使用

　　《補教名師王舒葳教你14天聽懂老外說的英語》要教你的是不同

於以往學習經驗的「塊狀意義」理解，不要再把聽和說的重點拘泥在幾個聽不懂的單字上，而應該善用以上所列連音、重音、正音、節奏等聽力技巧，以理解對方重點訊息、接收塊狀意義為目標，順利達成相互溝通，這樣不但不會給自己太多多餘的壓力，也可以逐漸建立起與外國人溝通的自信心。

　　《補教名師王舒葳教你14天聽懂老外說的英語》精心為讀者規劃了兩週14天的完整聽力課程，全書透過技巧講解與互動練習的方式，清楚明瞭地為你釐清你以往英語聽力的盲點和困惑，真正瞭解外國人說話的方式與習慣，重新打好英語聽力基礎，書中並補充許多精華句型與老外常用的話，相信絕對能夠幫助你的英語聽說能力往前跨一大步。

C目錄
ontents

DAY  辨別**發音相似**的母音
Cap, cop, 還是cup?

01-1~01-8

> **｜學習重點**

　　Cap, cop 還是 cup? 這三個字你說得對，分得清嗎?

　　可能從來沒有人告訴過你，想要輕鬆聽懂老外說英語，或要老外聽懂我們說什麼，第一件要做的事其實是正音。因為發音相似的英文母音，是造成我們說得不對，也聽不懂老外說什麼的因素之一。如果我們能確實分辨這些聲音發音的不同，並且自己也能說清楚，一定有助於聽力的改善喔!

　　本課我們替同學抓出容易混淆的母音，並多方向練習，幫助同學檢視自己的發音和辨音能力，進而打穩良好聽力的基礎喔!

Lesson 1 ▶ 聽聽看，說說看

▶ 舒葳老師說　(MP3) 01-1

　　你是否能準確地聽出不同的母音呢？先來測測自己的辨音能力吧！
請聽MP3，並從A, B選項中選出正確的關鍵字：

1. A. work　　B. walk
2. A. pan　　B. pen
3. A. collar　　B. color
4. A. sheep　　B. ship
5. A. cup　　B. cop
6. A. cap　　B. cape

● Answers

1.A　2.A　3.A　4.B　5.B　6.B

▶ 詳細解說　(MP3) 01-2

1. Why are you working in the dark?

　　你為什麼在黑暗中工作？

> A. work 工作 (正確答案)
>
> B. walk 散步
>
> 　　這裡他說的是 working，母音發 [ɜ˙]，有捲舌。答案B的

補教名師王舒薇教你
14天聽懂
老外說的英語

DAY
1

DAY
2

DAY
3

DAY
4

DAY
5

DAY
6

DAY
7

DAY
8

DAY
9

DAY
10

DAY
11

DAY
12

DAY
13

DAY
14

walking 母音則發 [ɔ]，沒有捲舌，嘴型張開。所以他問的是你為什麼要在暗處工作，而不是為什麼要在暗處走路喔！再仔細聽一次，working 和 walking是不是不一樣呢？比較下面的兩個句子並跟著說說看。

Why are you working in the dark? 你為什麼在黑暗中工作？
Why are you walking in the dark? 你為什麼在黑暗中走路？

❯ 焦點句型用語

Why are you...? 你為什麼要⋯？
in the dark 在黑暗之中；在暗處

❯ 老外時常這麼說

Why are they sitting in the dark? 他們為什麼坐在暗處？
Why are you dancing in the dark? 你們為什麼在黑暗中跳舞？

❯ 延伸活用例句

I'm afraid of the dark. 我怕黑。
She couldn't see anything in the dark. 她在黑暗中什麼也看不見。
I was kept in the dark. 我（那時）被瞞在鼓裡。

2. Could you pass me that pan over there, please?
可以請你把那個平底鍋遞給我嗎？

A. pan 平底鍋 (正確答案)
B. pen 筆

　　這裡他說的是pan [pæn] 平底鍋，母音發 [æ]，發音時嘴巴張

得較開而扁，pen的母音 [ɛ] 則比較含蓄。如果我們不知道 [æ] 和 [ɛ] 在發音上的差別，就很容易誤以為他說的是 pen[pæn]，而誤遞「筆」給他了。再仔細聽一次，pan 和 pen 是不是不一樣呢？比較下面的兩個句子並跟著說說看。

Could you pass me that pan over there, please?
可以請你把那個平底鍋遞給我嗎？

Could you pass me that pen over there, please?
可以請你把那支筆遞給我嗎？

▶ 焦點句型用語

Could you pass me the...? 可以請你把…遞給我嗎？

▶ 老外時常這麼說

Could you pass me the salt? 可以請你把鹽遞給我嗎？
Could you pass me the bread? 可以請你把麵包遞給我嗎？

聽到Could you pass me...? 就表示對方請你把某個東西遞給他。除了熟悉這個句型，還要聽清楚要遞的是什麼，才不會貽笑大方喔！

3. I think the collar of this shirt would suit you better.
我想這件的領子應該會比較適合你。

A. collar 領子（正確答案）
B. color 顏色

這裡他說的是 collar ['kɑlɚ] 領子，母音發 [ɑ]，發音時嘴巴張得

補教名師王舒葳教你
14天聽懂
老外說的英語

DAY
1

DAY
2

DAY
3

DAY
4

DAY
5

DAY
6

DAY
7

DAY
8

DAY
9

DAY
10

DAY
11

DAY
12

DAY
13

DAY
14

較大，答案 B 的color則發 [ʌ]，發音時嘴巴張得較小，音也發得稍短。所以他喜歡的是那件襯衫的「領子」而非它的「顏色」。再仔細聽一次，collar 和 color 是不是不一樣呢？比較下面的兩個句子並跟著說說看。

I think the collar of this one would suit you better.
我想這件的領子應該會比較適合你。

I think the color of this one would suit you better.
我想這件的顏色應該會比較適合你。

▶ 焦點句型用語

...suit you better 比較適合你
suit 就是適合某人的外表、個性等等。

▶ 老外時常這麼說

He suits you well. 他很適合妳。
That suits me fine. 我沒問題；對我來說很方便。
That color doesn't suit you at all. 那個顏色一點也不適合你。
Suit yourself. 隨便你。

▶ 延伸活用例句

Red is your color. 紅色真適合你。

聽到...suits you，或是...is your color. 就表示對方在compliment（讚美）你。這時候可以回應對方的讚美，說聲：

It's nice of you to say so. Thank you. 你這麼說真好，謝謝！

而如果對方說的是It doesn't suit you.，你可能便要反問：

You think so? 你這麼覺得嗎？
What's wrong with it? 什麼地方不對嗎？

4. Look! What a huge ship!
   看！好大的一艘船哪！

A. sheep 綿羊

B. ship 船（正確答案）

　　這裡他說的是 ship [ʃɪp] 船，母音發短音 [ɪ]，答案 A 的 sheep 則發長音 [i]。所以他指的是好大的「船」，而非好大的「綿羊」。再仔細聽一次，sheep 是不是聲音拉得比較長，ship 比較短呢？比較下面的兩個句子並跟著說說看。

Look! What a huge sheep!
看！好大的一隻綿羊哪！

Look! What a huge ship!
看！好大的一艘船哪！

❯ 焦點句型用語

What (a) + n.! 真是個…啊！

　　聽到What a...!，就知道對方要對某人、事、物的感覺表達他的看法，可以是正面也可以是負面。如果後面的名詞不可數，則不加冠詞"a"。

❯ 老外時常這麼說

What a lovely day! 多好的天氣啊！

What a business! 真是磨人的事！

What nonsense! 胡說八道！

❯ 延伸活用例句

How amazing! 多神奇啊！

補教名師王舒嫚教你
14天聽懂
老外說的英語

DAY
1
DAY
2
DAY
3
DAY
4
DAY
5
DAY
6
DAY
7
DAY
8
DAY
9
DAY
10
DAY
11
DAY
12
DAY
13
DAY
14

How ugly that building is! 那棟建築物真醜！

　　上面What (a) + n.! 是What 後面接名詞，表達對某件事物的讚嘆或不好的感覺。這裡的 How + adj.. 也是類似的用法，只是加的是形容詞。

　　回應對方的句子，如果你贊同，便說：

It surely is! 的確是！

　　不贊同則可以說：

Well, I think it's OK. 這個嘛，我覺得她還可以。

Well, I quite like it. 這個嘛，我倒是蠻喜歡的。

5. Where did you see the cup?
　 你在哪兒看到杯子的？

> A. cup 杯子
> B. cop 警察（正確答案）
>
> 　　這裡他說的是cup，母音發 [ʌ]，發音時嘴巴張得較小，答案 B 的警察 cop [kɑp] 則發 [ɑ]，發音時嘴巴張得較大。所以他問的是「警察」，可不要以為對方在問「杯子」喔。再仔細聽一次，cup 和 cop 是不是不一樣呢？比較下面的兩個句子並跟著說說看。
>
> Where did you see the cup? 你在哪兒看到杯子的？
> Where did you see the cop? 你在哪兒看到警察的？

> **焦點句型用語**

　　Where did you...? 你從哪…的？

> **老外時常這麼說**

Where did you get that idea from? 你怎麼會有那種想法？

Where did it go wrong? 哪裡出了錯？

6. Who is that woman wearing a cape?
   穿著斗篷的那個女人是誰？

A. cap 帽子

B. cape 斗篷（正確答案）

這裡他說的是 cape [kep]，母音發[e]，聲音要拉長。答案 A 的 cap 母音則發 [æ]，是嘴型扁而開的短音。所以他問的是「穿著斗篷的那個女人」而不是「戴著帽子的那個女人」。 再仔細聽一次，cape 是不是聲音較長、cap 聲音較短呢？比較下面的兩個句子並跟著說說看。

Who is that woman wearing a cap? 戴著帽子的那個女人是誰？

Who is that woman wearing a cape? 穿著斗篷的那個女人是誰？

❯ 焦點句型用語

Who is that ...wearing...? 穿…的那個…是誰？

問某人是誰時，常以他的穿著來說明指的是誰。這裡我們也可以說：Who is ...in / with...。

❯ 老外時常這麼說

Who is that woman wearing a yellow dress?

穿黃色洋裝的那個女人是誰？

Who is that girl in yellow?

穿黃色的那個女人是誰？

Who is that man with a beard and a moustache?

留鬍鬚的那個男人是誰？

DAY
1

DAY
2

DAY
3

DAY
4

DAY
5

DAY
6

DAY
7

DAY
8

DAY
9

DAY
10

DAY
11

DAY
12

DAY
13

DAY
14

beard指的是長在下巴上的山羊鬍，moustache則是嘴巴上方的鬍子。

舒葳老師小叮嚀

上面的練習你都做對了嗎？在日常生活中，我們聽不懂或聽錯老外的意思，常常是因為混淆了發音相似的字喔。因為很多字我們自己都念不正確，聽到時自然也就分辨不出，或誤以為是別的字。所以培養良好聽力的第一步便是把母音發得正確，自然也就聽得輕鬆囉！

Lesson 2 ▶ 自然發音

舒葳老師說

英語的字母和音標有緊密的關連性，我們只要掌握一些原則，大半的字看就會念，會念就會拼。念得準了，也聽得懂了。下面我們就一起來看看發音和拼字間的關係。

英文用26個字母來組成單字，却用另一套注音符號（音標）來標注這些字母。以第一個字母 a 來說，它的讀音用音標來表示是 [e]。反過來我們也可以說，音標 [e] 的發音就如同字母 a。這樣的規則，對我們來說反而是學正確發音的好方法。26個字母中的五個母音 a、e、i、o、u 的讀音用音標標示，分別如下表： (MP3) 01-3

字母	Aa	Ee	I i	Oo	Uu
讀音(音標)	[e]	[i]	[aɪ]	[o]	[ju]

從表上我們得知音標 [e] 讀若字母 Aa，[i] 若 Ee，以下類推。這五個音標是母音，而且是長母音。另外這五個母音字母還可以發音成短音，我們加入下表：

字母	Aa	Ee	I i	Oo	Uu
長母音	[e]	[i]	[aɪ]	[o]	[ju]
短母音	[æ]	[ɛ]	[ɪ]	[ɑ]	[ʌ]

至於五個母音a、e、i、o、u 分別在何種情況下讀長音，何種情況下讀短音，則有規則可循：（MP3）01-4

❯ 1. 短母音

● Rule：<u>單音節或重音節裡的單一母音發短母音</u>

a ➔ [æ] 如：　　ax 斧 n.　　　　bat 球棒 n.

　　　　　　　　rapid 快速的 adj　batman 蝙蝠俠 n.

e ➔ [ɛ] 如：　　egg 蛋 n.　　　　pet 寵物 n.

　　　　　　　　setup 安排 n./v.　rental 出租 n.；出租的 adj.

I ➔ [ɪ] 如：　　ink 墨水 n.　　　trip 旅途 n.

　　　　　　　　riddle 謎語 n.　　tickle 搔癢 v.；癢的感覺 n.

o ➔ [ɑ] 如：　　ox 公牛 n.　　　mop 拖地 v.；拖把 n.

　　[ɔ]　　　　problem 問題　　Boston 波士頓

　　　　　　　（O 短音有時發 [ɑ]，有時發 [ɔ]，這裡O 發 [ɔ]。）

u ➔ [ʌ] 如：　　bus 公車 n.　　　cut 切 v./割傷 n.

　　　　　　　　butter 奶油 n.　　umbrella 雨傘 n.

▶ | 2. 長母音

● Rule 1: 母音+子音+ e 的組合，母音發長音

a ➔ [e] 如：make 做 v.　　　　　　　　rate 率 n.

　　　　　　fake 假的 adj./做假 v./仿冒品 n.　classmate 同學 n.

e ➔ [i] 如：gene 基因 n.　　　　　　　scene 場景/背景 n.

　　　　　　theme 主題 n.　　　　　　mete 分配 n.

i ➔ [aɪ] 如：rice 米 n.　　　　　　　　hike 爬山 v.

　　　　　　spine 脊椎 n.　　　　　　file 檔案 n./歸檔 v.

o ➔ [o] 如：hope 希望 n./v.　　　　　　globe 地球/地球儀 n.

　　　　　　Pope 教宗 n.　　　　　　cone 圓錐形物 n.

u ➔[ju] 如：cute 可愛的 adj.　　　　　mute 沉默的/ 啞的 adj.

　　　[u] 如：crude 粗糙的/ 粗野的 adj.　flute 長笛 n.

● Rule 2: 兩個母音組合發前面母音的長音

ai , ay ➔ [e]

　　　如：rain 雨 n.；下雨 v.　　　mail 郵件 n.；寄信 v.

　　　　　play 玩樂 v.　　　　　halfway 中途的 adj.

ee, ea, ei ➔ [i]

　　　如：fee 費用 n.　　　　　　heel 腳後跟；鞋跟 n.

　　　　　flea 跳蚤 n.　　　　　realize 明白；瞭解 v.

　　　　　ceiling 天花板 n.　　　either 任一者的 adj.

ight, ie➔ [aɪ]

　　　如：sigh 嘆氣 n./v.　　　　delight 欣喜 n.；使高興 v.

　　　　　necktie 領帶 n.　　　　lie 說謊 v.；謊言 n.

oa, oe ➜ [o]

如： coat 大衣 n.　　　　　　loan 貸款 n./v.

　　toe 腳趾頭 n.　　　　　　foe 仇敵 n.

ue, ui ➜ [u]

如： true 真實的 adj.　　　　clue 線索 n.

　　suit 套裝 n.　　　　　　cruise 航遊 v./n.

● Rule 3: 雙母音

au, aw ➜ [ɔ]

如： fault 錯誤 n.　　　　　　naughty 頑皮的 adj.

　　law 法律 n.　　　　　　raw 生的；未加工的 adj.

ou, ow ➜ [au]

如： cloud 雲 n.　　　　　　bounce 跳躍 v./n.

　　clown 小丑 n.　　　　　town　城鎮 n.

（注意：ow 也可以發 [o]，如：snow 雪 n., glow 發光 v.；光輝n. 等。）

ew ➜ [ju] 或 [u]

如： few 少的 adj.　　　　　stew 燉煮、燜煮 v.；燉菜 n.

　　crew 工作人員 n.　　　　flew 飛

oo ➜ [u] 或 [ʊ]

　　　　　長　　短

如： moon 月亮 n.　　　　　fool 笨蛋 n.

　　cook 做菜 v.；廚師 n.　　foot 腳 n.

oi, oy ➜ [ɔɪ]

如： avoid 避免 v.　　　　　moisture 溼潤 n./v.

　　toy 玩具 n.　　　　　　loyal 忠誠的 adj.

補教名師王舒葳教你
1**4天聽懂**
老外說的英語

DAY
1

DAY
2

DAY
3

DAY
4

DAY
5

DAY
6

DAY
7

DAY
8

DAY
9

DAY
10

DAY
11

DAY
12

DAY
13

DAY
14

● Rule 4：加 "r" 的母音

ar ➜ [ɑr]

　　如：hard 難的、硬的 adj.　　garden 花園 n.

　　　　March 三月 n.　　　　　arch 拱門 n.；拱起、形成弧形 v.

or ➜ [ɔr]

　　如：fork 叉子 n.　　　　　　morning 早晨 n.

　　　　lord 君主、上帝 n.　　　sort 種類 n.；分類、整理 v.

er, ir, ur ➜ [ɝ]

　　如：clerk 辦事員 n.　　　　　herd 畜群 n.；放牧 v.

　　　　shirt 襯衫 n.　　　　　　flirt 調情 n./v

　　　　hurry 趕快 v.；急忙 n.　burden 負擔 n.；加負擔於…v.

air, are, ear ➜ [ɛr]

　　如：fair 公平的、皮膚白晰的 adj.；博覽會 n.　stair 樓梯 n.

　　　　fare 票價 n.　　　　　　dare 敢 v.；果敢行為 n.

　　　　wear 穿 v.　　　　　　　pear 梨 n.

ear ➜ [ɪr]

　　注意，ear 可以發 [ɪr]（如上），也可以發 [iə]。

　　如：year 年 n.　　　clear 清楚的、晴朗的 adj.；清除、使清楚 v.

　　dear 親愛的 adj.；親愛的人 n.　　　　fear 害怕 v./n

> | 3. Exercise　　　 01-5

依照自然發音的原則寫下你聽到的字

　　1. ___feel___

　　2. ___f___

　　3. _____

　　4. _____

5. boil

6. _____

現在請聽MP3，比較下面單字發音的不同，並跟著説説看。 🎵 01-6

fill 填滿 v.   feel 感覺 n./v.

fail 失敗v.   fell 掉落（fall的過去式）v.

chip 洋芋片、晶片   cheap 便宜的 adj.   chop 砍v./n.；肋排 n.

eel 鰻魚 n.   ill 生病的、不好的 adj.

bowl 碗 n.   boil 煮沸v.；沸騰n.   ball 球 n.

draw 畫、拖、領取v.   drew 畫、拖、領取（draw 的過去式）v.

▶ 舒葳老師小叮嚀

　　我們在上面介紹的這些規則可以幫助你抓到英文拼字與發音之間的關係，也就是説聽到聲音你便準確判斷對方説的是什麼字。

　　要特別説明的是，我們在這裡介紹的是大方向的原則，有些較較瑣碎的規則，我們在這裡則暫不介紹。雖然英文字發音不乏不符規則的例外，只要熟悉了大方向，抓住了發音的基本原則，就能為你將來的聽説能力打下紮實的基礎喔！

Lesson 3 ▶ 再聽聽看

▶ 舒葳老師說 🎵 01-7

　　在學會了自然發音後，現在你是否能準確的聽出不同的母音了呢？請聽MP3的問句，並從A, B選項中選出適當的回覆：

1. A. He was our neighbor from 1992 to1998.

　　 B. About half an hour ago.

2. A. Sure. Would you like the salt too?

B. Sure. And you have a pen there, don't you?

3. A. Oh, no! I left it on the dock

B. Oh, no! I left it on the baseball court.

4. A. Yes, of course. That's included in the company's

compensation package.

B. Give me a break. I'm just having a bad day, OK?

5. A. Do you think so? I thought it was a bit too sour.

B. It sure was. He's one of the best players I have ever seen.

6. A. Yeah, especially if we want to finish this project in time.

B. Yes, but we need to get the material ready first.

● Answers

1.B 2.A 3.A 4.A 5.B 6.A

> 詳細解說 01-8

1. When did he leave here?

他什麼時候離開這裡的?

> 　　這裡他問的是何時 leave 離開，因此恰當的回答應該是B. About
> half an hour ago. 這裡如果沒有注意，長短音分辨不清楚，很容易
> 把 leave 誤以為是 live，而完全誤解了對方的問題。比較下面的兩個
> 句子並跟著說說看。
>
> When did he leave here? 他什麼時候離開這裡的？
> When did he live here? 他什麼住在這裡的？

❯ 容易混淆的字

長母音 [i]	短母音 [ɪ]
sheep 綿羊	ship 船
sheet 一片、一張	shit 屎
heat 加熱	hit 打
lead 鉛	lid 蓋子
least 最少的	list 名單

❯ 老外時常這麼說

half an hour ago 半小時以前

half 是一半，所以半年就是 half a year。

a quarter of an hour　15分鐘

quarter 是四分之一。如果要說15分鐘除了一般的 fifteen minutes 以外，也可以說 a quarter of an hour。

例句：

I was there three quarters of an hour.

我在那裡待了四十五分鐘。

The train leaves a quarter to the hour.

火車每個四十五分時（三點四十五分、四點四十五分等等）出發。

a quarter (of a year) 三個月，也就是一年的四分之一。

There was a fall in unemployment in the third quarter of the year.

今年的第三季失業率有下降。

I get an electricity bill every quarter.

我每三個月收到一次電費帳單。

補教名師王舒懂教你
14天聽懂
老外說的英語

DAY
1

DAY
2

DAY
3

DAY
4

DAY
5

DAY
6

DAY
7

DAY
8

DAY
9

DAY
10

DAY
11

DAY
12

DAY
13

DAY
14

2. Can you pass me the pepper, please?

可以請你把胡椒遞給我嗎？

> 　　這裡他說的是 pepper，當然回覆應該是答應後再問需要鹽嗎。因此恰當的回答應是 A. Sure. Would you like the salt too? 這裡容易犯的錯，是把短母音的 [ɛ] 和 [e] 混淆，把 pepper 聽成了 paper。比較下面的兩個句子並跟著說說看。
>
> Can you pass me the pepper, please? 可以請你把胡椒遞給我嗎？
> Can you pass me the paper, please? 可以請你把紙遞給我嗎？

> ❯ 容易混淆的字

短母音 [ɛ]	長母音 [e]
let 讓	late 晚、遲
bet 賭	bait 誘餌
tell 說	tale 故事
fell 摔倒（過去式）	fail 失敗

3. Where did you put the bait?

你把魚餌放哪兒了？

> 　　這裡他說的是 bait，比較恰當的回覆應該是 A. Oh, no! I left it by the lake. 留在湖邊了。一般我們容易混淆的是長母音的 bait 和短母音的 bat 的發音。比較下面的兩個句子並跟著說說看。
>
> Where did you put the bait? 你把魚餌放哪兒了？
> Where did you put the bat? 你把球棒放哪兒了？

❯ 容易混淆的字

長母音 [e]	短母音 [æ]

rate 比率	rat 老鼠
pace 速度	pass 經過
tape 錄音帶	tap 輕敲
main 主要的	man 男人

4. Do you have any pension at all?
你有退休金保險嗎？

> 這裡他說的是 pension，回覆應該是 A. Yes, of course. That's included in the company's compensation package. 說明這是公司福利制度的一部份。這裡容易把同是短母音的 pension ['pɛnʃən] 聽成 passion ['pæʃən]，而誤以為對方在抱怨你一點熱情都沒有了。比較下面的兩個句子並跟著說說看。
>
> Do you have any pension at all? 你有退休金保險嗎？
> Do you have any passion at all? 你有一點熱情嗎？

❯ 容易混淆的字

短母音 [ɛ]	短母音 [æ]
pet 寵物	pat 輕拍
met 遇見（過去式）	mat 腳墊
head 頭	had 有（過去式）
left 離開	laughed 笑（過去式）

❯ 老外時常這麼說

Do you have any… at all? **你有任何的⋯嗎？**
at all 無論是在問句，或否定的回答，皆用來加強語氣。

例句：

補教名師**王舒薇**教你
14天聽懂
老外說的英語

DAY
1

DAY
2

DAY
3

DAY
4

DAY
5

DAY
6

DAY
7

DAY
8

DAY
9

DAY
10

DAY
11

DAY
12

DAY
13

DAY
14

I have had no food at all.
我一點東西也沒吃。

Why bother getting up at all when you have no job to go to?
反正也沒工作可做，為什麼還費事起床呢？

Do you have any pension? 你有退休金嗎？

pension就是退休金，也就是政府或私人公司在員工退休時付給員
工的一筆錢。

She won't be able to draw her pension until she's 65.
她要到六十五歲才能領到退休金。

5. That was a great pitch!
這顆球投得真好！

這裡他說的是 pitch，適當的回覆應該是針對投球這件事做回應，也
就是 B. It sure was. He's one of the best players I have ever seen.
這裡容易出現的狀況和第一題相同，長音 [i] 和短音 [ɪ] 不分，把
pitch 聽成了peach，還以為對方在稱讚桃子呢。比較下面的兩個句
子並跟著說說看。

That was a great pitch! 這顆球投得真好！
That was a great peach! 這顆桃子真好！

❯ 容易混淆的字

短母音 [ɪ]   **長母音 [i]**

knit 編織   neat 整齊

sit 坐   seat 座位

bit 一點   beat 打擊

bid 喊價   bead 珠子

❯ 老外時常這麼說

What a great pitch! 這顆球投得真好！

pitch 在這裡指的是棒球裡，投手投球給打擊手。

例句：
Who will be pitching first this evening?
今晚誰是先發投手？

She has a high-pitched voice. 她的聲音很高。

pitch 也指音調的高低。

6. We need to make a plan.
   我們必須做個計劃。

> 這裡他說的是 plan，回覆應該是與完成案子有關，也就是 A. Yeah, especially if we want to finish this project in time. 很多人常常會把 plan 和 plane 的發音發得一樣，原因和第二題是相同的，短音 [æ] 和長音 [e] 不分，於是聽老外說話時，便搞不清楚到底是 plan 還是 plane。對方說的是要做計劃，結果我們竟然去買了卡紙、漿糊，準備做飛機了呢。比較下面的兩個句子。
>
> We need to make a plan. 我們必須做個計劃。
> We need to make a plane. 我們必須做架飛機。

❯ 容易混淆的字

短母音 [æ]	長母音 [e]
pants 褲子	paints 顏料
lack 缺乏	lake 湖
fat 胖的	fate 命運
rap 饒舌樂	rape 強暴

DAY
1

DAY
2

DAY
3

DAY
4

DAY
5

DAY
6

DAY
7

DAY
8

DAY
9

DAY
10

DAY
11

DAY
12

DAY
13

DAY
14

❯ 聽力小祕訣

☺ 大略瞭解拼字與發音之間的關係，可以幫助自己發音上的準確。

☺ 母音的發音正確，或至少母音的聲音有正確的認知，才有可能聽懂老外用的字。

☺ 學任何新單字時，要大聲念出來，模仿老外的發音。千萬不要只有眼睛認得，耳朵卻不認得。

☺ 當聲音內化成你的一部份時，聽力自然會進步喔！

MEMO

MEMO

DAY 2 | 辨別**發音相似**的子音
Sing, thing, 還是thin?

02-1~02-8

> **學習重點**

是sing, thing, 還是thin？這三個字的差別，你聽得出嗎？

發音相似的英文子音，也同樣是我們聽錯、聽不懂的原因。今天，我們將一起來練習這些容易混淆的子音的辨音及發音，讓你聽得輕鬆，說得漂亮！

Lesson 1 ▶ 聽聽看，說說看

▶ 舒葳老師說 02-1

　　你是否能準確地聽出不同的子音呢？先來測測自己的辨音能力吧！
請聽MP3，並從A, B選項中選出正確的關鍵字：

1. A. think
   B. sink

2. A. say
   B. save

3. A. same
   B. sane

4. A. three
   B. tree

5. A. ships
   B. chips

6. A. roll
   B. rop

● Answers

1.B　2.B　3.A　4.B　5.B　6.A

▶ 詳細解說 02-2

1. The old man was sinking fast.
   老人快速地沉沒到海中。

A. think 思考。
B. sink 沉沒（正確答案）。

　　這裡他說的是 sinking fast「下沉得很快」，而不是 thinking
fast「思考地很快」。sink 開頭的發音 s 和 thinking 的 th 相似，

34

DAY
1

**DAY
2**

DAY
3

DAY
4

DAY
5

DAY
6

DAY
7

DAY
8

DAY
9

DAY
10

DAY
11

DAY
12

DAY
13

DAY
14

s 的發音就像注音符號ㄙ，而念 th 的時候舌頭會伸出來，在上下排牙齒之間。我們的同學常發得不正確，因此在聽的時候也很容易混淆。想想看，如果有人告訴塔台人員 "We are sinking."（我們正快速地下沈）， 向他求救，他卻回問："What are you thinking about?"（你們在想什麼？）豈不是鬧笑話事業小，誤了人命事大了嗎？比較下面的兩個句子並跟著說說看。

The old man was sinking fast. 老人快速地沉沒到海中。

The old man was thinking fast. 老人快速地思考該怎麼做。

❯ 焦點句型用語

sink 是沉沒、下沉的意思。王建民的伸卡球就叫sinker喔。

❯ 老外時常這麼說

The ship sank.

船沉了。

The country's image is sinking fast.

這個國家的形象在迅速下沉。

He sank back into the chair.

他癱倒在椅子上。

2. What did you save that for?

你為什麼儲存那個？

A. say 說
B. save 儲存（正確答案）

這裡他說的是 save，最後面的 v 因為是子音，下一個字 that 又以子音起始。這個 "v" 的聲音會弱化到你幾乎聽不見，但即便如此，你會發現說話者還是「做動作」，表示要發 v 這個聲音，因此會有一些停頓，才再繼續發下一個聲音 that。再仔細聽一次，是不是這樣呢？比較下面的兩個句子，第一個句子在 that 之前有停頓，第二個句子則無。

What did you save that for? 你為什麼儲存那個？

What did you say that for? 你為什麼那麼說？

▶ 焦點句型用語

save 在上面的句子中為儲存的意思：

What did you save in your cell phone besides phone numbers?

你手機除了電話號碼外，還儲存些什麼？

save 也是節用的意思。在此資源枯竭的時代，save幾乎是一個口頭禪：

What did you save today?

你今天節用了什麼？

What... for? …是做什麼用的？意思和why相同。聽到對方這麼說時，表示他不清楚某事物的用途或目的，或對某事物的存在不以為然。

▶ 老外時常這麼說

What is the party for? 為什麼要開這個晚會？

What did you do that for? 你為什麼這麼做？

以上兩句均有不以為然的意思。

What is this for? 這是做什麼？

出其不意地送人禮物時，對方可能便會這麼回答，表示客氣。

What are friends for? 朋友是做什麼的？

當某人受朋友幫助，表達感謝後，我們常常會聽到的回應就是What are friends for? 表示「朋友就是應該互相幫助的」。

3. **We have the same attitude towards this subject.**
我們對這件事有一樣的態度。

A. same 一樣的（正確答案）
B. sane 理智的，合乎情理的

這裡他說的是 the same，same 後面的 m 和 sane 的 n 聽起來很相似，我們很容易把 same 和 sane 混淆。m 字尾的 m 說的時候嘴巴要閉，因此聽得出來說話者在說下一個字 attitude 之前，嘴巴是閉起來的；而 n 則嘴巴不閉，而且會聽得到 n 的鼻音。再仔細聽一次，是不是這樣呢？台灣同學也常因 m, n 不分，使得老外摸不清你在說什麼喔！另外，a 和 the 在說得快的時候，聽起來也會很類似。比較下面的兩個句子並跟著說說看。

We have the same attitude towards this subject.
我們對這件事有一樣的態度。

We have a sane attitude towards this subject.
我們對這件事持理智的態度。

▶ 焦點句型用語

...have a ...attitude towards... …對…有…的態度。

the same attitude 是一樣的態度；**a sane attitude** 是理智、合乎情理的態度

❯|老外時常這麼說

It's important to have a positive attitude towards life.

對生命保持正面積極的態度是很重要的。

How do you keep sane in the insane world?

在這個沒有理智的社會裡要如何保持神智清醒？

4. The tree houses are located in a protected rainforest area.

這樹屋位於雨林保護區。

A. three 三間房子。

B. tree 樹屋（正確答案）

　　這裡他說的是 tree houses，而不是 three houses。tree 開頭的發音 tr 和 three 的 thr 相似，我們很容易混淆。Tr 的發音有點像注音符號ㄔ加上英文字母的 r，而念 thr 的時候舌頭會伸出來，在上下排牙齒之間。再仔細聽一次，是不是這樣呢？比較下面的兩個句子並跟著說說看。

The tree houses are located in a protected rainforest area.

這樹屋位於雨林保護區。

The three houses are located in a protected rainforest area.

這三棟房屋位於雨林保護區。

❯|焦點句型用語

are located 位於

in a protected rainforest area 雨林保護區

❯|老外時常這麼說

The shopping mall is located at the corner of Liberty Road and Main Street。

賣場位於自由路和緬因街的轉角。

The hotel is located at top of the hill.

旅社位於山頂上。

5. Chips are my favorite!

我最喜歡洋芋片了！

> A. ships 船。
> B. chips 洋芋片。（正確答案）
>
> 　　這裡他說的是 chips，而不是 ships。Chips 開頭的發音 ch 和 ships 的 sh 相似，乍聽之下，我們很容易混淆。Ch 的發音有點像注音符號ㄑ，sh 則像注音符號的ㄕ。再仔細聽一次，是不是這樣呢？比較下面的兩個句子並跟著說說看。
>
> Ships are my favorite! 我最喜歡船了！
> Chips are my favorite! 我最喜歡洋芋片了！

❯ 焦點句型用語

...are my favorite. 我最喜歡…了！
是表示最喜歡某事物的習慣說法。

❯ 老外時常這麼說

How sweet of you to buy me those chocolate chip cookies. They're my favorite.

你真貼心買巧克力餅乾給我，那是我最喜歡的。

DAY 1
DAY 2
DAY 3
DAY 4
DAY 5
DAY 6
DAY 7
DAY 8
DAY 9
DAY 10
DAY 11
DAY 12
DAY 13
DAY 14

6. Let's roll the wheels to the bike.

把這些輪胎滾到腳踏車那裡吧。

A. roll 滾動。（正確答案）
B. rope 用繩索綁在一起。

　　這裡他說的是 roll，答案 B 則是 rope。roll 字尾發音 [l] 和 rope 字尾發音 [p] 都很容易被忽略，因此也容易相互混淆。[l] 的發音舌尖必須頂到上顎牙齒後方。[p] 則是較輕的「氣音」。再仔細聽一次，是不是這樣呢？比較下面的兩個句子並跟著說說看。

Let's roll the wheels to the bike.

把這些輪胎滾到腳踏車那裡吧。

Let's rope the wheels to the bike.

把這些輪胎跟腳踏車用繩索綁在一起吧。

❯ 焦點句型用語

Let's... …吧。
聽到Let's... 就知道對方在提議做某事。

❯ 老外時常這麼說

Let's go out and eat. 我們出去吃東西吧。
Let's eat out tonight. 我們今晚在外面用餐吧。
Let's have Korean food. 我們去吃韓國菜吧。

She was on a roll. 她近來運氣很好。

　　on a roll 是片語，表示最近這一段期間很成功，運氣很好。
　　另一個聽起來很相似的也是片語on the ropes，則有完全不同的意

DAY
1

DAY
2

DAY
3

DAY
4

DAY
5

DAY
6

DAY
7

DAY
8

DAY
9

DAY
10

DAY
11

DAY
12

DAY
13

DAY
14

思，是用來表示事情做得不好且搖搖欲墜。

His business is on the ropes. 他的生意搖搖欲墜。

They are on a roll. 他們近來很順利。

They are on the ropes. 他們搖搖欲墜。

❯ 舒葳老師小叮嚀

發音相似的英文子音如 m, n、th, s、p, b 等，都是我們同學常常說不正確的發音。而一旦錯誤的發音說久了，便會誤以為自己說的才是正確的發音，結果是當老外說出正確的發音時，我們同學反而聽不懂。這也是為什麼有時候我們聽台灣人說英文反而比聽老外說英文聽得懂的原因了！因此，我們要趕緊糾正自己子音的發音，進而培養有效聽力、加強溝通喔！

Lesson 2 ❯ 自然發音

❯ 舒葳老師說

英文字裡的子音，字母與音標有一大半是一致的，不一致的也有規律可尋。下表是字母與音標的對照： (MP3) 02-3

有 聲 子 音			無 聲 子 音		
字母	音標	例 字	字母	音標	例 字
b	[b]	<u>b</u>oy, ca<u>b</u>	p	[p]	<u>p</u>en, la<u>p</u>

有 聲 子 音			無 聲 子 音		
字母	音標	例 字	字母	音標	例 字
g	[g]	pig, game	k/c/ck/ch	[k]	cook, school, check
d	[d]	send, desk	t	[t]	sent, take,
v	[v]	vine, live	f/gh/ph	[f]	fish, enough, phone
z	[z]	zoo, eyes	s/c/ce	[s]	star, center, nice
th	[ð]	those, bathe	th	[θ]	think, bath
s(u)	[ʒ]	vision, pleasure	sh	[ʃ]	wash, she
j, ge	[dʒ]	John, George, large	ch, tch	[tʃ]	church, watch,
l	[l]	kill, like			
m	[m]	come, man			
n	[n]	nice, ten			
ng	[ŋ]	sing, king			
r	[r]	poor, rope			
y	[j]	yes, yet, you			
h	[h]	how, hill			
w	[w]	we, weather			

補教名師王舒葳教你
14天聽懂
老外說的英語

DAY
1

DAY
2

DAY
3

DAY
4

DAY
5

DAY
6

DAY
7

DAY
8

DAY
9

DAY
10

DAY
11

DAY
12

DAY
13

DAY
14

　　加上我們在 Day 1 對母音字母與音標間的關係的認識，我們應知道英語的字母和音標有緊密的關連性，我們只要熟悉這些原則，大半的字看了就會念，會念就會拼字。也就是説，我們看到 bed 就會念 [bɛd]，會念 [bɛd] 就會拼 b-e-d。

　　這個法則可以幫助你學會新單字的發音，更可以幫助你檢視你現有的發音是否正確喔！下面我們就來看看同學常會發得不正確的子音。

▶ 1. 容易混淆的子音 (MP3) 02-4

	有聲子音字首	無聲子音字首	有聲子音字尾	無聲子音字尾
b/p	back	pack	hob	hop
g/c	gang	can	bag	back
d/t	doe	toe	feed	feet
v/f	vine	fine	save	safe
z/s	zip	sip	buzz	bus
th/th	then	thin	breathe	breath
dr/tr	drip	trip		
j/ch	joke	choke		

其他容易混淆的子音			
字首		字尾	
th/s	thank	sank	path	pass
sh/ch	shop	chop	cash	catch
m/n	map	nap	Sam	san
l/r	lice	rice	pool	poor
n/ng			thin	thing

▶ 舒葳老師小叮嚀

　　由於中文每個字都自成一個音節，沒有字尾音，在發音上，字尾音

也是中國學生最難發得漂亮的部份，常常會念得太重，甚至受中文注音符號的影響，把 b 發成ㄅ，把 t 發成ㄊ等，也就是錯誤地在子音後面加上一個母音。所謂的「台式英文」也因之而生。而發音的不正確，更直接影響了我們的聽力。

無聲子音只有氣音，聽的時候要注意聽才聽得到，因此念的時候也不要念得太用力。有聲子音則注意不要念太長，切忌如上述把子音音節化，無中生有的在子音後面加上一個母音（比如把 bag 念成「baㄍ」）。

❯ |2. 長母音加+子音字尾　🎵 02-5

長母音字尾	無聲子音字尾
sue	suit
bar	bark
play	plate
lie	light
we	weak
why	white
sea	seat
fee	feet

❯ 舒葳老師小叮嚀

而當字尾是無聲子音時，常因發音很小聲，或說的很快，很容易就被聽者忽略了。所以聽的時候要特別留意字尾。

不過事實上，這裡還有一個秘訣喔！如果比較上面兩欄，你會發現，雖然兩欄的字母音的發音都是一樣的，看起來好像唯一的不同就是

補教名師王舒葳教你
14天聽懂
老外說的英語

DAY 1

DAY 2

DAY 3

DAY 4

DAY 5

DAY 6

DAY 7

DAY 8

DAY 9

DAY 10

DAY 11

DAY 12

DAY 13

DAY 14

字尾的氣音，但如果你再仔細聽聽看，你會發現左欄的母音念起來的時候聲音稍長，而右欄的的母音念起來聲音稍短。這是因為當字尾有子音時，說話者要趕著去發字尾的子音，就只好把長母音念得稍微快一些。

　　再聽一次，熟悉它們不同的發音，並跟著說說看。

3. 其他容易混淆的字 🎵 02-6

● 字首相似的字

did 做（過去式）v.	didn't 沒做（過去式）v.
swim 游泳 n./v.	swing 搖擺 v./n.
fake 假的 adj.	fade 褪色、消退 v.
sit up 坐起來	sit down 坐下來
fun 有樂趣的 adj.	fund 資助、基金 n.
feed 餵食 v.	fit 適合 v./ n./adj.
respectively 分別的 adv.	respectfully 恭敬地 adv.
wind 上緊發條 v.	wine 紅酒 n.
supplies 供給 n./v.（單數為supply）	surprise 驚喜 n./v.

● 字尾相似的字

hand 手 n.	brand 品牌 n.
cab 計程車 n.	tab 標牌 v./n.
large 大的 adj.	charge 索價 v./n.
place 地方 n.	pace 速度 v./n.
grain 穀類 n.	drain 排水 v./n.
rest 休息 n./v.	guest 客人 n.
dine 吃飯 v.	fine 好的 adj.

date 約會 n./v.   rate 比率、等級、評價 v./n.

crazy 瘋狂的 adj.   lazy 懶惰的 adj.

inferior 次於的、較差的 adj.   superior 高等的、較優越的 adj.

interior 室內的 adj.   exterior 室外的 adj.

❯ │ 4. Exercise

請寫下你聽到的句子。

1. _____.

2. _____.

3. _____.

4. _____.

5. _____.

現在請聽MP3，比較下面的句子，並跟著說說看。

1. Come along. 一起來吧。
   Come alone. 獨自一個人來。

2. She ran. 她跑（過去式）。
   She rang. 她打電話（過去式）。

3. Nice place. 好地方。
   Nice play. 打得好（球）。

4. It's a pleasure. 那是個享受。
   It's a pressure. 那是個壓力。

5. It's a beautiful word. 這是個很美的字。
   It's a beautiful world. 這是個美麗的世界。

DAY
1

DAY
2

DAY
3

DAY
4

DAY
5

DAY
6

DAY
7

DAY
8

DAY
9

DAY
10

DAY
11

DAY
12

DAY
13

DAY
14

> **舒葳老師小叮嚀**

　　有些英文字在速度較慢、念得清楚時，聲音並不見得多麼相似，但當老外以自然速度說話時，因速度較快，若同學原本就不太熟悉這些字的用法，聽起來便很容易聽不清楚而誤以為對方說的是另一個字而無法理解。以上這些字是舒葳老師針對同學常見的聽力問題整理給大家練習。平時同學在學單字時也可以自己歸納發音類似的字，自己多念多做練習喔！

Lesson 3 > 再聽聽看

> **舒葳老師說**　 02-7

請聽MP3中句子，並選擇出正確回應：

1.　A. I thought the plot was great.
　　B. It has a beautiful floral design which I like very much.

2.　A.Yeah, that was really yummy.
　　B. No, sorry. It's still wet.

3.　A. Yeah, it's a real bargain.
　　B. Actually, I was hoping to get something better.

4.　A. Sure. Any specific brand or color?
　　B. Sure. I'll call right away.

5.　A. Especially on the green grass.
　　B. Especially in the summer lake.

6. A. You're joking. How can I miss it?

   B. Don't worry. I'll do that in a minute.

7. A. Don't worry. I have no intention to cut my feet.

   B. O.K. I will walk on the pavement.

● Answers

A.7　B.6　B.5　B.4　B.3　A.2　A.1

▶ 詳細解說　MP3 02-8

1. How did you like the play?

你覺得那齣劇如何？

A. I thought the plot was great.

　我覺得劇情很棒。（正確答案）

B. It has a beautiful floral design which I like very much.

　它有很漂亮的花樣設計，我很喜歡。

　　這裡他說的是 How did you like the play? 因此回應應是 A。plot 是「情節」、「故事架構」的意思。

　　play 和 plate 發音相似，容易混淆。play 母音 ay 拉長，字尾沒有子音。plate 字尾的 t 是無聲子音，念起來並不會清楚地聽見字尾 t，且你會發現 play 的母音較長，plate 的母音念的較短。比較下面的兩個句子並跟著說說看。

How did you like the play? 你覺得那齣劇如何？

How did you like the plate? 你覺得那個盤子如何？

▶ 容易混淆的字

DAY 1

DAY 2

DAY 3

DAY 4

DAY 5

DAY 6

DAY 7

DAY 8

DAY 9

DAY 10

DAY 11

DAY 12

DAY 13

DAY 14

字尾爲母音長音	字尾爲無聲子音
May 五月 n.	mate 伙伴 n.
hay 乾草 n.	hate 恨 v.
sigh 嘆氣 n./v.	sight 視力；景象 n.
tie 領帶 n.；綁 v.	tight 緊的 adj.

2. Did you try that?
你有試試看那個嗎？

A. Yeah, that was really yummy.　有啊，很好吃。（正確答案）

B. Actually, I was hoping to get something better.
沒有，抱歉。還是濕的。

這裡他說的是 Did you try that? try 是「嘗試」，也可以當「試吃」用。try 的字首 tr 因為和 dry 的 dr 發音相似，我們很容易把 try 和 dry 混淆。在這裡，tr 是無聲子音，dr 則是有聲子音。比較下面的兩個句子並跟著說說看。

Did you try that? 你有試試看那個嗎？

Did you dry that? 你有烘乾那個嗎？

❯ 容易混淆的字

字首爲 tr	字首爲 dr
trunk 樹幹；行李箱 n.	drunk 喝醉的 adj.
trip 旅途 n.	drip 滴下 n./v.
trill 顫動；顫音 n./v.	drill 鑽；訓練 n./v.

3. It's a good prize, isn't it?
這個獎項很好，不是嗎？

A. Yeah, it's a real bargain. 是啊，真是賺到了。

B. Actually, I was hoping to get something better.

事實上，我本來希望拿到更好的東西。（正確答案）

　　這裡他說的是 It's a good prize, isn't it?，所以回覆應與拿獎有關。這裡容易把 prize 聽成 price，而誤以為對方說的是價格很好了。prize 的尾音是有聲子音 [z]，price 則是無聲子音 [s]。比較下面的兩個句子並跟著說說看。

It's a good prize, isn't it? 這個獎項很好，不是嗎？

It's a good price, isn't it? 這個價格很好，不是嗎？

➤ 容易混淆的字

字尾爲無聲子音 [s]	字尾爲有聲子音 [z]
peace 和平 n.	peas 豌豆（複數）n.
ice 冰 n.	eyes 雙眼 n.
rice 米飯 n.	rise 上升；上漲 n./ v.
face 臉 n.	phase 階段；時期 n.

4. Could you get me a cab, please?

請幫我叫部計程車好嗎？

A. Sure. Any specific brand or color?

好的，任何特定的牌子或顏色嗎？

B. Sure. I'll call right away. 好的，我馬上打電話。（正確答案）

　　這裡他說的是 Could you get me a cab, please? 因此回應是 Sure. I'll call right away. 表示他馬上打電話叫車。cab 字尾的 b 因為和 cap 的 p 發音相似，我們很容易把 cab 和 cap 混淆。在這裡，b

補教名師王舒葳教你
1**4天聽懂**
老外說的英語

DAY
1

DAY
2

DAY
3

DAY
4

DAY
5

DAY
6

DAY
7

DAY
8

DAY
9

DAY
10

DAY
11

DAY
12

DAY
13

DAY
14

是有聲子音，但是因為在字尾，我們反而常會聽不見 b 的聲音。而 p 則是無聲子音，只聽得到「氣的聲音」。再仔細聽一次，是不是這樣呢？比較下面的兩個句子並跟著說看。在會話中，老外對句尾的子音常會做勢而不發。當你真的聽不出是 cab 或 cap 時，只得從上下文去體會了。

Could you get me a cap, please? 請幫我找頂帽子好嗎？

Could you get me a cab, please? 請幫我叫部計程車好嗎？

容易混淆的字

字尾為無聲子音 [p]

mop 拖把 n.；拖地 v.

tap 輕拍 n./v.；水龍頭 n.

rip 撕、扯 n./v.

字尾為有聲子音 [b]

mob 暴民 n.；聚眾滋事 v.

tab 標籤 n./v.

rib 排骨、肋骨 n.

5. Boys like to row.
男孩喜歡划船。

A. Especially on the green grass. 尤其在綠綠的草地上。

B. Especially in the summer lake. 尤其在夏天的湖裡。（正確答案）

　　這裡他說的是 row，指的是滑船。這裡 row 無子音字尾，很容易與字尾音不是那麼明顯的 roll 混淆。roll 的字尾音是 l，發音時舌尖要頂到上顎，我們同學一般發音時都沒有確實做到，聽的時候也往往就忽略了這個 l 音造成的聲音以及字意上差別。比較下面的兩個句子，第二個句子句尾會聽到舌尖要頂到上顎的 l 音。

Boys like to row. 男孩喜歡滑船。

Boys like to roll. 男孩喜歡打滾。

❯ 容易混淆的字

字尾爲 [o] [ɔ] 或 [ɔr]　　字尾爲 [ol] 或 [ɔl]

tow 拖吊 v./n.	toll 損失、死傷人數 n.
mow 除草 v./n.	mall 購物中心 n.
saw 看見（過去式）v.	soul 靈魂 n.
four 四 n.	fall 掉落 v./n.

6. Are you going to wash that?
你會洗那個嗎？

A. You're joking. How can I miss it?
你開玩笑。我怎麼能錯過？

B. Don't worry. I'll do that in a minute.
別擔心。我馬上就做。（正確答案）

　　這裡他說的是 wash，指的是洗。這裡 wash 字尾的 sh [ʃ] 和 watch 的 tch [tʃ] 相似，很容易混淆。要注意聽，否則還以為對方在問你看了什麼節目了呢。

比較下面的兩個句子並跟著說說看。

Are you going to watch that? 你會看那個嗎？
Are you going to wash that? 你會洗那個嗎？

❯ 容易混淆的字

wish 希望 v.	witch 女巫 n.
mush 軟的物質 n.	much 多 adj.
cash 現金 n.	catch 趕上 v.
share 分享 v.	chair 椅子 n.

sheep 綿羊 n.　　　cheap 便宜的 adj.

shop 購物 v.　　　chop 切、砍 v.

7. Be careful. Don't step on the glass.

小心。不要踩到玻璃了。

A. Don't worry. I have no intention to cut my feet.

別擔心，我一點也不想割到我的腳。（正確答案）

B. O.K. I will walk on the pavement.

好，我會走在步道上。

　　這裡他說的是 glass，指的是玻璃。答案的 have no intention to 是「無意」的意思。這裡 glass 字首的 gl [gl] 很容易與會聽成 grass 的 gr 混淆。gr 有輕微的捲舌音 r，gl 則無。這也是一般中國學生在發音時容易忽略的音，而直接地影響到聽力。比較下面的兩個句子並跟著說說看。

Be careful. Don't step on the glass. 小心。不要踩到玻璃了。

Be careful. Don't step on the grass. 小心。不要踩到草皮上了。

▶ 容易混淆的字

字首為 [gl] [cl] 或 [pl]

glow 發光 v./n.

clash 不合、利害衝突 v./n.

pleasant 愉悅的 adj.

play 玩耍 v./n.

clown 小丑 n.

字首為 [gr] [cr] 或 [pr]

grow 種植 v.

crash 衝撞、墜毀 v./n.

present 禮物 n

pray 祈禱 v./n.

crown 皇冠 n.

▶ 聽力小秘訣

DAY 1
DAY 2
DAY 3
DAY 4
DAY 5
DAY 6
DAY 7
DAY 8
DAY 9
DAY 10
DAY 11
DAY 12
DAY 13
DAY 14

☺ 子音的發音正確與否同樣會影響自己對英文聲音的認知，進而影響你的聽力。

☺ 熟悉本課介紹容易混淆的聲音，多加練習。將來聽老外説話時並能有更迅速正確的反應。

☺ 平時練習聽力時若有將一個字聽成另一個字的情形，一定要找出這兩個字的正確發音並反覆練習。

MEMO

DAY 3 字尾消失原則
You won't believe it!

MP3
03-1~03-6

> **學習重點**

　　請先念念看這裡的標題，再聽聽看MP3怎麼説。你有沒有發現won't的 t 不會説出來，it 的 t 也只有氣音呢？事實上，在英文裏，" t " 字尾都是不會大聲念出來的。同學如果不熟悉這個字尾音消失的規則，自然就會產生聽力上的障礙了喔！

　　今天我們就來學習英文字尾消失的規則吧。多聽，多念，以後聽到老外説這類字的時候才能正確反應喔！

DAY **3** 字尾消失原則
You won't believe it!

MP3
03-1~03-6

Lesson 1 > 聽聽看，寫寫看

> **舒葳老師說** 03-1

你是否能準確地聽出MP3在說什麼呢？請聽MP3，並寫下你聽到的句子：

1. _____.

2. _____.

3. _____.

4. _____.

5. _____.

6. _____.

● Answers

5. What's that look on your face?　6. Shall we leave a tip?

3. I have a date tonight.　4. Put my hat back.

1. You can't beat that.　2. Let him do it.

> **詳細解說** 03-2

1. You can't beat that.
   這已經是最便宜的了。

補教名師王舒葳教你
14天聽懂
老外說的英語

DAY 1
DAY 2
DAY 3
DAY 4
DAY 5
DAY 6
DAY 7
DAY 8
DAY 9
DAY 10
DAY 11
DAY 12
DAY 13
DAY 14

這句話乍聽之下聽起來像：You can be that. 但事實上，他說的是：You can't beat that. 這句話字面上的意思是「你沒辦法打敗這個了。」也就是說，當客人在討價還價時，老闆可以說："You can't beat that." 表示「這已經是最便宜的了」的意思。

要注意的是，雖然 can't 和 beat 的 t 消音了，在說話的時候還是會留下短暫的停留時間，只是不會把 t 發出來而已。再聽一次，練習跟著說說看。

▶ 延伸活用例句

That's my best offer. 那是我可以給的最好的價錢了。

2. Let him do it.
讓他做吧。

Let 的 t 消音，it 的 t 則發氣音，說得快時也可能消音，因此如果不熟悉這個規則，乍聽之下就會不知道對方在說什麼。要注意的是，雖然 t 消音了，在說話的時候還是會留下短暫的停留時間，只是不會把 t 發出來而已。再聽一次，練習跟著說說看。

3. I have a date tonight.
我今晚有約會。

date 的 t 消音，tonight 的 t 這裡發氣音，說得快時也可能消音。date 在這裡是約會的意思，但乍聽之下，你可能以為他說的是：I have a day tonight. 而摸不著頭腦了。date也可以當約會對象用。再聽一次，練習跟著說說看。

▶ | 延伸活用例句

My friend set me up on a blind date. 我朋友替我安排了一個相親。

How was your date? 你的約會順利嗎？

Will you be my date? 你願意當我的女／男伴嗎？

4. Put my hat back.

把我的帽子放回去。

> Put 的 t 和 hat 的 t 都消音，不只如此，back 的 ck 也消音喔。雖然我們前面聽到的例子都是 t 消音，但事實上，字尾發 [p] 或 [k] 時也會有消音的現象喔！要注意的是，[p] 或 [k] 在發音時，嘴巴都要做到動作，只是聲音不用發出來喔！再聽一次，練習跟著說說看。

5. What's that look on your face?

你那是什麼表情？

> that 的 t 消音，look 的 k 也消音。如果你第一次聽的時候沒有聽懂，有可能是你不了解消音的現象，也有可能是你不熟悉這個句型。再聽一次，練習跟著說說看。發 [k] 的時候嘴巴要做到動作，只是不要把聲音發出來，所以聽的時候會覺得中間有短暫的停頓。

▶ | 延伸活用例句

Don't give me that look. 不要給我那種表情。

Don't look at me like that. 不要那樣看我。

Why the long face? 為什麼拉長著臉？

補教名師王舒葳教你
14天聽懂
老外說的英語

DAY
1

DAY
2

**DAY
3**

DAY
4

DAY
5

DAY
6

DAY
7

DAY
8

DAY
9

DAY
10

DAY
11

DAY
12

DAY
13

DAY
14

6. Shall we leave a tip?

我們要不要給個小費？

> tip 的 p 會發氣音或消音，leave a tip 是「給小費」的意思。
> Shall we...? 表示「我們要不要⋯？」是問對方意見的意思。再聽一
> 次，練習跟著説説看。

〉延伸活用例句

Do we leave a tip? 我們該給小費嗎？

Don't forget to leave a tip for the server. 別忘了給服務生小費。

〉舒葳老師小叮嚀

上面的練習你都做對了嗎？我們在這課學到了字尾的 [t]，[p] 和 [k]
在自然的英語中是會消音的，對這個現象有了解後，便能幫助你的聽
力更進一步喔！然而 [t] 的聲音在英文中相當特別，除了在字尾消音之
外，還有一些其他的變化喔！下面我們就針對 t 的消音規則做更進一步
的分析與練習，同時也介紹另一個聲音規則 - [h] 的消音。

Lesson 2 〉 消失的子音 🎧 03-3

〉1. 消失的 "t"

● Rule 1 - "t" 字尾消音

Si(t) down. 坐下。

Le(t) me see. 讓我看。

He wen(t) the nex(t) day. 他隔天去了。

Wha(t) migh(t) happen? 可能會發生什麼事？

Pa(t) was qui(te) righ(t), wasn'(t) she? Pat 蠻對的，不是嗎？

Wha(t)? Pu(t) my ha(t) back! 什麼？把我的帽子放回去！

● Rule 2 － [t] 或 [d] 在 [n] 之前消音

The hikers went in the mountains. 登山者進了山。

She's certain that he has written it. 她確定他已經寫了。

The cotton curtain is not in the fountain. 棉質窗簾不在噴水池裡。

The frightened witness had forgotten the important

written message. 驚嚇過度的目擊者已忘了這個重要的文字訊息。

Students study Latin in Britain. 學生在英國學拉丁文。

I couldn't do it. 我做不下去。

● Rule 3 － [t] 或 [d] 在 [n] 之後也消音

He had a great in(t)erview. 他的面談很順利。

Sorry to in(t)errupt. 抱歉打斷你。

She's at the in(t)ernational center. 她在國際中心。

Don't take advan(t)age of her. 不要佔她便宜。

There are twen(t)y of them. 他們有二十個人。

Try to en(t)er the information. 試試看輸入訊息。

● Rule 4 － "want to" 發成 "wanna"， "going to" 發成"gonna"

I wanna go. 我要去。(I want to go.)

I wanna see it. 我要看。(I want to see it.)

Don't you wanna try? 你不想試試看嗎？(Don't you want to try?)

I'm gonna go. 我會去。(I am going to go.)

DAY
1

DAY
2

DAY
3

DAY
4

DAY
5

DAY
6

DAY
7

DAY
8

DAY
9

DAY
10

DAY
11

DAY
12

DAY
13

DAY
14

He's gonna love it. 他會愛死這個。(He's going to love it.)

What're you gonna do? 你要怎麼辦？

(What are you going to do?)

● Rule 5 – "t" 在兩個母音之間時發 [D]

在這裡，[D] 是「彈舌音」的意思，跟[d]的發音類似。聽 MP3，跟著說説看。

Here's your letter.

這是你的信。

She had a little bottle.

她有一個小瓶子。

Betty bought some butter.

貝蒂買了點奶油。

Get a better water heater.

買一個好一點的熱水器。

Put all the data in the computer.

把所有的資料放在電腦裏。

Insert a quarter in the meter.

把一個二十五分錢的硬幣放進收費器裏。

注意，後三句的 Get 和 a，Put 和 a，和 Insert 和 a，雖然都是分開的兩個字，但是因為 [t] 仍是處於兩個母音之中，因此也發彈舌音 [D]。

▶ 2. 消失的 "h"

在英文口語中，説話説得快的時候要發[h]這個音會較吃力，因此在句子中的[h]也消音。

Did (h)e go? 他有去嗎？

I'll tell (h)im. 我會告訴他。

Give (h)er the message. 給他這個訊息。

Is (h)is work good? 他的工作表現好嗎?

Did you take (h)er pen? 你有拿她的筆嗎?

He won't let (h)er. 他不讓她(做這件事)。

上面的這幾個句子也包含了「連音」的聲音規則在內,連音我們在Day 7會再進一步介紹。

▶ |3. Exercise 03-4

聽聽看下面的短文,留意 t 的字尾,並跟著說說看

I'm studying this Pronunciation an(d) Lis(t)ening course. There's a lo(t) to learn, bu(t) I find i(t) very enjoyable. I think I will find i(t) easier and easier to lis(t)en to native speakers speak English, bu(t) the only way to really improve is to practice all of the time.

Now I can distinguish differen(t) vowels and consonants tha(t) sound similar, and I also pay more attention to stresses when I lis(t)en than I used to. I have been talking to a lot of native speakers of English la(t)ely and they tell me that I'm easier to understand. Anyway, I could go on and on, bu(t) the impor(t)an(t) thing is to lis(t)en well and sound good. And I hope I'm getting better and better!

▶ 舒葳老師小叮嚀

我們一直強調,對英文聲音的正確瞭解是提升聽力的第一步。希望讀到這裡,你對英文聲音已有更進一步的認識了喔!認識了聲音的規則後,還需要充分的練習,才能把這些知識「內化」,在未來說英文或聽

補教名師王舒葳教你
14天聽懂
老外說的英語

DAY
1

DAY
2

DAY
3

DAY
4

DAY
5

DAY
6

DAY
7

DAY
8

DAY
9

DAY
10

DAY
11

DAY
12

DAY
13

DAY
14

英文時都能自然地使用出來喔！

Lesson 3 ▶ 再聽聽看

▶ 舒葳老師說   03-5

請聽MP3中的句子，並選擇出正確回應。

1. A. Sure. Come with me.
   B. So why didn't you?

2. A. No, he isn't.
   B. No, she isn't.

3. A. Don't worry. I won't bother her anymore.
   B. Don't worry. I won't bother him anymore.

4. A. Oh, really? Why are you leaving so early?
   B. OK. I hope you'll enjoy it.

● Answers
1.A 2.A 3.B 4.B

▶ 詳細解說   03-6

1. I wanna go.

> A. Sure. Come with me. 當然，跟我一起來。（正確答案）
> B. So why didn't you? 那麼你為什麼沒去呢？

63

這裡他說 I wanna go. 就是 I want to go. 的意思。所以你恰當的回應應該是：Sure. Come with me. 請比較練習下面兩個句子。在第二句的 I wanted to go. 中，[t] 發彈舌音。

I wanna go. 我要去。

I wanted to go. 我本來想去的。

2. Is he the one?
他就是那個人嗎？

A. No, he isn't. 不，他不是。（正確答案）
B. No, she isn't. 不，她不是。

這裡他說 Is he the one? 其中 h 消音。你恰當的回應應該是：No, he isn't. 請比較練習下面兩個句子。

Is he the one? 他就是那個人嗎？

Is she the one? 她就是那個人嗎？

3. Leave him alone.
不要煩他。

A. Don't worry. I won't bother her anymore.
不用擔心，我再也不會打擾她了。

B. Don't worry. I won't bother him anymore.
不用擔心，我再也不會打擾他了。（正確答案）

這裡他說 Leave him alone. 其中 h 消音。你恰當的回應應該是：Don't worry. I won't bother him anymore. 請比較練習下面兩個句子。

DAY
1

DAY
2

DAY
3

DAY
4

DAY
5

DAY
6

DAY
7

DAY
8

DAY
9

DAY
10

DAY
11

DAY
12

DAY
13

DAY
14

> Leave her alone. 不要煩她。
>
> Leave him alone. 不要煩他。

4. I got to go.

我得走了。

> A. Oh, really? Why are you leaving so early?
>
> 喔,真的嗎?你為什麼這麼早就要離開?
>
> B. OK. I hope you'll enjoy it. 好的,希望你玩得愉快。(正確答案)
>
> 　　這裡他說 I got to go. 其中第一個 t 消音,第二個 t 便可以視為
> 介於兩個母音o的中間,因此發彈舌音 [D]。I got to go. 就是 I have
> to go.,是「我得走了」的意思。因此,你恰當的回應應該是:Oh,
> really? Why are you leaving so early? 請比較練習下面兩個句子。
>
> I got to go. 我得走了。
>
> I'm gonna go. 我會去。

▶ 聽力小秘訣

☺ 英文中有許多消音的現象,瞭解消音規則,可以幫助自己發音上的
準確。

☺ 把消音規則融入自己平時的發音中,聽老外說英文時才較能迅速反
應。

☺ 養成常聽英文的習慣,嘴巴跟著說,長期培養對聲音的正確認知。

☺ 當聲音內化成你的一部份時,聽力自然會進步喔!

MEMO

DAY 4 掌握字的重音

compete, competition,
competitive, competency

04-1~04-5

　　在英文單字裡，重音是字意不可分割的一部分。重音也幫助我們辨識我們聽到的是什麼字。有時候我們明明學過一個字，看也看得懂，但經由老外的口中說出就硬是鴨子聽雷。這常常是因為我們把重音放錯了位置，聽到正確的發音反而聽不懂。

　　那麼我們該如何掌握字的重音呢？其實重音的位置也是有規則的喔，現在就讓我們來看看這些規則吧！

Lesson 1 > 聽聽看，說說看

> 舒葳老師說 04-1

你是否能準確地發出不同重音的字呢？先來測測自己對重音的認識是否正確吧！請說出下列各組的字：

1. extreme extremely
2. famous infamous
3. equal equality
4. admire admirable admiration
5. economy economic economical
6. compete competitive competitor competition competence

現在聽MP3，你念得正確嗎？

> 詳細解說 04-2

1. extreme 極端的；極度的 adj.；極端 n.

   extremely 極端地；極度地 adv.

> 這兩個字，一個是形容詞，一個是副詞，重音都在同一個位置。

> 延伸活用例句

You gave me extreme joy. 你給我極大的快樂。

We should avoid extremes. 我們應該避免走極端的路線。

We get on extremely well. 我們相處地極好。

I'm never an eloquent person and I can be extremely quiet sometimes.

我從來不是個能言善道的人，而且有的時候可以非常地安靜。

2. famous 有名的 adj.

　 infamous 聲名狼藉的；惡名昭彰的 adj.

> 　　infamous 和 famous 一樣，都是「有名的」的意思，但是 infamous 是因不好的名聲而有名，也就是「惡名昭彰」，跟 notorious（見P65）是一樣的意思。
>
> 　　由於 infamous 由 famous 延伸而來，因此很多同學會理所當然地把重音放在 fa 而念成 infamous，但這是不正確的喔！當你的重音念錯時，老外就會較難理解你說的話，你也聽不懂老外說什麼了。

延伸活用例句

I want to be famous.

我想成名。

The restaurant is famous for its seafood.

這間餐廳的海鮮很有名。

The infamous murderer was sentenced to death.

惡名昭彰的謀殺者被判死刑。

He wrote an essay on the infamous Watergate scandal.

他寫了一篇關於那不名譽的水門案的文章。

DAY 1
DAY 2
DAY 3
DAY 4
DAY 5
DAY 6
DAY 7
DAY 8
DAY 9
DAY 10
DAY 11
DAY 12
DAY 13
DAY 14

3. equal 平等的 adj.

　　unequal 不平等的 adj.

　　equality 平等 n.

　　inequality 不平等 n.

> equality 是 equal 的名詞，如果你以為 equality 的重音也在第一個音節可就錯了喔！equality 和 inequality 的重音都在 qua，練習說說看。

▶ 延伸活用例句

All men are created equal.

人生而平等。

Men and women had unequal education opportunities in the old days.

在古早時代，男性和女性是沒有平等的教育機會的。

Everybody had an equal chance.

每個人都有均等的機會。

Income inequality in our society is continuously increasing.

我們社會的貧富差距現象持續升高。

4. admire 仰慕；欽佩 v.
　　admirable 令人仰慕與欽佩的 adj
　　admiration 仰慕；欽佩 n.

> admirable 是 admire 的形容詞，因此很多同學會以為 admirable 的重音也在 mi，而把這個字念成了 admirable。以聽

DAY
1

DAY
2

DAY
3

DAY
4

DAY
5

DAY
6

DAY
7

DAY
8

DAY
9

DAY
10

DAY
11

DAY
12

DAY
13

DAY
14

力的角度來說，因為 admirable 的重音在第一個音節，聽起來跟 admire 不像，所以造成了同學就算認識 admire 這個字，在聽到老外說admirable時，也完全反應不過來，不知道其實就是 admire 的詞性變化而已，還以為是什麼從來沒聽過的新單字呢！另外，admiration 是名詞，重音在 ra，也要特別注意喔！

▶ 延伸活用例句

I admire him for his courage.

我欽佩他的勇氣。

His honesty is admirable.

他的誠實令人景仰。

I have a lot of admiration and respect for him.

我對他有非常多的仰慕和尊敬。

5. economy　經濟 n.
　/ɪ/
　economic　經濟的 adj.

　economical　節約的 adj.

　economics　經濟學 n.

economy 是經濟的意思，重音在 co。economic 是經濟的形容詞，而 economical 則是在使用資源上很經濟的，也就是很節省、很省錢的意思。兩個形容詞的重音都在 no。另外，economics 是名詞，是經濟學的意思，重音也在 no。

▶ 延伸活用例句

The world economy is going down.

世界經濟正在走下坡。

The experts believe that China's economic growth will continue.

專家相信中國的經濟會持續成長。

What's the most economical way of traveling around Taiwan?

什麼是在台灣環島旅行最經濟節省的方式？

She studied economics at college.

她在大學讀經濟學。

6. compete 競爭 v.

   competitive 好競爭的；有競爭力的 adj.

   competitor 競爭對手 n.

   competition 競爭者、競賽 n.

   competent 有能力的；能勝任的 adj.

   competence 能力；勝任 n.

> compete是競爭的意思，延伸出數個詞類變化。注意各個詞類變化的重音，練習説説看。

❯ 延伸活用例句

You need good language ability to compete in the job market.

你需要好的語言能力才能在職場上與人競爭。

Mary is a very competitive person.

瑪莉是個很好勝的人。

City café has become Starbucks' competitor.

城市咖啡已經成了星巴客的競爭對手。

We are in a market with no competition.

我們在一個沒有競爭者的市場。

He entered a singing competition and finished second.

他參加一個歌唱比賽得到第二名。

Workers who are incompetent can get fired.

能力不好的人會被炒魷魚。

Managers who hire people at work look for people with competence.

雇用人員的經理要找的是有能力的人。

> 舒葳老師小叮嚀

　　英文字的詞類變化常會有不同的重音，因此常會有聽得懂一個字的動詞，卻聽不懂它的名詞或形容詞的狀況。要克服這個問題、聽懂不同重音的詞類變化，可是有小撇步的喔！下一課就讓我們來學習重音變化的基本規則吧。

Lesson 2 > 字的重音規則

> 舒葳老師說　　(MP3) 04-3

　　字的重音變化是有規則可循的。雖然不是所有的字都符合以下的規則，瞭解這些基本規則仍可以幫助你掌握重音的原則，改善發音及聽力！

● Rule 1: 兩個音節的名詞，通常重音在第一音節

present 禮物 n.　permit 許可證 n.　product 產品 n. butter 奶油 n.

curtain 窗簾 n.　album 相本 n.　novel 小說 n.　liqueur 酒 n.

1k81

● Rule 2: 兩個音節的形容詞，通常重音在第一音節

pretty 漂亮的 adj.　fancy 花俏的 adj.　ugly 醜的 adj.　shining 發光的 adj.

shocking 令人震驚的 adj.　tempting 有誘惑力的 adj.

peaceful 和平的 adj.　perfect 完美的 adj.

● Rule 3: 兩個音節的動詞，通常重音在第二音節

present 呈現 v.　permit 許可 v.　produce 製造 v.　seduce 引誘 v.

combine 合併 v.　create 創造 v.　inhale 吸氣 v.　replace 取代 v.

注意，請比較這部份的前三個動詞及 **Rule 1** 的前三個名詞。

● Rule 4: 以 tion, sion, cian 結尾的字，通常重音在倒數第二音節
（ic, tion, sion, cian 前一音節）

solution 解決方案 n.　information 資訊 n.　operation 運作 n.

decision 決定 n.　permission 允許 n.　precision 明確性；精確度 n.

physician 內科醫生 n.　Christian 基督教徒 n.　magician 魔術師 n.

● Rule 5: 以 ic, ical 結尾的字，通常重音在倒數第三音節
（ical 前一音節）

realistic 現實的 adj.　aerobic 有氧的 adj.　strategic 策略性的 adj.

critical 批判的 adj.　economical 有經濟效益的 adj.　comical 喜劇的 adj.

political 政治的 adj.　cubical 立方體的 adj.　radical 激進的 adj.

● Rule 6: 以 ious, eous 結尾的字，通常重音在倒數第三音節
（ious, eous 前一音節）

curious 好奇的 adj.　notorious 惡名昭彰的 adj.　furious 火冒三丈的 adj.

dangerous 危險的 adj. instantaneous 即時的 adj.

outrageous 無法無天的；可憎的 adj.

● Rule 7: 以cy, ty, phy, gy 結尾的字，通常重音在倒數第三音節
（cy, ty, phy, gy前兩個音節）

democracy 民主 n. policy 政策 n. bureaucracy 官僚制度 n.

possibility 可能性 n. personality 人格 n. creativity 創造力 n.

philosophy 哲學 n. photography 攝影 n. geography 地理 n.

technology 科技 n. biology 生物學 n. psychology 心理學 n.

● Rule 8: 複合字。如果兩個英文字合起來成了一個獨立的新字，它
就是複合字。複合字無論連起來寫成一個字，或分成兩個字，在
意義上都是一個意思。

a. 複合名詞，通常重音在第一部份

greenhouse 溫室 n raincoat 雨衣 n. smoking room 吸煙室 n.

phone book 電話簿 n. high school 高中 n. rice cooker 電鍋 n.

b. 複合形容詞，通常兩個部份皆為重音

bad-tempered 脾氣壞的 adj.

old-fashioned 過時的 adj.

well-designed 設計良好的 adj.

well-mannered 有教養的；有禮貌的 adj.

poorly-made adj. 做得粗糙的 adj.

ill-fitting 不適宜的；不合的 adj.

c. 複合動詞，通常重音在第二部份的原重音

DAY
1

DAY
2

DAY
3

DAY
4

DAY
5

DAY
6

DAY
7

DAY
8

DAY
9

DAY
10

DAY
11

DAY
12

DAY
13

DAY
14

understand 瞭解 v.　underestimate　低估 v.

overlook 忽視 v.　overemphasize　過度強調 v.

❯|舒葳老師小叮嚀

　　如前所說，這些規則提供了我們英文字重音的基本原則，但是你可能也已經發現，還有許多字是無法套用於這些規則的。碰到了重音不確定的字，最好的方式是查字典，務必在新學一個單字時就確實掌握它正確的發音。如此一來，才能在剛開始就養成正確的發音習慣，也才能聽得正確囉！

Lesson 3 ❯ |標出重音節，並唸唸看

❯|舒葳老師說　(MP3) 04-4

　　請將下列各組單字標出重音節，並唸唸看。然後聽MP3，比較一下與老外的發音。

1.　suspect
　　suspect
　　suspicious
　　suspicion

2.　character
　　characteristic
　　characterization

3.　technology
　　technological
　　technician

4.　subscribe
　　subscriber
　　subscription

5.　courage
　　discourage
　　courageous

6.　a turn off
　　to turn off

DAY 1
DAY 2
DAY 3
DAY 4
DAY 5
DAY 6
DAY 7
DAY 8
DAY 9
DAY 10
DAY 11
DAY 12
DAY 13
DAY 14

▶ 詳細解說 04-5

1. sus**pect** 嫌疑犯（名詞）　　**sus**pect 懷疑（動詞）
　suspicious 疑心的（形容詞）　sus**pic**ion 疑心（名詞）

> suspect 可以是名詞，嫌疑犯，重音在前面（見 Lesson 2 Rule 1）；也可以是動詞，懷疑，重音在後面（見 Lesson 2 Rule 3）。

▶ 延伸活用例句

The prime suspect in the case committed suicide.

這件案子的主要嫌疑犯自殺了。

Who do you suspect stole the car?

你懷疑是誰偷了這台車？

I have a suspicion that he asked me out simply because you asked him to.

我懷疑他約我出去只是因為你叫他這麼做。

Don't be so suspicious.

不要疑心病這麼重。

2. **char**acter 性格（名詞）
　charac**ter**istic 特性（形容詞、名詞）
　characteri**za**tion 具有…的特性，電影、小說的人格塑造（名詞）

> character 是名詞，重音在第一音節；characteristic 因字

77

尾是 ic，重音節在 ic 的前一個音節（見 Lesson 2 Rule 5）；characterization 字尾是 tion，重音節在 tion 的前一個音節（見 Lesson 2 Rule 4）。

❯ 延伸活用例句

It would be very out of character for her to lie.

她如果說謊就太不像她的個性了。

She dealt with it with characteristic dignity.

她以一貫的自尊處理這件事。

A big nose is a family characteristic.

大鼻子是家族特徵。

3. technology 科技（名詞）

technological 科技的（形容詞）

technician 技師（名詞）

technology 字尾是 gy，重音在 gy 的前兩個音節（見 Lesson 2 Rule 7）；technological 因字尾是 ical，重音節在 ical 的前一個音節（見 Lesson 2 Rule 5）；technician 字尾是 cian，重音節在 cian的前一個音節（見 Lesson 2 Rule 4）。

❯ 延伸活用例句

Modern technology is simply amazing.

現代科技令人讚嘆。

We've seen tremendous technological changes over the last 20 years.

DAY
1

DAY
2

DAY
3

**DAY
4**

DAY
5

DAY
6

DAY
7

DAY
8

DAY
9

DAY
10

DAY
11

DAY
12

DAY
13

DAY
14

過去的二十年我們看到了劇烈的科技變化。

He works as a lab technician.

他是實驗室工程師。

4. subscribe 訂閱 v.
   subscriber 訂閱者 n.
   subscription 訂閱 n.

> subscribe 是兩音節的動詞，重音在第二個音節（見 Lesson 2 Rule 3）；subscriber 是 subscribe 的人，重音節仍在 scri；subscription 是指訂閱的這件事、這個動作，字尾是 tion，重音節在 tion 的前一個音節（見 Lesson 2 Rule 4）。

❯ 延伸活用例句

To subscribe to our newsletter, simply fill out this form here.

如果你要訂閱我們的通訊報，只要填這個表格就好了。

I am a subscriber of *National Geographic Magazine*.

我是《國家地理雜誌》的訂戶。

You can pay your subscription fee online.

你可以在網上付訂閱費用。

5. courage 勇氣 n.
   discourage 使洩氣；阻止 v.
   courageous 有勇氣的 adj.

> courage 是兩音節的名詞，重音在第一個音節（見 Lesson

> 2 Rule 1）；discourage 前面加 dis 是否定的意圖，重音節仍在 cour；courageous 字尾是 eous，重音節在 eous 的前一個音節（見 Lesson 2 Rule 6）。

▶ 延伸活用例句

I didn't have the courage to tell the truth.

我（那時）沒有勇氣說實話。

I was discouraged by what he said.

他說的話使我氣餒。

That was a very courageous thing to do.

那麼做需要非常大的勇氣。

6. to turn off 關掉

a turnoff 令人失去興趣的事

> 這裡 to turn off 是片語，是「關」的意思，turn 和 off 兩個字都是重音。a turnoff 中，turnoff 是複合名詞，如果有個人或事把你「關起來」了，就表示這個人或這件事是「令你失去興趣、令你倒胃的人／事／物」，重音在第一部份（見 Lesson 2 Rule 8, a.）。

▶ 延伸活用例句

Could you turn that light off, please?

可以請你把那盞燈關掉嗎？

His bad habits were a real turnoff.

他的壞習慣著實讓我對他失去興趣。

DAY
1

DAY
2

DAY
3

DAY
4

DAY
5

DAY
6

DAY
7

DAY
8

DAY
9

DAY
10

DAY
11

DAY
12

DAY
13

DAY
14

聽力小祕訣

☺ 學習單字時，務必確實找出正確的重音位置。

☺ 找到正確重音位置後，反覆大聲念出正確的發音能幫助你熟悉這個字的聲音。

☺ 有時候我們並不一定能確實聽清楚對方說的每個音節，但重音節能幫助你掌握一個字大致聽起來的音調，幫助你判斷出聽到的是什麼字喔。

MEMO

MEMO

DAY 5 句子的**重音與節奏**
It's a BEAUtiful DAY!

05-1~05-6

> **學習重點**

　　當同學在聽老外說英文時，常會希望聽清楚每一個字、每一個音，而一旦聽不清楚某幾個字，便開始驚慌失措，更加無法專心理解對方在說什麼了。但是你可能不知道，聽老外說英文時，其實並不需要聽懂每一個字！

　　今天，舒葳老師就要帶同學來學習如何善用句子重音和節奏聽出老外所要表達的重點喔！

Lesson 1 ▶ | 聽聽看，說說看

▶| **舒葳老師說** 05-1

請聽MP3，標出他說得最大聲、最清楚的音節／字：

1. Excellent!
2. It's a beautiful day!
3. It's hard to tell.
4. He's planning to resign.
5. Can I have some milk with my tea?
6. I don't think he'll do it.

▶| **詳細解說** 05-2

1. Excellent!
   太好了！

> 　　這個字的重音是 **Ex**，除了重音之外，你是否也有感覺到這個重音節也拉得特別長，反之，第二和第三個音節相對而言就說得較短呢？再聽聽看下面的句子，模仿 MP3 跟著說說看。所有的重音節都會拉得比較長喔！

▶| 延伸活用例句

Interesting!
有趣了！

DAY
1

DAY
2

DAY
3

DAY
4

DAY
5

DAY
6

DAY
7

DAY
8

DAY
9

DAY
10

DAY
11

DAY
12

DAY
13

DAY
14

Incredible!

真不可思議！

It's ridiculous!

太扯了！

It's unbelievable!

真不敢相信！

That's amazing!

真是太驚人了！

He's a man of determination.

他是個堅定的人。

2. It's a beautiful day!

天氣真好！

這個句子的重音是 beautiful 的 beau 和 day。你是否有感覺到這兩個音節拉得比較長，反之，其他的字或音節就說得較短呢？再聽一次，模仿 MP3 跟著說說看。再聽聽看下面的句子，模仿 MP3 跟著說說看。所有的重音節都會拉得比較長喔！

> 延伸活用例句

It's a wonderful thought!

真是個太好的想法了！

That's a brilliant idea!

真是個好主意！

It's a depressing day.

真是令人沮喪的一天。

That's a terrible joke.

真是個令人不舒服的笑話。

3. It's hard to tell.

很難說；很難分辨得出來。

這個句子的重音是 hard 和 tell。你是否有感覺到這兩個音節拉得比較長，反之，其他的字或音節就說得較短，也較不清楚呢？再聽一次，模仿 MP3 跟著說說看。再聽聽看下面的句子，模仿 MP3 跟著說說看。所有的重音節都會拉得比較長喔！

▶ │延伸活用例句

It's hard to believe.

很難相信。

It's impossible to tell.

不可能知道的。

It's likely to happen.

很有可能發生。

It's a stupid question to ask.

那是個很笨的問題。

It's a terrible thing to do.

那是很糟糕的行為。

4. He's planning to resign.

他計劃要辭職。

DAY
1

DAY
2

DAY
3

DAY
4

DAY
5

DAY
6

DAY
7

DAY
8

DAY
9

DAY
10

DAY
11

DAY
12

DAY
13

DAY
14

　　這個句子的重音是 planning 的 plan 和 resign 的 sign。你是否有感覺到這兩個音節拉得比較長，反之，其他的字或音節就說得較短、也較不清楚呢？再聽一次，模仿 MP3 跟著說說看。再聽聽看下面的句子，模仿 MP3 跟著說說看。所有的重音節都會拉得比較長喔！

▶ 延伸活用例句

He's going to quit.

他要辭職。

I'm going to propose.

我會求婚。

He's going to present.

他要做簡報。

I'm planning to study Engineering.

我計劃要讀工程學。

I'm happy to help.

我很樂意幫忙。

I've been meaning to tell you.

我一直想告訴你。

5. Can I have some milk with my tea?
可以在我的茶中加點牛奶嗎？

　　這個句子的重音是 milk 和 tea。你是否有感覺到這兩個音節拉得比較長，反之，其他的字或音節就說得較短、也較不清楚呢？再聽一次，模仿 MP3 跟著說說看。再聽聽看下面的句子，模仿 MP3

跟著說說看。所有的重音節都會拉得比較長喔！

▶ 延伸活用例句

Can I have some pepper with my soup?

我可以在湯中加點胡椒嗎？

I'd like some sugar with my coffee.

我的咖啡要加點糖。

You should drink some hot tea with honey.

你應該喝熱茶加點蜂蜜。

6. I don't think he'll do it.
   我不認為他會這麼做。

這個句子的重音是 don't think 和 do。你是否有感覺到這幾個音節拉得比較長，反之，其他的字或音節就說得較短呢？再聽一次，模仿 MP3 跟著說說看。再聽聽看下面的句子，模仿 MP3 跟著說說看。所有的重音節都會拉得比較長喔！

▶ 延伸活用例句

I don't remember him saying.

我不記得他這麼說過。

I didn't say it would be easy.

我沒有說會容易做。

I said it would be worth it.

我說會值得做。

DAY
1

DAY
2

DAY
3

DAY
4

**DAY
5**

DAY
6

DAY
7

DAY
8

DAY
9

DAY
10

DAY
11

DAY
12

DAY
13

DAY
14

He doesn't think he'll win the game.

他不覺得他會贏得這場比賽。

I don't believe he's telling the truth.

我不相信他說的是實話。

> **舒葳老師小叮嚀**

　　老外在說英文的時候並不是每個字都說得一樣重，因此同學在聽不清楚說得較輕的字時常會很緊張、會慌，反而聽不懂對方說的話。事實上，老外加重加長的字就是句子的重點，聽到了這些字，其實也就足夠了喔！下面我們就來瞭解英文句子重音的變化和如何能利用這些規則幫助我們聽得更輕鬆吧！

Lesson 2 > 句子重音與節奏的規則

> **舒葳老師說**

　　一個句子會強調的重音，一定是特別重要、需要對方聽清楚的字。而加重的音，也自然都會拉得比較長，比較容易聽得清楚喔！因此，我們在聽老外說話時，只要能掌握這些重且長的音，基本的意思也就抓到了。這課我們就來看看在一般的英語言談中，哪些類別的字特別容易強調拉長。

> **1.「內容字」與「架構字」**

　　英文句子中的字可以分成「內容字」和「架構字」兩類。「內容字」為帶有「意義」，也就是主導句子含意的字，包括：名詞、動詞、

否定助動詞、副詞、形容詞、疑問詞等。因為是整個句子所要傳達訊息的重點所在，這些字通常也是句子的重音所在，幫助我們聽到重要的資訊。

反之，「架構字」便不帶有這麼豐富的意義，包括：代名詞、介系詞、慣詞、be 動詞、連接詞。這些字的功能只是保持句子的文法正確而已，因此就算沒聽見，通常也不會影響我們的理解，因此不帶重音，說話時也是快快帶過。

● 內容字：

名　　　詞：meeting, book, bike, 等

動　　　詞：talk, read, go, 等

否定助動詞：don't, can't, won't, 等

副　　　詞：now, later, quickly, 等

形　容　詞：happy, beautiful, horrible, 等

疑　問　詞：who, what, where, when, why, how

● 架構字：

代名詞：he, she, it, 等

介系詞：in, of, to, 等

連接詞：and, but, because, 等

冠　詞：a, the be

動　詞：is, am, was, 等

● 例句練習　MP3 05-3

a.

This is my cat.（名詞）

What does it eat?（疑問詞）（動詞）

Please do it quickly.（副詞）（動詞）（副詞）

You did an excellent job.（形容詞）（名詞）

Why did you ask that question?（疑問詞）（動詞）（名詞）

Why didn't you write that letter?（疑問詞）（否定助動詞）（動詞）
（名詞）

　　你是否有發現上面的粗體字不僅說得比較大聲，花的時間也較其他字長呢？現在，請不要看書，再聽一次。把注意力放在重音即可，感受你是否能從重音及句子節奏抓到所要表達訊息的重點。

b.

Men like online games.

Men like the on-line games.

The men might like the on-line games.

Some of the men might have liked the on-line games here.

Some of the men might have liked some of the on-line games here.

　　注意，上面的從第一句延伸出來的各個句子，雖然句子越加越長，但加進去的都是「架構字」，因此句子的重音皆未改變，節奏也都與第一句 Men like computer games. 大致相同。這裡 might 加重音是因為 might 是「情態助動詞」強調可能的意思，是「內容字」。除此之外，其他的字都快快帶過，聽不清楚，對意思的理解也影響不大。

　　現在，請不要看書、再聽一次。把注意力放在重音即可，感受你是否能從重音及句子節奏抓到所要表達訊息的重點。

DAY 1
DAY 2
DAY 3
DAY 4
DAY 5
DAY 6
DAY 7
DAY 8
DAY 9
DAY 10
DAY 11
DAY 12
DAY 13
DAY 14

c.

Women like clothes.

The women like beautiful clothes.

The women like to dress themselves with beautiful clothes.

The women don't like to dress themselves with beautiful clothes.

Why don't the women like to dress themselves with beautiful clothes?

　　注意上面從第一句延伸出來的句子。後面加的字有內容字也有架構字，因此當句子變長，句子的重音節奏也有了變化。所有的粗體字都會説得清楚且大聲。反之，非粗體字部份聽不清楚並無大礙。

　　現在，請不要看書、再聽一次。把注意力放在重音即可，感受你是否能從重音及句子節奏抓到所要表達訊息的重點。

❯❯ | 2. Exercise: 05-4

　　聽聽看下面的短文，並模仿MP3跟著説説看。再聽一次，練習把注意力放在重音即可。

I'm studying this Pronunciation an(d) Lis(t)ening course. There's a lot to learn, but I find it very enjoyable. I think I will find it easier and easier to listen to native speakers speak in English, but the only way to really improve is to practice all of the time.

Now I can distinguish different vowels and consonants that sound similar, and I also pay more attention to stresses when I listen than I used to. I have been talking to a lot of native speakers of English lately and they tell me I'm easier to understand. Anyway, I could go on and on, but the important thing is to listen well and sound good. And I hope I'm getting better and better!

DAY 1
DAY 2
DAY 3
DAY 4
DAY 5
DAY 6
DAY 7
DAY 8
DAY 9
DAY 10
DAY 11
DAY 12
DAY 13
DAY 14

舒葳老師小叮嚀

　　英文句子中並不是每個字都說得一樣大聲一樣久的。影響句子意義的重要字詞會說得長、說得重，而只有文法功能，不影響意義傳達的字詞自然不需要太花力氣去強調。在這課我們介紹了英文句子重音與節奏的基本規則，只要能掌握這些句子中的重音、長音，我們在聽老外說話的時候，就不需因為漏聽了幾個字而慌張了。也就是說，聽力變得輕鬆多了，只要聽到重音就等於聽到全貌了喔！

Lesson 3 ▶ 再聽聽看

舒葳老師說 05-5

聽MP3，寫下重音字。

1. _____.

2. _____.

3. _____.

4. _____.

5. _____.

● Answers

5. How long have you been doing this sore of work?
4. University students pay a lot of money for their books.
3. Do you like the paintings in the conference room?
2. Sorry but I can't make it on Monday because I'm working late.
1. Thanks for inviting me.

▶ 詳細解說 05-6

1. Thanks for inviting me.
謝謝你邀請我。

> 　　這個句子的重音是 Thanks 和 inviting，其中 inviting 的重音又在vi。除了要養成聽重音的習慣，我們也要確保耳朵認識在句子中的inviting 這個字。為什麼這麼説呢？因為我們即使眼睛認識inviting這個字，在聽對方説話時，卻常因為對方説話速度快，我們只聽到vi 的重音而一時聽不出對方説的是 inviting。當重音在非第一音節的時候尤其容易聽不出來，這也是造成聽力困難的常見原因之一喔。
>
> 　　聽聽看下面的幾個句子，先不要看書並專注聽重音，你聽得出來他在説什麼嗎？多聽幾次，模仿 MP3 跟著説説看。
>
> This soup is delicious.
> 這湯真美味。
>
> He's so irresponsible.
> 他真不負責任。
>
> Turn left at the next intersection.
> 下個十字路口左轉。

2. Sorry but I can't make it on Monday because I'm working late.

94

抱歉我星期一不能去，因為我得加班。

> 這個句子的重音是 Sorry, can't make, Monday, working 和 late。其中 Monday 的重音又在 mon，working 的重音在 work。make it 是「做得到、去得了、趕得到」的意思。如果你剛才在做練習題時寫下了這些字，你是否就能抓到他要告訴你的訊息了呢？
>
> 聽聽看下面的幾個句子，先不要看書並專注聽重音，你聽得出來他在說什麼嗎？多聽幾次，模仿 MP3 跟著說說看。
>
> I didn't make it to the meeting last Friday.
> 我上週五沒趕得及參加會議。
>
> Do you think you'll make it to the party tonight?
> 你覺得你今晚能參加派對嗎？

3. Do you like the paintings in the conference room?
   你喜歡在會議室的畫嗎？

> 這個句子的重音是 like, paintings, conference 和 room。其中 paintings 的重音在 paint，conference 的重音在 con。conference room是「會議室」的意思。如果你剛才在做練習題時寫下了這些字，你應該就能抓到他要告訴你的訊息了。
>
> 聽聽看下面的幾個句子，先不要看書並專注聽重音，你聽得出來他在說什麼嗎？多聽幾次，模仿 MP3 跟著說說看。
>
> Have you met the new assistant in the payroll department?
> 你見過薪資部門那個新來的助理了嗎？
>
> Did you see the notice they put up the other day about postponing the meeting?
> 你看到他們那天張貼關於會議延期的佈告了嗎？

DAY 1
DAY 2
DAY 3
DAY 4
DAY 5
DAY 6
DAY 7
DAY 8
DAY 9
DAY 10
DAY 11
DAY 12
DAY 13
DAY 14

95

4. University students pay a lot of money for their books.
   大學生花很多錢在書上。

這個句子的重音是 University, students, pay, lot, money 和 books。其中 University 的重音在 ver，你可能會覺得 Uni 聽起來也像是重音，那是因為句首的第一個字如果是「內容字」時，聽起來會比較高昂。student 的重音在 tu，money 的重音在 mon。如果你剛才在做練習題時寫下了這些字，你應該就能抓到他要告訴你的訊息了。

聽聽看下面的幾個句子，先不要看書並專注聽重音，你聽得出來他在説什麼嗎？多聽幾次，模仿MP3跟著説説看。

He spends a lot of time online.
他花很多時間上網。

I know I spend a lot of time thinking about trying to save money.
我知道我花很多時間思考如何可以省錢。

Many of us dream of having thousands and thousands of dollars to spend on anything we desire.
我們很多人都夢想擁有百萬千萬的錢可以用來買任何我們想要的東西。

---

5. How long have you been doing this sort of work?
   這類的工作你做多久了？

這個句子的重音是How, long, doing, sort 和work。其中doing的重音在ing。如果你剛才在做練習題時寫下了這些字，你應該就能抓到他要告訴你的訊息了。

聽聽看下面的幾個句子，先不要看書並專注聽重音，你聽得出來他在説什麼嗎？多聽幾次，模仿MP3跟著説説看。

How long has he been the CEO of the company?

DAY
1

DAY
2

DAY
3

DAY
4

DAY
5

DAY
6

DAY
7

DAY
8

DAY
9

DAY
10

DAY
11

DAY
12

DAY
13

DAY
14

他當這個公司的執行長有多久了？

How often **do you** go **to this** sort **of place**?

你多常去這類的場所？

6. Do you **think it's** harder **to** speak **or to** understand **English**?

你覺得說英文和（聽）懂英文哪一個難？

這個句子的重音是 **think, harder, speak, understand** 和 **English**。其中 **harder** 的重音在 **hard**，**understand** 的重音在 **stand**。如果你剛才在做練習題時寫下了這些字，你應該就能抓到他要告訴你的訊息了。

聽聽看下面的幾個句子，先不要看書，你聽得出來他在說什麼嗎？多聽幾次，模仿 MP3 跟著說說看。

Do you **think it's** better **to** fly **or to** take **a train**?

你覺得坐飛機還是搭火車去比較好？

Which **is** easier, **to** learn bass **or** electric guitar?

哪一個比較容易，學貝斯還是電吉他？

> **聽力小秘訣**

☺ 不要嘗試聽到或聽懂每一個字，因為這不但是非常難以達成的目標，更常為我們帶來不需要的挫折感。

☺ 每一個人在說話時，都會自然地把希望對方聽到的重要訊息說得比較大聲、比較長，比較清楚。這些也是我們需要專注聽到的訊息。

☺ 把注意力放在抓到重音字，根據你能聽懂的數個重音字，便能快速拼湊對方要表達訊息的全貌。利用英文句子的重音與節奏能幫助你聽得更輕鬆。

☺ 如果聽見了重音仍是不能理解，便可能是單字或慣用語不足的問題，要趕緊加強這些不會的單字或慣用語。

☺ 自己平時說英文也應該利用重音與節奏，幫助老外更能理解你的英文。久而久之，你便能將自然的英文聲音內化，聽說都自然喔！

MEMO

DAY 6 非重點字的**弱化**—
Let's Rock'n Roll!

06-1~06-6

> **學習重點**

　　Day 5我們帶同學一起練習聽英文句子的重音，也就是所謂的「關鍵字」或句子的重點。今天我們便要來看看那些非重音的字，在老外的口中會起什麼樣的變化。一旦我們瞭解平時為什麼不容易聽懂這些字的原因，我們便能更進一步突破自己聽力上的障礙喔！

　　而在熟悉老外說話的習慣後，不僅你的聽力會進步，你的發音和口語表達也會更容易讓老外聽懂了！

也要加油已！

Lesson 1 ▶ 聽聽看，說說看

▶ 舒葳老師說 06-1

　　請練習說說看下面的句子。然後聽 MP3，比較看看你的發音跟
MP3 中老外發音有何不同。

1. I have bread and butter for breakfast.
2. I don't like any of them.
3. What do you mean?
4. Who's to blame?
5. More or less.
6. I've had enough of her.

▶ 詳細解說 06-2

1. I have bread and butter for breakfast.
我早餐都吃麵包塗奶油。

> 　　這個句子的重音字是 have, bread, butter 和 breakfast。除了
> 這幾個重音之外，你是否有注意到其他的字相對而言就說得較短，
> 母音也發得較不確實呢？再聽聽看下面的句子，模仿 MP3 跟著說
> 說看。重音字會拉得比較長，輕音字的母音則會弱化，念得又快又
> 短。

▶ 延伸活用例句

DAY
1

DAY
2

DAY
3

DAY
4

DAY
5

**DAY
6**

DAY
7

DAY
8

DAY
9

DAY
10

DAY
11

DAY
12

DAY
13

DAY
14

I had toast and jam for breakfast.

我今天早餐吃土司塗果醬。

I'll have cream and sugar with my coffee.

我的咖啡要加糖和奶精。

2. I don't like any of them.

這些我都不喜歡。

　　這個句子的重音是 don't, like 和 any。除了這幾個重音之外，你是否有注意到其他的字相對而言就說得較短，母音也發得較不確實呢？再聽聽看下面的句子，模仿 MP3 跟著說說看。重音字會拉得比較長，輕音字的母音則會弱化，念得又快又短。

▶ 延伸活用例句

I only know one of them.

我只認識他們的其中一個。

I really enjoy working with some of my colleagues.

我真的很喜歡跟我某些同事一起工作。

3. What do you mean?

你是什麼意思？

　　這個句子的重音是 What 和 mean。除了這幾個重音之外，你是否有注意到其他的字相對而言就說得較短，母音也發得較不確實呢？再聽聽看下面的句子，模仿 MP3 跟著說說看。重音字會拉得比較長，輕音字的母音則會弱化，念得又快又短。

❯ 延伸活用例句

Where did you go?

你去了哪裡？

Which one do you like?

你喜歡哪一個？

4. **Who's to blame?**

誰該為此負責？這件事該怪誰？

> 這個句子的重音是 **Who** 和 **blame**。除了這幾個重音之外，你是否有注意到其他的字相對而言就說得較短，母音也發得較不確實呢？再聽聽看下面的句子，模仿 **MP3** 跟著說說看。重音字會拉得比較長，輕音字的母音則會弱化，念得又快又短。

❯ 延伸活用例句

Who's to blame for the financial crisis?

誰該為財務危機負責？

We're all to blame.

我們都有責任。

I have no one to blame.

我不能責怪任何人。

5. **More or less.**

多多少少。

> 這個句子的重音是 **More** 和 **less**。除了這兩個重音之外，你是否有注意到 **or** 這個字相對而言就說得較短，母音也發得較不確實呢？再聽聽看下面的句子，模仿 **MP3** 跟著說說看。重音字會拉得

比較長，輕音字的母音則會弱化，念得又快又短。

❯ 延伸活用例句

Are you talking about John or Mary?

你在說的是約翰還是瑪莉？

It's now or never.

現在不做就沒機會了。

6. **I've had enough of her.**
我受夠她了。

這個句子的重音是 had 和 enough。除了這兩的重音字之外，你是否有注意到其他的字相對而言就說得較短，母音也發得較不確實呢？再聽聽看下面的句子，模仿 MP3 跟著說說看。重音字會拉得比較長，輕音字的母音則會弱化，念得又快又短。

❯ 延伸活用例句

Have you had enough to eat?

你有吃飽嗎？

He isn't good enough for you.

他配不上妳。

❯ 舒葳老師小叮嚀

老外在說英文的時候並不是每個字都說得一樣重，重要的字講得大聲，不重要的字會相對弱化，同學也常會因為聽不清楚或聽不懂這些說得較輕的字而緊張慌亂。但是現在我們已經知道，原來我們常聽不清楚

DAY 1 DAY 2 DAY 3 DAY 4 DAY 5 DAY 6 DAY 7 DAY 8 DAY 9 DAY 10 DAY 11 DAY 12 DAY 13 DAY 14

這些字，有很大的原因是因為老外在說這類字的時候發音弱化了。跟我們原本想像的發音不同，也難怪我們會聽不懂。下面我們就來進一步了解，到底這些輕音的字，老外會怎麼說吧！

Lesson 2 ▶ 弱化的聲音

▶ 舒葳老師說

　　一個句子中不需強調的輕音字會弱化，因為對方是否聽得清楚都不是很重要，因此就會說得較快、較輕、較短，而產生了弱化的現象。這些弱化的聲音都會發 [ə] 的聲音。這課我們就來練習弱化音的發音，讓自己聽得更懂、說得也更標準。請注意，以下均使用*斜體字*表示弱化的音節。

▶ 1. 弱音規則　　🎧 06-3

● Rule 1: 單字弱音節的弱化音

在單字中，弱音節弱化。

ban*a*n*a*

Europ*e*

wom*a*n

surf*ace*

*a*ddition

*e*conom*i*cs

● Rule 2: 句子弱音字的弱化

在句子中，重音字的輕音節或輕音字母音皆弱化。

As usual.

Look at this.

Which one do you want?

There are as many as two thousand.

You are the sunshine of my life.

Leave them at the door

以下是常聽見的弱化字。聽MP3，練習説説看。

to

See you tonight. 今晚見。

He went to work. 他去工作了。

Don't jump to conclusions. 不要妄下結論。

You've got to pay to get it. 要付費才能使用。

Let's go to lunch. 去吃午餐吧。

So to speak. 好比説。

and

ham an(d) eggs 火腿蛋

gold an(d) jewelry 黃金和珠寶

Coffee? With cream an(d) sugar? 咖啡？加糖和奶精嗎？

They watched it again an(d) again. 他們看了一次又一次。

They kept going back an(d) forth. 他們不停地來來回回。

We learned by trial an(d) error. 我們從嘗試與錯誤中學習。

or

Soup or salad? 湯還是沙拉？

One or two? 一個或兩個？

DAY
1
DAY
2
DAY
3
DAY
4
DAY
5
DAY
6
DAY
7
DAY
8
DAY
9
DAY
10
DAY
11
DAY
12
DAY
13
DAY
14

Now *or* later? 現在還是等會？

More *or* less. 多多少少。

For here *or* to go? 這邊用還是帶走？

Are you going up *or* down?（電梯中）你往上還是往下？

can

I *can* do it. 我辦得到。

Can it wait? 可以等嗎？

No one *can* fix it. 沒有人能修得好。

What *can* I do? 我能怎麼辦？

They *can* afford the house. 他們買得起這棟房子。

I don't think you *can* open the cans.

我不覺得你可以打開這些罐頭。

of

all *of* them 他們全部

the rest *of* it 剩下的

That's the best *of* all! 那真是最好的！

As a matter *of* fact, ... 事實上⋯

Get out *of* here. 滾出去。

What's the name *of* the game? 這遊戲叫什麼？

are

What *are* you doing? 你在做什麼？

Where *are* you going? 你要去哪裡？

What *are* you planning on doing? 你打算怎麼做？

Those *are* no good. 那些不好。

How *are* you doing? 你好嗎？

The*y are* all back. 他們都回來了。

● Rule 3: 縮音

你讀到的是…	你聽到的是…
I am	I'm
he is that is there is he is not he has he has not	he's that's there's he isn't he's he hasn't
I would I should I would not I would not	I'd I'd I'd not I wouldn't
I do not I cannot I will I will not I will not	I don't I can't I'll I'll not I won't
I have we have they have I had	I've we've they've I'd

DAY
1

DAY
2

DAY
3

DAY
4

DAY
5

DAY
6

DAY
7

DAY
8

DAY
9

DAY
10

DAY
11

DAY
12

DAY
13

DAY
14

I would have	I'd've
I wouldn't have	I wouldn't've
I should have	I should've
I shouldn't have	I shouldn't've
I could have	I could've
I couldn't have	I couldn't've
I might have	I might've

▶ | 2. Exercise 06-4

再聽聽看下面的短文，注意弱化音的發音，並跟著說說看。

I'm studying this Pronunciation *and* Listening course. There's a lot *to* learn, but I find it very enjoyable. I think I will find it easier and easier *to* listen *to* native speakers speak in English, but the only way *to* really improve is *to* practice all *of* the time.

Now I *can* distinguish different vowels *and* consonants that sound similar, *and* I also pay more attention *to* stresses when I listen than I used to. I have been talking *to* a lot *of* native speakers *of* English lately *and* they tell me I'm easier *to* understand. Anyway, I could go on *and* on, but the important thing is *to* listen well *and* sound good. And I hope I'm getting better *and* better!

▶ 舒葳老師小叮嚀

　　英文句子中並不是每個字都說得一樣大聲、一樣久的。影響句子意義的重要字詞會說得長、說得重，而只有文法功能不影響意義傳達的字詞自然不需要太花力氣去強調。在這課我們帶同學一起發

現與體會老外在弱音字的發音方式，只要能掌握這些句子中的重音與弱音分別是如何說的，我們在聽老外說話的時候，就更容易掌握對方說的話了！

Lesson 3 ❯ 再聽聽看

❯ 舒葳老師說　🎵 06-5

寫出你聽到的句子：

1. _____.

2. _____.

3. _____.

4. _____.

5. _____.

6. _____.

● Answers

6. We've eaten.

5. They've gone.

4. I've cut the bread.

3. I'd've come if I'd known.

2. I wouldn't've have done it without you.

1. You should've told her.

DAY
1

DAY
2

DAY
3

DAY
4

DAY
5

**DAY
6**

DAY
7

DAY
8

DAY
9

DAY
10

DAY
11

DAY
12

DAY
13

DAY
14

▶詳細解說 (MP3) 06-6

1. You should've told her.
   你應該告訴她的。

> You should have told her. 會說成 You should've told her. 意思是說「你應該告訴她的（你卻沒告訴她）」。請比較下面的句子並練習跟著說說看。
>
> You should've told her. 你應該要告訴她的。
>
> You shouldn't've told her. 你不該告訴她的。

2. I wouldn't have done it without you.
   沒有你我是不可能做得到的。

> I wouldn't have done it. 會說成 I wouldn't've done it. 這整句話的意思是說「沒有你我是不可能做得到的（但是因為有你的幫忙，所以做到了」。請比較下面的句子並練習跟著說說看。
>
> I would've done it. 我本來應該做得到的。
>
> I wouldn't've done it. 我本來應該做不到的。

3. I'd've come if I'd known.
   我要是早知道，我就會來了。

> I would have come if I had known. 會說成 I'd've come if I'd known. 是「我要是早知道我就會來了（但是我不知道所以也沒來）」的意思。請比較下面的句子並練習跟著說說看。
>
> I'd've come if I'd known. 我要是早知道，我就會來了。

I wouldn't've come if I'd known. 我要是早知道，我就不會來了。

4. I've cut the bread.
我已經切好麵包了。

I have cut the bread. 會說成 I've cut the bread. 請比較下面的句子並練習跟著說說看。

I've cut the bread. 我已經切好麵包了。

I'll cut the bread. 我等會會切麵包。

5. They've gone.
他們已經走了。

They have gone. 會說成 They've gone. 這裡的重點是要熟悉 gone 是 go 的過去分詞。請比較下面的句子並練習跟著說說看。

They've gone. 他們已經走了。

They'll go. 他們會去。

6. We've eaten.
我們吃過了。

We have eaten. 會說成 We've eaten. 這裡的重點是要熟悉 eat 是 eaten 的過去分詞。另外，你是否有發現，eaten 的 t 消音了呢？請比較下面的句子並練習跟著說說看。

We've eaten. 我們吃過了。

We'll eat. 我們會去吃。

DAY 1
DAY 2
DAY 3
DAY 4
DAY 5
DAY 6
DAY 7
DAY 8
DAY 9
DAY 10
DAY 11
DAY 12
DAY 13
DAY 14

❯ 聽力小秘訣

☺ 老外說話時，會把重點放在重要的內容字。而不那麼重要的字，也就是架構字，便會自然地弱化。

☺ 在口語中，弱化字的母音皆會發 [ə] 的聲音，跟我們單獨念那個單字本身的時候，發音其實是有些不同的。

☺ 熟悉弱化字的發音方式會幫助我們聽得更懂。

☺ 自己平時說英文也應該學習老外說話的方式，強化內容字、弱化架構字。當你說話的方式更接近老外的說話方式，他們也就更能理解你的英文了。

MEMO

DAY 7 連音變化

Tele ri mi ser? Tell her I miss her!

07-1~07-6

> **學習重點**

　　我們先看看這章的標題。你知道 **"Tell her I miss her."** 在老外口中，聽起來會像是 **Tele ri mi ser.** 嗎？為什麼會這樣呢？

　　事實上，不只是這句話，很多時候老外說的話會令我們摸不著頭腦，都是因為在一般英文口語中，說話一說得快，便會產生所謂的「連音」現象。原本是分開的字聲音連在了一起，也難怪我們會聽不懂了。

　　今天，我們就來看看各種連音的現象。瞭解了英文連音變化的規則後，聽力自然會進步喔！

you can't understand while reading those dots separately. When u look behind, you will discover that all these dots will be connected into a line — that is, your life.

~ by Steve Jobs

Lesson 1 ▶ | 聽聽看，寫寫看

▶ 舒葳老師說　**MP3** 07-1

請聽MP3，寫下你聽到的句子。

1. _____.

2. _____.

3. _____.

4. _____.

5. _____.

6. _____.

● Answers

1. I'm sick of it.　2. Here's a bag of candy.　3. We agree.　4. I'll deal with it.　5. We have a deep pot.　6. As soon as you can.

▶ 詳細解說　**MP3** 07-2

1. I'm sick of it.
我厭倦透了。

> I'm sick of it. 聽起來會像是 I'm si cko fi(t). 最後的 t 會消音或

只發氣音。再聽聽看下面的句子，模仿 MP3 跟著說説看。

❯ 延伸活用例句

I'm tired of it.

我厭倦透了。

I'm sure of it.

我很確定。

2. Here's a bag of candy.

這裡是一袋糖。

> Here's a bag of candy. 聽起來會像是 Here'sa bagof candy. 再聽聽看下面的句子，模仿 MP3 跟著說説看。

❯ 延伸活用例句

Can you get me a pack of cigarettes? 你可以幫我買一包煙嗎？

Ther(e) is a carton of milk in the fridge. 冰箱有一盒牛奶。

3. We agree.

我們同意。

> We agree. 聽起來會像是 Wea gree. 再聽聽看下面的句子，模仿 MP3 跟著說説看。

❯ 延伸活用例句

We oppose it. 我們反對這件事。

He enjoyed it. 他很喜歡。

DAY
1

DAY
2

DAY
3

DAY
4

DAY
5

DAY
6

DAY
7

DAY
8

DAY
9

DAY
10

DAY
11

DAY
12

DAY
13

DAY
14

4. I'll deal with i(t).

我會處理。

> I'll deal with it. 聽起來會像是 I'll deal withi(t).最後的 t 會消音。
再聽聽看下面的句子，模仿 MP3 跟著説説看。

❯ 延伸活用例句

I can't cope with it.

我無法承受。

Can you manage it?

你處理得來嗎？

5. We hav(e) a deep po(t).

我們有一只較深的鍋子。

> We have a deep pot. 聽起來會像是 We hav(e)a deepo(t).
have 的 e 不發音，最後的 t 也會消音。再聽聽看下面的句子，模仿
MP3 跟著説説看。

❯ 延伸活用例句

Stop pushing me around.

不要一直指使我做這個做那個。

I hav(e) a black cat.

我有一隻黑貓。

6. As soon as you can.

儘快。

DAY
1

DAY
2

DAY
3

DAY
4

DAY
5

DAY
6

**DAY
7**

DAY
8

DAY
9

DAY
10

DAY
11

DAY
12

DAY
13

DAY
14

As soon as you can. 聽起來會像是 A ssoonasyou can. 再聽聽看下面的句子，模仿 MP3 跟著說說看。

> 延伸活用例句

We'll go as soon as (h)e comes.

他一來我們就走。

I'll come back as soon as possible.

我們儘快回來。

> 舒葳老師小叮嚀

　　英文的連音是造成同學聽不懂老外說的主音之一。但我們在學校學英文時，卻很少有老師會特別教我們連音的規則。事實上，連音的道理很簡單，話說得快了，音也自然就連在一塊了！但話又說回來，我們如果不瞭解連音形成的方式，就是想說快也快不了。長久以來，我們說英文的習慣便與老外不同，聽到老外說話也就較不容易反應得過來了。因此，有系統地學習連音的方式和規則對我們的發音和聽力都會有很大的幫助喔！

Lesson 2 > 連音規則

> 舒葳老師說　🎵 07-3

　　老外在說話時，可不是每一個字都是獨立分開的。反之，字與字之間會自然連貫在一起。英文的連音可以分為三大類：子音與母音的連音，母音與母音的連音，以及子音與子音的連音。我們現在

就分別來看看這三類連音的規則吧！

● 1.Consonant-to-Vowel　子音接母音的連音

當前一個字尾音是子音、後一個字的字首是母音時，便會產生子音接母音的連音。請看下例：

a. 短句

1. Stop it. 不要這樣。

2. Prov(e) it. 證明給我看。

3. Com(e) on. 別這樣。

4. Watch out! 小心！

5. I'll ask. 我問問看。

6. Hav(e) a look. 看一下。

b. 長句

1. Can I help you? 需要幫忙嗎？

2. Did we los(e) anything? 我們有掉任何東西嗎？

3. Switch off the light. 關燈。

4. You can always chang(e) your mind. 你總是可以改變主意的。

5. Do you want to shar(e) a taxi? 你要共乘一輛計程車嗎？

6. It didn't work out. 沒成功。

c. t + 母音的連音：t 彈舌音（見Day 3, p.61）

1. What a mess. 真是一團亂。

2. Put it on. 穿上；戴上。

DAY
1

DAY
2

DAY
3

DAY
4

DAY
5

DAY
6

**DAY
7**

DAY
8

DAY
9

DAY
10

DAY
11

DAY
12

DAY
13

DAY
14

3. Not at all. 一點也不會。

4. He's a lot of fun. 他很有趣。

5. That is what I mean. 我就是那個意思。

6. It's been quit(e) a long time. 已經有好一段時間了。

d. h 消音後的連音（見Day 3, p.61）

1. Is this (h)is book? 這是他的書嗎？

2. I think (h)e is the one. 我覺得就是他。

3. We need (h)im now. 我們現在需要他。

4. Did you tell (h)im about Michael? 你有跟他說麥可的事嗎？

5. Why don't you tak(e) (h)er to that new restaurant? 你何不帶她
去那間新餐廳？

6. Did you ask (h)er about that? 你有問她那件事嗎？

● 2. Vowel-to-Vowel 母音接母音的連音

當前一個字尾音是母音，後一個字的字首也是母音時，便會產
生母音接母音的連音。要注意的是，母音和母音連音的時候，聽起
來常常會像是中間多了一個子音喔。請看下例：

a. 當第一個字字尾母音發 [o]、[aʊ]、[u]、[ʊ]、[ju] 時，與下一個
字的字首母音間以 (w) 連接

你讀到的是這樣…	你聽到的是這樣…
do it	do wit
do I	do wl
how often	how woften
no other	no wother

you ought	you wought
due in	due win
know if	know wif
so I'll	so wI'll

b. 當第一個字字尾母音發 [i]、[ɪ]、[aɪ]、[eɪ] 時，與下一個字的字首母音間以 [j] 連接

你讀到的是這樣…   你聽到的是這樣…

see it	see yit
may I	may yI
she is	she yiz
we ought	we yought
high up	hi yup
the end	the yend
be in	be yin
I am	I yam

c. 例句

1. Do I know this guy?

   我認識這個人嗎？

2. How often do you think this happens?

   你覺得這種事多久會發生一次？

3. I don't know how to do it.

   我不知道怎麼做。

4. Don't you see it?

DAY
1

DAY
2

DAY
3

DAY
4

DAY
5

DAY
6

**DAY
7**

DAY
8

DAY
9

DAY
10

DAY
11

DAY
12

DAY
13

DAY
14

你還看不清嗎？你還不明白嗎？

5. We've finally come to the end of the tunnel.

我們終於來到黑暗的盡頭了；辛苦的日子終於快過去了。

6. She is the one I told you about.

她就是我告訴你的那個人。

● 3. Consonant-to-consonant　子音接子音的連音

　　當前一個字的字尾是子音，後一個字的字首也是子音時，便可能會產生子音接子音的連音。子音與子音的連音包括下面幾種情形：

a.　前一個子音與後一個子音發音相同時，兩個子音當一個聲音發

1. Do you want to? 你想這麼做嗎？

2. Open the red door. 打開那道紅色的門。

3. I wish she'd come. 我真希望她能來。

4. That's a bad dog. 那是一隻壞狗。

5. Our luck could change. 我們的運氣可能會改變。

6. Leav(e) it to me. 交給我。

b.　t + y 的連音

1. I'll meet you there. 我跟你在那裡見面。

2. He's gonna beat you. 他會揍你。

3. Don't you like it? 你不喜歡嗎？

4. I hat(e) you. 我恨你。

121

5. I went there last year. 我去年去的。

6. I don't care what you say. 我不在乎你說什麼。

c. d + y 的連音

1. Would you come? 你會來嗎？

2. Could you say that again? 你可以再說一次嗎？

3. Did you hear that? 你聽到了嗎？

4. Where did you get that from? 你那是哪來的？

5. How would you like your steak? 你的牛排要幾分熟？

6. How could you do that? 你怎麼可以那麼做？

● 4. Exercise： 07-4

再聽聽看下面的短文，注意連音，並跟著說說看。

I'm studying this Pronunciation and Listening book. There's a lot to learn, but I find it very enjoyable. I think I will find it easier and easier to listen to native speakers speak in English, but the only way to really improve, is to practice all of the time.

Now I can distinguish different vowels and consonants that sound similar, and I also pay mor(e) attention to stresses when I listen than I used to. I have been talking to a lot of native speakers of English lately and they tell me I'm easier to understand. Anyway, I could go on an(d) on, but the important thing is to listen well and sound good. And I hop(e) I'm getting better and better!

DAY 1

DAY 2

DAY 3

DAY 4

DAY 5

DAY 6

DAY 7

DAY 8

DAY 9

DAY 10

DAY 11

DAY 12

DAY 13

DAY 14

> 舒葳老師小叮嚀

　　熟悉連音的規則，可以幫助我們在說英文時說得既順又快喔！不過同學要記得，學會了規則後還得要常常練習，才會讓連音成為你平時說話時自然的習慣。同學不妨多聽廣播或任何有錄音的英文文章或對話，一邊聽一邊畫下連音記號，多聽幾次並跟著念。平時自己閱讀文章時，也可以試試看自己是否能自然地把字與字連在一起喔！

Lesson 3 **>** 再聽聽看

> 舒葳老師說　 07-5

請聽MP3，寫下你聽到的句子。

1. _____.

2. _____.

3. _____.

4. _____.

5. _____.

6. _____.

7. _____.

8. _____.

9. _____.

10. _____.

● Answers

（以下為上下顛倒印刷之文字）

1. Can you tell me your office hours?
2. That wasn't a fair answer.
3. I'm in a rush I'm afraid.
4. When did (h)e go there?
5. He is practicing as much as (h)e can.
6. What you see is what you get.
7. Have you heard of this singer?
8. It's due in two weeks.
9. I'll be in in a minute.
10. It'll be over in an hour.

 詳細解說　07-6

1. Can you tell me your office hours?
你可以告訴我你們的上班時間嗎？

office hours 會說成 office(h)ours，其中 h 消音，因此 ce [s] 會直接連到 ours [aʊrz]；用連音記號表示就是：Can you tell me your office (h)ours? office hours 就是「上班時間、營業時間」，也可以說成 business hours。請唸唸看下面的句子，聽 MP3，練習跟著說說看。

Our business (h)ours are from nin(e) am to fiv(e) pm Monday through Friday.
我們的營業時間是週一到週五，早上九點到下午五點。

U.S. Postal Service reduces offic(e) (h)ours to offset reduced volume.
美國的郵政服務減少營業時間以減少需求量降低的影響。

How long does it take to get there during rush (h)our?

DAY
1

DAY
2

DAY
3

DAY
4

DAY
5

DAY
6

DAY
7

DAY
8

DAY
9

DAY
10

DAY
11

DAY
12

DAY
13

DAY
14

尖峰時刻到那裡要多久？

2. That wasn't a fair answer.
那麼說不公平。

wasn't a 會說成 wasn'ta，fair answer 會說成 fairanswer；用連音記號表示就是：That wasn't a fair answer. 請唸唸看下面的句子，再聽 MP3，練習跟著說說看。

He isn't a good cook. 他不是個好廚師。

It isn't a bad idea. 那不是個壞主意。

3. I'm in a rush I'm afraid.
很抱歉我在趕時間。

這句話說得快時，除了a 和rush 不連音外，每個字都會跟前一個字連音，因此這句話可以說成 Imina rushimafriad. 用連音記號表示就是：I'm in a rush I'm afraid. in a rush 就是「趕時間」；I'm afriad是「恐怕」的意思，用在告訴對方壞消息、表達歉意時。請唸唸看下面的句子，再聽MP3，練習跟著說說看。

I won't be availabl(e) I'm afraid. 恐怕我不會有空。

We'r(e) in a hurry. 我們在趕時間。

I'm in a very difficult position. 我立場很困難。

4. When did he go there?
他什麼時候去那裡的？

125

did he 可以說成 did(h)e，其中因為 h 消音，did 的尾音 d [d] 會直接連到 he 的 e [i]；用連音記號表示就是：When di̲d (h)e go there? 請唸唸看下面的句子，再聽 MP3，練習跟著說說看。

How di̲d (h)e do i̲(t)? 他是怎麼辦到的？

When i̲s (h)e going to ge(t) married? 他何時才要結婚？

5. He is practicing as much as he can.
   他現在一有空就練習。

He is 中 He 的 e [i] 和 is 的 i [I] 連音，母音與母音的連音中間可加上 [j]，幫助連音連得更順，說成 He(y)is，as much as he 說成 as muchas(h)e，h 消音，因此 as 的 s [s] 會直接連到 he 的 e [i]。用連音記號表示就是：He̲ is practicing as muc̲h a̲s (h)e can. as much as 就是「儘可能、儘量多」；as much as he can 就是「他只要有機會就會做」的意思。請唸唸看下面的句子，再聽 MP3，練習跟著說說看。

She can hav̲(e) as muc̲h a̲s she wants.
她要有多少就可以有多少。

We should communicat̲(e) as muc̲h a̲s possible.
我們應該儘可能地常溝通。

6. What you see is what you get.
   你看到的就是你會得到的。

What you 的 t 和 y 連音會發 [tʃ]，see is 連音則可以說成

DAY
1

DAY
2

DAY
3

DAY
4

DAY
5

DAY
6

DAY
7

DAY
8

DAY
9

DAY
10

DAY
11

DAY
12

DAY
13

DAY
14

see(y)is 。這句話用連音記號表示就是：What you see is what you ge(t). 這句話的意思就是「你現在看到的就是你能得到的」，表示你眼前的一切都是真實的，不會改變，不會有假；這句話也可以用來表示「我就是這樣的一個人，你不用想要改變我」。

小甜甜布蘭妮有一首歌的歌名就叫做 *"What You See is What You Get"* 喔！請唸唸看下面的句子畫上連音記號，再聽MP3，練習跟著說說看。

I mean what I say. 我說的話是真心的。

You asked for i(t); you got i(t). 你要求的，現在你得到了。

To see is to believe. 眼見為真。

7. Have you heard of this singer?
你有聽過這個歌手嗎？

Have you 中 have 的 v (e消音) 和 you 的 y 連音，說成 havyou；heard of 的 d 和 o 連音，說成 heardof；this singer 中 this 的尾音 s 和 singer 的字首 s 連音，說成 thisinger。 這句話用連音記號表示就是：Hav(e) you heard of this singer? 請唸唸看下面的句子畫上連音記號，再聽 MP3，練習跟著說說看。

We both think it's good. 我們兩人都覺得好。

Pleas(e) say you love me. 請說你愛我。

8. It's due in two weeks.
兩週後到期。

due in 的 ue [ju] 和 in 的 i [I] 連音，母音與母音的連音中間可

加上 [w] 的聲音，幫助連音連得更順，發成 due(w)in。這句話用連音記號表示就是：It's due in two weeks. due 的意思是「到期」，in two weeks 是「兩週後」，所以這句話的意思就是「兩週後到期」，通常用來指兩週後要完成某項工作。請唸唸看下面的句子，再聽 MP3，練習跟著說說看。

The bank loan is due in a month. 銀行貸款一個月後就到期了。

Her train is due at 8 a.m. 她的火車預定早上八點到。

9. I'll be in in a minute.
我馬上進去。

be 的 e [i] 和 in 的 i [I] 連音，母音與母音的連音中間可加上 [j] 的聲音，幫助連音連得更順，發成 be(y)in。in 和 in 連音，in 和 a 又連音，因此這句話會說成：I'll be(y)inina minute. 用連音記號表示就是：I'll be in in a minute. 在這裡，I'm be in. 的意思就是「我會進去」，可以用來表示「進辦公室」；in a minute 就是「一分鐘後」，其實就是「很快」的意思。請唸唸看下面的句子，再聽 MP3，練習跟著說說看。

Will you be in? 你會在嗎？

Ill be ou(t). 我會出去。

10. It'll be over in an hour.
一個小時之內就會結束。

be 的 e [i] 和 over 的 o [o] 連音，母音與母音的連音中間可加上 [j] 的聲音，幫助連音連得更順，發成 be(y)over。此外，over 和

DAY
1

DAY
2

DAY
3

DAY
4

DAY
5

DAY
6

DAY
7

DAY
8

DAY
9

DAY
10

DAY
11

DAY
12

DAY
13

DAY
14

in 連音，in 和 an 連音，an 和 hour 又連音，因此這句話會說成：It'll be(y)overinan(h)our. 用連音記號表示就是：It'll be over in an (h)our. 在這裡，I'm be in. 的意思就是「我會進去」，可以用來表示「進辦公室」；in a minute 就是「一分鐘後」，其實就是「很快」的意思。請唸唸看下面的句子，再聽 MP3，練習跟著說說看。

It's not over yet. 還沒結束。

It's all over now. 全完了；都結束了。

Start it all over again. 再從頭開始一次。

〉 聽力小秘訣

☺ 老外說話時，會自然地把字連在一起說。耳朵須能熟悉連音的聲音，才不會反應不過來而聽不懂老外在說什麼。

☺ 多聽英文的MP3，一邊看稿子，一邊聽。體會老外連音的使用，並跟著模仿，讓耳朵和嘴巴都能習慣各種組合的連音。一旦聽過了，也熟悉了，未來再聽到時就不會聽不懂了。

☺ 平時在閱讀英文時，也可以利用連音的規則，讓自己練習用連音讀出英文句子。長期下來可以讓自己在平時說英文時也能自然地使用連音。如此一來，你的英文聽說能力就都能有長足的進步了喔！

MEMO

DAY 8 | 語調與弦外之音
What would you like?

08-1~08-5

我們先看看這章的標題。這句話的重音應該放在哪裡呢？試著説説看。

你知道嗎？當重音放在不同的地方的時候，也會改變這句話的意思喔！如果你能掌握重音位置所傳達的意義，也會幫助你聽得更容易、了解更順暢呢！

現在，我們就來看看英文中音調的各種改變所代表的意義。了解了英文音調的變化規則，不但聽力會進步，你也能説出更道地的英文喔！

"我愛你"

Lesson 1 ➤ 聽聽看，說說看

➤ 舒葳老師說　08-1

請聽MP3，想想看起來A、B與C 各組中，每個句子各表達什麼意思。

A. 1. What would you like?

   2. What would you like?

   3. What would you like?

   4. What would you like?

B. 1. I didn't hire Jane.

   2. I didn't hire Jane.

   3. I didn't hire Jane.

   4. I didn't hire Jane.

C. 1. Where can we go?

   2. Where can we go?

   3. Where can we go?

   4. Where can we go?

➤ 詳細解說　08-2

A. What would you like?

DAY
1

DAY
2

DAY
3

DAY
4

DAY
5

DAY
6

DAY
7

**DAY
8**

DAY
9

DAY
10

DAY
11

DAY
12

DAY
13

DAY
14

What would you like? 這句話一般而言，句子的最重音會放在 like，也就是上面的最後一句：What would you like? 意思是說：「你想來點什麼？」用在替人點餐的時候。不過，這句話如果重音放在不同的位置，想強調的意思也不同喔！

上面第一句中，重音放在 What，What would you like? 強調「你想來點什麼？」。可能是他在說這句話時對方聽錯了而回答了「他想要某個人之類的」，因此問問題的人再次強調他問的是他想要「什麼」。

第二句，重音放在 would，What would you like? 強調「你想來點什麼？」，翻成中文就有「你到底想要什麼」的意思，表示對方已經說了他不要這個，也不要那個，似乎給他什麼他都不能滿意。因此問話的人這麼說，意思是：「那你到底要什麼」。這樣的語氣，有抱怨的意思喔！

第三句，重音放在 you，What would you like? 強調「你想來點什麼？」，表示別人已經點過餐了，該你點了。那「你」要什麼呢？

是不是很有趣呢？懂得聽老外的音調和重音，才能正確掌握對方要表達的意思喔！下面我們再聽一次 MP3，練習說說看吧！

聽說練習與整理

1. What **would** you like? = 我不是問「誰」，我問的是「什麼」。

2. What **would** you like?

   = 你已經說了你不要什麼了，那到底什麼你才會想要呢？

3. What would **you** like? = 其他人已經點餐了或已經表達他們的喜好

了，現在該你點餐或表達你的喜好了。

4. What would you like? = 一般性問題，你想要來點什麼。

B. I didn't hire Jane.

上面的這句話，重音放在不同的位置，想強調的意思也不同喔！

第一句，重音放在I，I didn't hire Jane. 強調「我沒有雇用珍」。強調雇用她的人不是我，是別人。

第二句，重音放在didn't，I didn't hire Jane.「我沒有雇用珍」，表示珍可能從頭到尾都沒有被雇用，這件事情根本沒有發生。

第三句，重音放在 hire，I didn't hire Jane.「我沒有雇用珍」，強調我也許是面試了她、跟她談過或甚至討論是否顧用她的這個可能性，但我從未做「雇用」她的這個決定或舉動。

最後一句，重音放在 her，I didn't hire Jane.「我沒有雇用珍」，要表達的是「我雇用的不是珍，而是別人，你們可能搞錯了」。

是不是很有趣呢？懂得聽老外的音調和重音。才能正確掌握對方要表達的意思喔！下面我們再聽一次MP3，練習說說看吧！

▶ 聽說練習與整理

1. I didn't hire Jane. = 是別人雇用她的，不是我。

2. I didn't **hire** Jane.

= 完全不是事實，我根本沒雇用她（她可能根本沒被雇用）。

3. I didn't **hire** Jane.

= 她也許是我面試的，但我沒有做雇用她的決定或動作。

4. I didn't **hire** Jane. = 我雇用的人不是珍，是另有其人。

C. Where can we go?

Where can we go? 這句話一般而言，句子的最重音會放在go，也就是上面的最後一句：Where can we **go**? 意思是說：「我們可以去哪裡？」不過，這句話如果重音放在不同的位置，想強調的意思也不同喔！

第一句，重音放在Where，**Where** can we go? 強調「我們可以去哪裡？」。我問的是哪裡，而不是其他事情。

第二句，重音放在can，Where **can** we go. 「我們可以去哪裡？」。表示我們好像哪兒都不許去。重點在問那到底有什麼地方是我們「可以」去的嗎？

第三句，重音放在we，Where can **we** go? 「我們可以去哪裡？」。他們，或你們，已經知道可以去哪裡了。那我們呢？這句的重點在於：輪到告訴我們，我們可以去哪了吧？

最後一句，重音放在 Where can we **go**? 「我們可以去哪裡？」，是一般性問題。 沒有特別要強調什麼意義，只是單純地問「我們可以去哪裡?」的時候，重音就會放在最後一個內容字：go。

▶ 聽說練習與整理

1. Where can we go? = 我想知道的是「哪裡」，不是「什麼時間」或

DAY 1
DAY 2
DAY 3
DAY 4
DAY 5
DAY 6
DAY 7
DAY 8
DAY 9
DAY 10
DAY 11
DAY 12
DAY 13
DAY 14

「怎麼去」等等。

2. **Where can we go?** = 我們好像哪裡都去不得。到底有什麼地方是我們可以去的嗎？

3. **Where can we go?** = 他們可以去那些地方，那我們呢？我們可以去哪裡？

4. **Where can we go?** = 一般性問題，我們可以去哪？

❯ 舒葳老師小叮嚀

　　英文重音及語調的變化會影響所要表達的語意。如果同學不知道語調對語意的影響，永遠都只照字面上去聽、去理解，可能還是沒辦法正確抓到對方想表達的意思喔！也難怪有的時候，我們即便是每個字都聽清楚了，卻彷彿還是覺得前後邏輯不通，或語意合不太起來，原來就是因為我們不瞭解「語調」所傳達的「弦外之音」！下面，我們就來進一步了解英文重音和語調的變化和其所要表達的意涵吧！

Lesson 2 ❯ 語調變化

❯ 舒葳老師說　　MP3 08-3

　　老外會自然地經由強調句子中不同的字，來表達不同的意思。中文其實也有一樣的現象喔！以 Lesson 1 舉的例子「我沒有雇用她」這句話為例，如果你試試看把重音放在不同的位置說說看，是否也會有不同的效果呢？如下：

我沒有雇用她。

1 補教名師王舒懿教你
4天聽懂
老外說的英語

DAY
1

DAY
2

DAY
3

DAY
4

DAY
5

DAY
6

DAY
7

DAY
8

DAY
9

DAY
10

DAY
11

DAY
12

DAY
13

DAY
14

我沒有雇用她。

我沒有雇用她。

我沒有雇用她。

　　這是英文語調變化的最基本出發點－加重你最需要強調的字。這課我們就來認識英文不同類別的重音及語調的變化，並練習聽聽看、說說看。

▶ 1.句子的重音規則

　　每一個句子都會有很多的「內容字」，也因此會有很多的重音。但每一個句子都會有句子的最重音，也就是句子的重點。句子重音的變化便造成了音調的改變，也改變了所要傳達的意義。句子重音與音調的變化有以下幾種類別。

● Rule 1: 句子的最重音通常在最後一個內容字

What's the matter? 有什麼問題？

What are you doing? 你在做什麼？

That rat is bigger than the cat. 　那隻老鼠比這隻貓還大。

I find learning a new language difficult.

我覺得學習一個新的語言蠻難的。

I have something for you. 我有東西要給你。

Put the coffee in it. 把咖啡倒進去。

　　注意，在後兩句中，因為句子的最後一字 you 和 it 都是「架構字」。「架構字」因不帶重要字義，我們不會特別強調（「架構字」和「內容字」的分辨，請見 Day 5）。something 和 coffee 分別是兩個句子的最後一個內容字，因此為句子的重音。

● Rule 2: 句子的最重音有時不只一個

I lost **my** purse. 我弄掉了我的錢包。

The **scooter** ran the **red** light. 那輛摩托車闖紅燈。

I lost the **battle**, not the **war**. 我輸了這場戰役，但可還沒輸了這場戰爭。

❯❘2. 語調的變化

● Rule 1: 新訊息要加重音

　　雖然一般而言，句子的重音都在最後一個「內容字」，但當我們說出新訊息，也就是對方還不知道的資訊時，我們一定也希望對方能聽見、聽清楚。因此，當這個新訊息不在最後一個內容字時，我們便會把重音放在這個新的訊息，以免對方沒聽見喔！

A.

Woman: I have lost my **coat**.　我掉了我的外套。

　　　（coat 是最後一個關鍵字）

Man: **What** kind of coat?　什麼樣的外套？

　　　（我們已經知道是coat了，這裡kind 是新的重點。）

Woman: It was a **raincoat**.　是雨衣。

　　　（raincoat 是最後一個關鍵字，也是新訊息）

Man: What **color** was your raincoat? 什麼顏色的雨衣？

　　　（顏色是這個問題的新重點）

Woman: It was **gray**. Gray with **floral** patterns. 灰色。灰色有花的圖
　　　　案。

　　　（前半句中 gray 是最後一個關鍵字，也是重點。後半句中，
　　　　我們已經知道是灰色了，因此 floral patterns 變成新的重點）

B.

Woman: I could use a drink.　我想喝點酒。

Man: What kind of drink?　你想喝哪種酒？

Woman: I'd love some wine.　葡萄酒會不錯。

Man: What type of wine do you prefer?　你喜歡哪種酒？

Woman: Any white wine will do. Any white, but not a very dry white.
　　　任何白酒都好。白酒，但不要太澀的白酒。

Man: Let's have some white wine in the pub.
　　　我們去酒吧喝點白酒吧。

● Rule 2: 更正錯誤訊息時，正確訊息加重音

　　當對方説錯了什麼，我們要加以糾正時，自然也是希望對方聽得清清楚楚。因此，當我們説出正確的訊息以糾正對方時，也會把這個正確的訊息加重。

1.

Woman: Did you go on Thursday?　你週四去的嗎？

Man: No, I went on Thursday and Friday. 不，我週四和週五都去了。

　　（不但是週四，還有週五喔！）

2.

Woman: You should've worked harder. 你應該努力點的。

Man: I did work hard. 我有努力啊。

　　（這裡用助動詞 did 強調「我的確有」。）

3.

Woman: It seems expensive.　好像有點貴。

DAY 1
DAY 2
DAY 3
DAY 4
DAY 5
DAY 6
DAY 7
DAY 8
DAY 9
DAY 10
DAY 11
DAY 12
DAY 13
DAY 14

Man: It doesn't seem expensive to him. 他可不覺得貴。

（你覺得貴，但他可不這麼覺得。）

4.

Woman: I heard you have lived in Taiwan for 10 years.

我聽説你在台灣住十年了。

Man: Actually, I have livered here for 15 years.

事實上，我已經在這裡住十五年了。

（不只十年，已經十五年了。）

5.

Woman: We all forgot about mom's birthday. 我們都忘了媽的生日。

Man: I didn't. 我可沒忘。

（那是你們忘了，我可沒忘。）

6.

Woman: Where's your bike? Did someone borrow it?

你的腳踏車／機車呢？借人了嗎？

Man: No. Someone stole it.

不是。被偷了。

（不是讓人借了，是讓人給偷了。）

● Rule 3: 確認對方訊息時，所要確認的訊息加重音

當不確定自己是否已聽清楚對方所説訊息而欲確認時，也會將想確認的部份加重音。

1.

Woman: You did want two Cokes, didn't you?

你説要兩杯可樂，沒錯吧？

（確定是要兩杯嗎？）

Man: No, I didn't. Just one. 不是。一杯就好。

2.

Woman: Did you say you will speak to them about the new project?

你是説你會跟他們談新案子，對嗎？

（你會去談，不用我或別人再去談了吧？）

Man: Yes, that's right. Leave it to me.

是的，沒錯。交給我處理。

3.

Woman: It cost me six thousand to buy this dress.

這件洋裝花了我六千塊。

Man: Six thousand? 六千？

（是六千嗎？不是六「百」？除了確認外，還有不以為然或不可置信之意。）

4.

Woman: Tina's already quit.　Tina辭職了。

Man: She has?　她已經這麼做了嗎？

（原本就知道她可能會辭職，但已經辭了嗎？有表示驚訝之意。）

5.

Woman: Alan has done some beautiful drawings of his dream

house.　Alan 畫了些畫，畫他夢想中的房子。

Man: So he has finished them!　所以他已經完成了啊！

（原本就知道他在畫，但已經完成了嗎？）

DAY 1

DAY 2

DAY 3

DAY 4

DAY 5

DAY 6

DAY 7

DAY 8

DAY 9

DAY 10

DAY 11

DAY 12

DAY 13

DAY 14

6.

Woman: You'll have to visit Tarako National Park sometime.
　　　　It really is amazing!

　　　　你有空一定得去太魯閣國家公園看看。真的很令人驚豔！

Man: Oh, so you did go there for your holiday!

　　　喔，所以你們真的去那裡渡假了！

　　　（事前可能就知道對方要去那裡渡假，所以是真的去了囉。）

● Rule 4: 重音改變時，意思也跟著改變

1. I have two. / I have, too. / I have to.

a) 請練習說説看以下問答。重音在哪？

How many kids do you have? 你有幾個小孩？
I have two. 我有兩個。

I have tried my best. 我已經盡力了。
I have, too. 我也盡力了。

Why do you work so hard? 你為什麼工作那麼努力？
I have to. 我必須這麼做。

**b) 你知道 I have two. I have, too. 和 I have to. 聽起來有什麼
不一樣嗎？現在聽 MP3 跟著說説看。**

I have two. 我有兩個。
重點在 two，因此重音在 two.
I have, too. 我也有。
強調你有，我也有。因此重音在我，和也。
I have to. 我得這麼做。

have 在這個句子中是強調的動詞「必須」，也是最後一個內容字。

2. thought

a) 請練習説説看下面句子。重音在哪？

A.

Man: I thought you'd enjoy it. 我以為妳會喜歡。

Woman: So did I. It was too cold though. 我也是啊。但是真的是太冷了。

Man: I thought you'd enjoy it. 我早知道妳會喜歡。

Woman: Yeah, the beach resort is the bomb.

　　　　是啊，那個海灘渡假勝地真是太棒了。

B.

Man: I thought it was going to rain. 我以為會下雨。

Woman: So did I. I'm glad it didn't though.

　　　　我也是。不過我很高興沒下。

Man: I thought it was going to rain. 我就知道會下雨。

Woman: I know. The weather is terrible. 是啊。天氣真的太糟了。

b) 現在請聽MP3 跟著説説看。

A.

Man: I thought you'd enjoy it.（結果對方並不喜歡。）

Woman: So did I. It was too cold though.

Man: I thought you'd enjoy it.（對方也真的喜歡。）

DAY 1
DAY 2
DAY 3
DAY 4
DAY 5
DAY 6
DAY 7
DAY 8
DAY 9
DAY 10
DAY 11
DAY 12
DAY 13
DAY 14

Woman: Yeah, the beach resort is the bomb.

B.
Man: I thought it was going to rain.（結果並未下雨。）
Woman: So did I. I'm glad it didn't though.

Man: I thought it was going to rain.（真的下雨了。）
Woman: I know. The weather is terrible.

　　thought 是一個有趣的字，它是 think 的過去式。 當過去式用的時候是「我本來／過去這麼想」的意思，可以當「我原本以為（但其實我想錯了）」用，也可以當「我原本就有想到（所以我是對的）」。當我們以正常的語調說話，也就是把重音放在最後一個內容字時，這時 thought 仍然是重音，因為他原本就是「內容字」，thought 的意思當「以為」用；而當我們又更特別強調thought 這個字時，便是要表達「我早就想到了吧！」

　　再聽一次，你是否能體會不同重音想傳達的不同感覺呢？

▶ │3. 句子重音改變影響意義

a) 請練習說說看下面句子。重音在哪？

1. didn't say he stole the money. Someone else said it.
   我沒有說他偷了錢。別人說的。

2. I didn't say he stole the money. That's not true at all.
   我沒有說他偷了錢。這完全不是真的。

3. I didn't say he stole the money. I only suggested the possibility.

我沒有說他偷了錢。我只是暗示了這個可能性。

4.　I didn't say he stole the money. I think someone else took it.

我沒有說他偷了錢。我想是別人拿的。

5.　I didn't say he stole the money. Maybe he just borrowed it.

我沒有說他偷了錢。也許他是借的。

6.　I didn't say he stole the money, but rather someone other

　　money.

我沒有說他偷了這些錢，而是其他的錢。

7.　I didn't say he stole the money. He maybe have taken some

　　jewelry.

我沒有說他偷了錢。也許他只是拿了些珠寶。

b) 現在請聽MP3 跟著說說看。

1.　I didn't say he stole the money. Someone else said it.

　　（強調「我」沒有說，因此強調 I。）

2.　I didn't say he stole the money. That's not true at all.

　　（強調我「沒有」說，因此強調 didn't。）

3.　I didn't say he stole the money. I only suggested the

　　possibility.

　　（強調我沒有「說」，因此強調 say。）

4.　I didn't say he stole the money. I think someone else took it.

　　（強調我沒有說是「他」，因此強調 he。）

5.　I didn't say he stole the money. Maybe he just borrowed it.

　　（強調我沒有說他「偷」，因此強調stole。）

6.　I didn't say he stole the money, but rather someone other money.

（強調我沒有説他偷「這些」錢，因此強調 the。）

7. I didn't say he stole the money. He might have taken some

jewelry.

（強調我沒有説他偷這些「錢」，因此強調 money。）

❯ 舒葳老師小叮嚀

　　英文中以重音加強所要強調重點的表達方式，其實和中文並無不同。但是同學卻往往因為英文是一個「外國語」，一味地背誦文法單字，反而忽略了這個語言溝通時最自然、最基本的元素。一旦習慣讓聽重音、聽語調成為聽英文的一部份，你會發現你更能以平常心面對説英文的老外喔！你會更輕易地抓住對方想表達的意思和感覺，不只如此，你自己在説英文的時候，也會更自然呢！

Lesson 3 ❯ 再聽聽看

❯ 舒葳老師說 08-4

請聽MP3，並選擇最適當的回應。

1. A. Oh, I thought you wanted tea.
   B. Oh, I thought you wanted one.

2. A. No, I also bought a dress and a pair of shoes.
   B. Come on. It's an expensive bag. I had to think carefully.

3. A. Oh, so who did?

DAY
1

DAY
2

DAY
3

DAY
4

DAY
5

DAY
6

DAY
7

DAY
8

DAY
9

DAY
10

DAY
11

DAY
12

DAY
13

DAY
14

B. Oh, so which song did you write?

4. A. Oh, sorry. I thought you were asking about the salmon. No,
   it's on the table.
   B. No, it's on the table. It doesn't require refrigeration.

5. A. Yeah, I enjoyed some sports but not football.
   B. Yeah, I can't enough of televised sports.

6. A. No, this is my first time.
   B. Yes, I love this place.

● Answers

1. B   2. B   3. A   4. A   5. A   6. B

> 詳細解說   08-5

1. But we asked for two coffees!
但我們要的是兩杯咖啡！

這裡他強調的是 "two"，表示對方可能是弄錯了數量，說話者才
需要強調是兩杯，而不是其他的數目，因此，可能的回應應該是 B.
Oh, I thought you wanted one.（我以為你要的是一杯）。

下面我們聽聽看強調不同的重點時，語調會有什麼樣的不同變
化。請跟著練習說說看。

W: But we asked for two coffees! 但我們要的是兩杯咖啡！
M: Oh, I thought you wanted one. 噢，我以為你要的是一杯。

W: But we asked for two coffees! 但我們要的是兩杯咖啡！

> M: Oh, I thought you wanted tea. 噢，我以為你要的是茶。

2. You spent 4 hours just to buy this bag?

妳花了四小時買這個袋子？

> 　　這裡她強調的是"4 hours"，表示對方覺得不可思議的是「四小時」這麼長的時間。因此較適合的回應應是針對時間做解釋，也就是選項 B. Come on. It's an expensive bag. I needed to think carefully.
>
> 　　下面我們聽聽看強調不同的重點時，語調會有什麼樣的不同變化。請跟著練習說說看。
>
> M: You spent 4 hours just to buy this bag?
>
> 　　妳花了四小時就為了買這個袋子？
>
> W: Come on. It's an expensive bag. I needed to think carefully.
>
> 　　不要這樣嘛。這個袋子很貴，我得考慮清楚。
>
> M: You spent 4 hours just to buy this bag?
>
> 　　妳花了四小時就買這個袋子？
>
> W: No, I also bought a dress and a pair of shoes.
>
> 　　不是，我還買了一件洋裝和一雙鞋子。

3. I didn't write that song.

我沒有寫那首歌。

> 　　這裡她強調的是"I"，表示對方可能以為是她，但事實上不是她，因此說話者才需要強調「我」沒寫。較適合這個情境的回應應該是 A. Oh, so who did?
>
> 　　下面我們聽聽看強調不同的重點時，語調會有什麼樣的不同變

DAY 1
DAY 2
DAY 3
DAY 4
DAY 5
DAY 6
DAY 7
DAY 8
DAY 9
DAY 10
DAY 11
DAY 12
DAY 13
DAY 14

化。請跟著練習説説看。

W: I didn't write that song. 我沒有寫那首歌。
M: Oh, so who did? 噢,那是誰寫的?

W: I didn't write that song. 我沒有寫那首歌。
M: Oh, so which song did you write? 噢,那妳寫的是哪一首?

4. Is the cured ham in the fridge?

火腿在冰箱嗎?

這裡説話者強調的是"cured ham",表示對方可能以為他問的是別的食物,但事實上不是她,因此説話者才需要強調「火腿」。因此較適合這個情境的回應應該是 A. Oh, sorry. I thought you were asking about the salmon. No, it's on the table.

下面我們聽聽看強調不同的重點時,語調會有什麼樣的不同變化。請跟著練習説説看。

W: Is the cured ham in the fridge?
火腿在冰箱嗎?
M: Oh, sorry. I thought you were asking about the salmon. No, the ham is on the table.
噢,抱歉,我以為妳問的是鮭魚。不,火腿在桌上。
W: Is the cured ham in the fridge?
火腿在冰箱嗎?
M: No, it's on the table. It doesn't require refrigeration.
不,火腿在桌上。它不需要冰。

5. I thought you like sports.

我以為你喜歡運動比賽。

　　這裡他以正常的語調說這句話，也就是強調所有「內容字」，最重音在 sports。因此這裡的 thought 指的是「以為」，表示對方似乎不喜歡運動比賽，因此 A. Yeah, I enjoy some sports but not football. 是恰當的回應。

　　下面我們聽聽看強調不同的重點時，語調會有什麼樣的不同變化。注意第一句重音也可以放在 like，強調我以為你「喜歡」，但你似乎不太喜歡？請跟著練習說說看。

W: I thought you liked sports. 我以為你喜歡運動比賽。
M: Yeah, I enjoy some sports but not football.
　　我是喜歡某些運動比賽，但我不喜歡足球。
W: I thought you like sports. 我就知道你喜歡運動比賽。
M: Yeah, I can't get enough of televised sports.
　　是啊，電視轉播的運動比賽我怎麼看都看不夠。

---

6. I thought you'd been here before.
我就知道你來過這裡。

---

　　thought 可以當「我原本以為（但其實我想錯了）」，也可以當「我原本就有想到（所以我是對的）」用。這裡他強調的是 thought，當後者，也就是「我就知道」用，表示對方的確來過，因此 B. Yes, I love this place. 是恰當的回應。

　　下面我們聽聽看強調不同的重點時，語調會有什麼樣的不同變化。請跟著練習說說看。

M: I thought you'd been here before. 我以為你來過這裡。
W: No, this is my first time. 不，這是我第一次來。

M: I thought you'd been here before. 我就知道你來過這裡。
W: Yes, I love this place. 是啊，我愛極這地方了。

▶ 聽力小秘訣

☺ 老外在說話時，除了單字句型外，語調也是重要的傳達意義的工具。瞭解語調背後的意義，才能真正聽懂英文。

☺ 英文的語調和中文一樣，都是加重特別需要強調的字詞，包括強調新訊息、更正對方的誤解或確認對方所說之訊息。也因此當一個句子的重音位置不同時，也代表對方想表達的重點也不同。

☺ 英文的重音就是聲調提得較高，在重音的部位說得也較慢、較清晰，以確保聽話者聽得清楚。

☺ 平時聽英文的時候，便練習體會老外在說每一句話時的節奏，何時輕何時重，何時拉得長何時快快帶過。相信你很快地就能在聽老外說英文時如魚得水喔！

DAY 1
DAY 2
DAY 3
DAY 4
DAY 5
DAY 6
DAY 7
DAY 8
DAY 9
DAY 10
DAY 11
DAY 12
DAY 13
DAY 14

MEMO

DAY 9 語意單位&英文筆記
I don't think I know.
I don't think. I know.

MP3
09-1~09-6

> 學習重點

　　你知道嗎？老外在説話時，不同的地方停頓、換氣，也會產生不同的意思喔！看看本課的標題，I don't think I know. 和 I don't think. I know. 意思是否不同呢？（請見本課 p.163）

　　理解老外語句的聲調及停頓的位置所代表的意義，不但能夠幫助你更能聽懂老外在説什麼，在聽長篇聽力的時候還能幫助你跟上老外的節奏，避免只聽得懂前兩句，然後就只能鴨子聽雷的窘境。

　　除了聽懂外，同學也常會有需要用英文做筆記的機會，如聽英文演講、聽英文簡報、跟老外開會、甚至是在考試時，如托福、IELTS、及其他的劍橋英檢等考試都需要考生有做英文筆記的能力。但你可能不知道，聽懂聲調及停頓語句也是訓練自己做英文筆記的重要方法之一喔！今天我們就來帶同學一起學習如何利用語句段落聽懂老外的話，又如何聽英文、做筆記吧！

DAY 9 語意單位&英文筆記

I don't think I know.
I don't think. I know.

09-1~09-6

是穿給別人炫耀用的～

Lesson 1 聽聽看，寫寫看

> 舒葳老師說   09-1

　　請聽聽看，試著做筆記、寫下你聽到的句子。請練習快速寫下重點即可，不需要寫出完整的句子。

1. _____.

2. _____.

3. _____.

4. _____.

5. _____.

6. _____.

● Answers

1. It's J-O-S-E-P-H-I-N-E.
2. 886-2-2393-4939
3. suwei.wang@msa.hinet.net
4. 5F, No.7, Alley 8, Lane 111, Moon Lake Road Section 3, Taipei, Taiwan.
5. We need sugar, flour, milk, butter and a dozen eggs.
6. I have been to, Germany, France, Belgium, England, Spain and Greece.

> **詳細解說** 🎵 09-2

1. It's J-O-S-E-P-H-I-N-E.

在這一題中，説話者拼出一個名字：Josephine. 你是否有發現到，她在拼字的時候，説完每一個字母音調都提高，一直到最後才落下呢？

當你聽到老外聲調上揚時，你便知道他還沒拼完，便要趕緊跟上去注意聽；反之，當你聽到他的聲調落下時，便知道他已經説完了。

在聽英文時，最怕就是一閃神，聲音就過了，聽不見也來不及。如果能事先知道對方是否會繼續説下去，也會增加你聽的能力喔！

再聽一次試試看，是不是這樣呢？

2. 886-2-2393-4939

在這一題中，説話者説出一個電話號碼。值得一提的是，數字説起來簡單，聽老外説一整串的數字還得寫下來時，同學們卻常常都是反應不及。因此，平時常練習聽數字並寫下來是很重要的練習喔！

除了確實熟悉數字並能迅速反應外，聲調和「語意單位」也能幫忙你在聽老外説話時有好的臨場反應喔！老外在説電話號碼時，和我們在説中文的時候一樣，會自動替數字分組，以免説得上氣不接下氣。這一小組的數字就是所謂的「語意單位」。「語意單位」不僅能幫助説話者説得較輕鬆，也能幫助聽話者聽得較清楚喔！你是否也有注意到，説話者在説完每一個數字音調都提高，一直到一小組數字説完時，聲調才會落下呢？

再聽一次試試看，是不是這樣呢？

DAY 1
DAY 2
DAY 3
DAY 4
DAY 5
DAY 6
DAY 7
DAY 8
DAY 9
DAY 10
DAY 11
DAY 12
DAY 13
DAY 14

3. suwei.wang@msa.hinet.net

在這一題中，說話者說出一個電子郵件信箱。在現代生活裡，拼姓名、說電話和電子郵件信箱都已經是日常生活中頻繁的事了。我們在聽老外說這些基本資料時，也都往往需要能把聽到的正確迅速地記下來，在這裡，語調和停頓同樣也能幫助你。

如同上一題替數字分組，在說其他訊息時我們也同樣會替文字或訊息分組，幫助說話者不至說得上氣不接下氣，也幫助聽話者聽得較輕鬆、較清楚。因此說話者在說完每一個字時音調也會提高，直到說完一個「語意單位」時才落下。

以這題為例，他語氣的停頓如下（斜線表示停頓）：

suwei/.wang@/msa/./hinet/.net

在聽英文時，最怕就是一閃神，聲音就過了，聽不見也來不及。如果能事先知道對方的節奏，也會增加你聽的能力喔！再聽一次試試看，是不是這樣呢？

4. 5F, No.7, Alley 8, Lane 111, Moon Lake Road Section 3, Taipei, Taiwan.

聽地址並能夠正確地記錄也是我們常會需要做的事。

同樣的，你也會發現老外在每說完一個部份時，音調都會提高，並做短暫停頓，直到說完一個「語意單位」時才落下。

以這題為例，他語氣的停頓如下（斜線表示停頓）：

5F,/ No.7,/ Alley 8,/ Lane 111,/ Moon Lake Road/ Section 3,/

Taipei,/ Taiwan.

再聽一次，練習跟著說話者一起說，模仿他的呼吸與節奏。

5. We need sugar, flour, milk, butter and a dozen eggs.

這裡，說話者告訴你他需要哪些東西，而你必須記下來。這時，你必須養成挑「重點」，也就是挑「關鍵字」寫的習慣。以這題為例，你只要寫下需要的東西即可，但即便如此，你都還是可能來不及。因此，你可以利用語氣停頓的空格，每個字都只先拼一半，看得懂即可，等對方說完了，你在回去把字拼完整、寫好。

甚至你也可以寫中文或寫注音喔！畢竟重要的是聽懂了、記下來了。什麼方法對你管用，就是最好的方法。

當然，如同上面的幾題，你也應該用聲調來預知他後面是否還有更多的東西要說，幫助你專心並掌握對方節奏。一旦聲調落下了，你便可以回頭把剛才的筆記重新寫好、寫清楚。

上面這句話，他語氣的停頓如下：
We need sugar,/ flour,/ milk,/ butter/ and a dozen eggs.

再聽一次，練習跟著說話者一起說，模仿他的呼吸與節奏。

6. I have been to Germany, France, Belgium, England, Spain and Greece.

這裡，說話者告訴你他去過哪些國家，而你必須記下來。這

DAY 1
DAY 2
DAY 3
DAY 4
DAY 5
DAY 6
DAY 7
DAY 8
DAY 9
DAY 10
DAY 11
DAY 12
DAY 13
DAY 14

時，你同樣只須挑「重點」，也就是挑「關鍵字」寫的習慣。以這題為例，你只要寫下去過的國家即可。你可以利用語氣停頓的空檔，每個字都只先拼一半，看得懂即可，等對方說完了，你在回去把字拼完整、寫好。你也可以寫中文或寫注音喔。

如同上面的幾題，你也應該用聲調的上揚來預知他後面是否還有更多的東西要說，幫助你專心並掌握對方節奏。一旦聲調落下了，你便可以回頭把剛才的筆記重新寫好、寫清楚。

上面這句話他語氣的停頓如下：
I have been to Germany,/ France,/ Belgium,/ England,/ Spain/ and Greece.

再聽一次，練習跟著說話者一起說，模仿他的呼吸與節奏。

▶ 舒葳老師小叮嚀

老外在說話時，即便是速度快的時候，也是會喘息呼吸、會停頓的。這些停頓對英語學習者有兩層意義：第一，這些停頓配合聲調，能幫助我們知道對方說到哪裡了，是說到一半？還是已經說完並準備開始說下一個重點了？掌握及預測對方的節奏能幫助我們的聽力。第二層意義，則是句中停頓的位置，有時也是會改變語意的。因此，下一課我們就一起來看看英文「語意單位」能如何幫助我們提升聽力，以及他又是如何影響說話者的語意吧！

Lesson 2 ❯ 語意單位

DAY 1

DAY 2

DAY 3

DAY 4

DAY 5

DAY 6

DAY 7

DAY 8

DAY 9

DAY 10

DAY 11

DAY 12

DAY 13

DAY 14

❯ 舒葳老師說　🎧 09-3

　　「語意單位」是幫助想邁向聽力「進階班」、聽長篇聽力的同學的好工具及重要的技巧。

　　「語意單位」的意義，是讓我們藉由聲調及停頓的位置判斷說話者的語句是否已經完成。如果語調上揚並停頓，表示針對這個部份，後面還有重要訊息要補充，這時我們便知道我們必須繼續專心聽，不能鬆懈；反之，如果對方語調落下，則表示這個語句已經完成，我們便要準備下一個新的句子或新的訊息。

　　我們一直強調聽力最難的地方，便在它「稍縱即逝」。一個閃神，對方已經說完了，沒聽見也來不及了。掌握「語意單位」，便是幫助我們跟上對方的節奏，一個不小心沒聽懂前一句話時，也要能追上下一個句子。下面我們便來看看我們究竟應該怎麼聽吧。

● 1. 數字和名字：上揚、上揚、落下

106

94768

May 11, 1974

September 21, 1999

0933 909 226

886 2 2394 1666

LA

IBM

MRT

ASAP

X, Y, Z

Nicole

Sophia

Hoffman

　　一連串的數字或字母，老外皆會將之分為幾段來説。如果是名字，則通常會以音節做為分段的標準。而在段落結束或整串數字或字母結束前，語調皆上揚，因此當我們在聽的時候可以知道對方尚未説完，要繼續專心聽下去。當對方語調下降時，便表示對方已經説完了。

● 2. 一連串的人、事、物：上揚、上揚、落下

They sell Fords, Buicks, and Toyotas.
他們賣福特、別克和豐田汽車。

There are only three primary colors: red, yellow and blue.
只有三個原色：紅、黃和藍。

I'd like two hamburgers, soup and salad, and a drink.
我要漢堡、湯和沙拉，和一杯飲料。

I bought a tie, two shirts, underwear, and a pair of pants.
我買了一條領帶、兩件襯衫、內衣褲、和一條褲子。

I watched TV, played on-line games, did some work and slept a bit.
我看了電視、玩了線上遊戲、做了點工作還睡了一下。

We grow basil, lemon grass, lavenders, and rosemary.
我們種羅勒、檸檬草、薰衣草和迷迭香。

　　當老外在説一連串的事物時，説到前面幾個事物時語調皆會上

揚，因此當我們在聽的時候可以知道對方尚未說完，要繼續專心聽下去。當對方說 and 並且語調下降時，表示對方已經說完了。

● 3. 語意未完，語調上揚；語意結束，語調落下

She works for I'm Publishing. 她在我識出版社工作。

上面這句話語氣完結了，因此語調落下。

現在請比較下面這組句子。每組都有兩個相似的句子，只是第二句的後面較第一句多了段補充說明。請注意兩句話語調的不同。

I enjoy playing card games. 我喜歡玩牌。
（語句結束，語調直接落下）。
I enjoy playing card games with my family. 我喜歡跟家人玩牌。
（因為後半部還再進一步加註了更多的訊息，說完後，語調變成先上揚，最後補充完後語調才落下）。

下面是更多例子。注意第一句和第二句語調的變化：

I remembered to bring the notebook.
我記得帶筆記本。
I remembered to bring the notebook, but I forgot my pen.
我記得帶筆記本，但我忘了帶我的筆。

She's going to come back.
她會再上門的。
She's going to come back with her friends.
她會帶她朋友一起再上門的。

DAY 1
DAY 2
DAY 3
DAY 4
DAY 5
DAY 6
DAY 7
DAY 8
DAY 9
DAY 10
DAY 11
DAY 12
DAY 13
DAY 14

I'm planning to get a Master degree.

我計劃讀碩士。

I'm planning to get a Master degree in the United Kingdom.

我計劃去英國讀碩士。

Babies like to play with sounds.

嬰兒喜歡玩聲音。

Babies like to play with the sounds that they are making.

嬰兒喜歡玩他們自己發出來的聲音。

● 4. 一段語意的開始,語調會提高;一段語意的完成,口氣會稍加停頓(以下斜線 "/" 代表短暫停頓, "//" 代表較長停頓,也就是一段語意的完成。)

I really want to learn to play the guitar.// It has a great sound/ and there are a lot of great songs/ I want to learn.// The best thing about the guitar/ is that it's easy to carry!// I play the piano and I like it,/ but I can only play at home.// I would love to be able to play anywhere.// With a guitar,/ I could take it to my friends' house/ or to the park.// It would give me more time/ to practice/ and to improve my singing.//

　　在同一個句子中則會因「語意單位」的結束而做短暫的停頓(" / "),這可以幫助我們依照意思分割對方說的句子,增進理解。而在每一句話結束時,說話者的語氣都會稍稍停頓,幫助讀者準備聽下一個重點。並且,在新的一句話開始時,句子中的第一個內容字聲調也會較高昂,以吸引我們的注意喔。因此,當你聽到語氣停頓、聲調提高的時候,你就知道一個新的主題或重點又要開始了。

　　這個技巧在你已不幸錯過了前一句的重點,並且已經不知道老

外在說什麼的時候最能派上用場。只要你能掌握下一個重點開始的地方，並專心聽，你還是有機會能再次掌握到重點，抓到大部份的訊息喔！

請再聽一次。這次不要看書，用耳朵體會語氣停頓和聲調的變化。

● 5. 語意單位與意義改變

I don't think I know.
I don't think. I know.

上面兩句話的意思有何不同呢？第一句話是一個完整的「語意單位」，說話者一氣呵成，意思是：「我不認為我知道。」也就是：「我不知道」的意思。

第二句則是兩個「語意單位」：I don't think. 和 I know. 因此說話者會在 I don't think. 後面先停頓，再接著說 I know. 那麼這又是什麼意思呢？I don't think. I know. 的意思就變成了：「我不用思考，我不用想。我就是知道。」

所以聽老外說話時，聽清楚停頓的地方也很重要喔！

● Exercise (MP3) 09-4

請不要看書，聽聽看下面的短文。注意音調，什麼時候後面還有未完的語句？什麼時候已經說完了？什麼時候又是一個新的重點？

I'm studying this Pronunciation and Listening book.// There's a lot

DAY
1

DAY
2

DAY
3

DAY
4

DAY
5

DAY
6

DAY
7

DAY
8

DAY
9

DAY
10

DAY
11

DAY
12

DAY
13

DAY
14

to learn,/ but/ I find it very enjoyable.// I think I will find it easier/ and easier to listen to native speakers speak in English,/ but the only way to really improve, is to practice all of the time.//

Now I can distinguish different vowels/ and consonants/ that sound similar,// and I also pay more attention to stresses when I listen/ than I used to.// I have been talking to a lot of native speakers of English lately/ and they tell me I'm easier to understand.// Anyway,/ I could go on and on,/ but the important thing is to listen well and sound good.// And I hope I'm getting better and better!//

❯ 舒葳老師小叮嚀

　　英文聽力會困難的主要原因之一，是因為聲音一下就過去了，若是沒抓到也沒辦法再回來了，與閱讀可以一看再看相當不同。這課的重點之一，是幫助同學藉由注意「語意單位」正確聽懂對方的意思，避免誤解。另一個重點，即是練習聽出說話者何時會說完，何時要開始新的重點。這樣的技巧能幫助我們在聽的時候知道何時要格外專心，何時稍加鬆懈也無傷大雅。下面我們來實際練習看看。

Lesson 3 ❯ | 再聽聽看 MP3 09-5

A.
請聽MP3，並依指示選擇正確的答案。

1. 誰笨？ ("Dave," said the boss, is stupid.)

A. Dave.
B. The boss.

2. 他賣什麼？ (He sold his houseboat and farm.)
A. Houseboat and farm.
B. House, boat and farm.

3. 他吃了什麼？ (I had pie and apples.)
A. Pineapples.
B. Pie and apples.

B.
請聽聽看，寫下你聽到的句子。請練習一邊聽即一邊快速寫下重點即可不需要寫出完整的句子。

1. _____

2. _____

3. _____

● Answers

B.
1. I bought tissues, two toothbrushes, toothpaste, slippers, mineral water, and batteries.
2. The teachers are from Japan, Taiwan, Spain, Brazil, Greece, and France.
3. I knew I was going to be late for work, so I drove too fast and got a speeding ticket.

A.
1.A   2.A   3.B

DAY 1
DAY 2
DAY 3
DAY 4
DAY 5
DAY 6
DAY 7
DAY 8
DAY 9
DAY 10
DAY 11
DAY 12
DAY 13
DAY 14

▶ 詳細解說 🎵 09-6

A.

1. "Dave," said the boss, "is stupid!"

「大衛」，老闆說，「是笨的。」

請注意，在這句話中，說話者在什麼地方有稍微停頓換氣呢？換氣表示一段「語意單位」已經結束了。在這裡，他說的是（/表示停頓換氣）：

Dave/ said the boss/ is stupid.

這表示 said the boss 是一個獨立的單位，也就是「老闆說」，是插入語。說什麼呢？ "Dave is stupid."。反之，下面的第二句中，The boss is stupid. 就是一完整的語句，中間並無停頓或換氣。因此這裡的正確答案應是 A. Dave.

請比較下面兩句並練習跟著說說看。

"Dave," said the boss, "is stupid!"
「大衛」，老闆說，「是笨的。」

Dave said, "The boss is stupid!"
大衛說：「老闆是笨的。」

---

2. He sold his houseboat, and farm.
他賣了他的船屋和農場。

請注意，在這句話中，說話者在什麼地方有稍微停頓換氣呢？在這裡，他的 houseboat 是 連在一起說的。表示 houseboat 是一個獨立的單位，也就是「船屋」。反之，下面的第二句 He sold his house, boat, and farm. 中，house 語調上揚，house 和 boat 中有

DAY
1

DAY
2

DAY
3

DAY
4

DAY
5

DAY
6

DAY
7

DAY
8

**DAY
9**

DAY
10

DAY
11

DAY
12

DAY
13

DAY
14

停頓，因此這裡的 house 和 boat 是兩個獨立的東西，正確答案應是 A. Houseboat and farm.

請比較下面兩句並練習跟著說說看。

He sold his houseboat, and farm.
他賣了他的船屋和農場。
He sold his house, boat, and farm.
他賣了他的船、房子和農場。

3. I had pie and apples.
   我吃了派和蘋果。

在這句話中，重音在哪？說話者在什麼地方有稍微停頓換氣呢？在這裡，他的重音在 pie 和 apple，表示 pie 和 apple 是兩個獨立的單位，也就是「派」和「蘋果」。反之，下面的第一句 I had pineapples. 中，重音在 pine，pineapple 中也未停頓，因此 pineapples 是一個獨立的東西。正確答案應是 B. Pie and apples.

請比較下面兩句並練習跟著說說看。

I had pineapples. 我吃了鳳梨。
I had pie and apples. 我吃了派和蘋果。

B.
1. I bought tissues, two toothbrushes, toothpaste, slippers, mineral water, and batteries.
   我買了衛生紙、牙膏、拖鞋、礦泉水和電池。

在這裡，他說的是（"/" 表示停頓）：

I bought tissues,/ two toothbrushes,/ toothpaste,/ slippers,/ mineral water,/ and batteries.

練習邊聽邊寫下一兩個英文字母或中文翻譯代表每一個字,並藉由聽語調提升瞭解對方尚未説完,以繼續專心聽接下來要説的訊息。一連串的事物後接 and 再加上語調落下,表示語句完成,可回頭整理筆記。

2. The teachers are from Japan, Taiwan, Spain, Brazil, Greece, and France.

這些老師們來自日本、台灣、西班牙、巴西、希臘和法國。

在這裡,他説的是("/" 表示停頓):

The teachers are from Japan,/ Taiwan,/ Spain,/ Brazil,/ Greece,/ and France.

練習邊聽邊寫下一兩個英文字母或中文翻譯代表每一個字,並藉由聽語調提升瞭解對方尚未説完,以繼續專心聽接下來要説的訊息。一連串的事物後接 and 再加上語調落下,表示語句完成,可回頭整理筆記。

3. I knew I was going to be late for work, so I drove too fast and got a speeding ticket.

我知道我要遲到了,所以我開車開太快,結果被開罰單。

在這裡,也可以説("/" 表示停頓):

I knew I was going to be late for work,/ so I drove too fast/ and got a speeding ticket.

DAY
1

DAY
2

DAY
3

DAY
4

DAY
5

DAY
6

DAY
7

DAY
8

DAY
9

DAY
10

DAY
11

DAY
12

DAY
13

DAY
14

> 　　每次語氣的停頓，都代表了一個「語意單位」。練習邊聽邊利用一兩個英文字寫下每一的「語意單位」的重點，並藉由聽語調提升了解對方尚未說完，以繼續專心聽接下來要說的訊息。語調落下，表示語句完成，可回頭整理筆記。

〉聽力小秘訣

☺ 一個英文的句子中可能有數個「語意單位」，老外在說話時會以短暫換氣或停頓來代表一個「語意單位」的結束。

☺ 「語意單位」使說話者得以在正確的地方換氣，也幫助聽話者藉由一段一段的「語意單位」，清楚正確地了解對方所傳達的訊息。我們在聽老外說話時，注意對方的聲調和「語意單位」，可以幫助我們跟上老外的節奏，知道現在說到了哪裡。

☺ 每一個新的句子的開頭，聲調都會特別提高。這也是我們需要特別專心聽的地方。

☺ 當說完一個「語意單位」，語調卻上揚時，表示句子還沒說完。

☺ 當語調落下，表示句子完成，可準備新句子的開始。

MEMO

DAY**10** | 慣用語的使用

10-1~10-5

> **學習重點**

　　前面九天，我們幫同學整理了英文中最常造成同學聽力的「聲音」問題。同學聽力不好，往往是因為一直在用眼睛學英文，並用中文的聲音系統去理解英文的聲音，自然一直無法突破。在前面，我們一起了解了英文聲音的運作並多加練習後，同學的聽力必定可以大大提升！

　　但在掌握了「聲音」的因素後，我們還得學習英文中的成語、慣用語和片語，才不會功虧一簣喔！這是因為老外在說話時使用的字句和寫文章時是非常不同的。有許多口語常用的成語、慣用語及片語都是我們在閱讀英文時不會看到的，也因為如此，當我們突然需要聽老外說話，他又滿口「口語英文」時，我們當然就有聽沒有懂啦！

　　現在我們就一起來看看常用的成語、慣用語及片語，熟悉口語英文，戰勝英文聽力！

DAY 10 慣用語的使用

Lesson 1 ▶ 聽聽看，寫寫看

▶ 舒葳老師說 MP3 10-1

聽聽看MP3中的對話，並選擇第二個人回應所表達的意思。

1. _____   a. It'll just take a minute.

2. _____   b. It's easy.

3. _____   c. It's a regular part of his job.

4. _____   d. It's best to get it over with now.

5. _____   e. It' s a good idea to work together.

6. _____   f. It's good that you went at all.

● Answers

1.b 2.c 3.e 4.d 5.a 6.f

▶ 詳細解說 MP3 10-2

1. Man: Man, I have to do all the homework for chapter 6 tonight!

　　　我今晚要做完所有第六章的功課！

Woman: Don't worry about it. It's a piece of cake.

　　　別擔心，小意思而已。

> 正確答案：b. It's easy. 很容易。
>
> 　　It's a piece of cake. 就是「小意思、很容易，難不倒人」的意

補教名師王舒薇教你
1**4**天聽懂
老外說的英語

DAY
1

DAY
2

DAY
3

DAY
4

DAY
5

DAY
6

DAY
7

DAY
8

DAY
9

DAY
10

DAY
11

DAY
12

DAY
13

DAY
14

思。 另一個類型用法的成語是 "as easy as pie"，同樣也是「易如反掌」的意思。

▶ 老外時常這麼說

Man: How was the test? 考試考得如何？

Woman: A piece of cake! 太簡單了。

2. Man: Thanks for the coffee. That was really great service.
謝謝這個咖啡。你的服務真好。

Woman: It's all in a day's work. 這是我工作份內的事。

正確答案：c. It's a regular part of his job. 這是他平時工作的一部份。

　　It's all in a day's work. 就是「這是我工作份內的事」，用來形容某些事雖然困難或聽起來很奇特，但其實是這個人日常工作的一部份。

▶ 老外時常這麼說

Drinking champagne with Hollywood stars is all in a day's work for top celebrity reporters.
對於專門訪問名人的記者而言，和好萊塢明星們喝香檳只是日常工作的一部份。

We worked till twelve last night on the presentation. It's all in a day's work for an executive at my company.
我們昨晚準備簡報工作到十二點. 對我們公司的管理人來說這只是日常工作的一部份。

3. Man: Maybe we should work on this project together.

也許我們應該一起做這個案子。

Woman: Yes, two heads are better than one.
是啊，三個臭皮匠勝過一個諸葛亮。

正確答案：e. It's a good idea to work together. 一起做是個好主意。

Two heads are better than one. 兩個頭好過一個頭，其實就是中國人說的：「三個臭皮匠勝過一個諸葛亮」的意思。用來表示兩個人的合作或腦力激盪，會比一個人努力或苦思成果來得好。這句話也可以用在形容「寡不敵眾」喔！

▶ 老外時常這麼說

Two heads are better than one when it comes to solving complex political issues.
要解決複雜問題的時候，兩個人一起想會比一個人獨立做來得好。

4. Man: I've got to get started on the report or I'll never finish
   it today.
   我得趕緊開始寫報告，不然的話我今天絕對寫不完的。

Woman: There's no time like the present. 不現在做還等待何時。

正確答案：d. It's best to get it over with now. 現在就把它完成是最好的方式。

There's no time like the present. 就是「不現在做還等待何時」，表示說話者認為應該立即行動。present 是「禮物」，也是「現在」，所以我們會說「現在」就是任何人給你最好的禮物。因為只要能把握現在，live in the present，也可以說 live in the

補教名師王舒葳教你
14天聽懂
老外說的英語

DAY
1

DAY
2

DAY
3

DAY
4

DAY
5

DAY
6

DAY
7

DAY
8

DAY
9

DAY
10

DAY
11

DAY
12

DAY
13

DAY
14

present moment，你就能夠創造無限可能喔！

▶ 老外時常這麼說

A: When do you think I should phone Mr. Davison about that job?

你覺得我應該什麼時候打電話給Davison先生，詢問關於那份工作的事？

B: Well, there's no time like the present.

這個嘛，不如現在就行動吧。

Live in the present. Do not look back and grieve over the past.

活在當下。不要回頭看或為過去懊惱悲傷。

5. Woman: Could you be a dear and give me a hand with these boxes?

你可以好心幫我搬這些箱子嗎？

Man: No sooner said than done. 馬上就做。

正確答案：a. I'll start right away. 馬上就做。

　　No sooner said than done. 就是「馬上就做」，意思是對方在提出請求的同時，這件事就可以完成了。這句話是用來表示馬上就會去做，或這件事已經幾乎要完成了。類似表達熱忱與效率的說法還有："Consider it done." 或直接說："Done."

▶ 老外時常這麼說

A: Would you mind closing the window? 你介意把窗戶關上嗎？

B: No sooner said than done. 馬上關。

Just ask and consider it done. 只要你開口，我們就能幫你辦好。

6. Man: I was late for class on Friday. I had a doctor's appointment.

我星期五上課遲到。我去看醫生。

Woman: Better late than never. 遲到總比沒去好。

正確答案：f. It's good that you went at all. 你有去就已經很好了。

Better late than never.「遲到總比沒發生好」，就是「雖然晚了，但至少你做了，總比什麼都沒做來得好」。

▶ 老外時常這麼說

A: Cathy's card arrived 10 days after my birthday.

Cathy的卡片在我生日過了十天後才到。

B: Oh well, better late than never.

這個嘛，遲來的卡片總比沒有卡片好。

> 舒葳老師小叮嚀

　　有的時候我們聽老外講話時，明明聽懂了每個字，卻還是搞不懂對方的意思，不明白這些字為什麼在這個情境下被組合在一起。這時，很可能是因為老外用了英文的成語。和中文一樣，成語所表達的意思常不一定和字面的意思相同，或另有弦外之音。這時候，如果我們對這些用語不熟悉，就有可能摸不清對方所指為何了。除了成語之外，要聽得懂老外說話，我們還得多多學習英文的慣用語及片語。英文中的成語、慣用語及片語數量繁多，下面我們先介紹一些比較常聽到的吧。

補教名師王舒藏教你
14天聽懂
老外說的英語

DAY
1

DAY
2

DAY
3

DAY
4

DAY
5

DAY
6

DAY
7

DAY
8

DAY
9

DAY
10

DAY
11

DAY
12

DAY
13

DAY
14

Lesson 2 > | 成語、慣用語及片語

> 1. 成語及慣用語 (MP3) 10-3

　　英文的片語及慣用語很多，我們不可能一一說明。在這裡，我們只能先介紹一些常用的，讓同學先體會一下老外在英文口語中時常掛在嘴邊的成語慣用語，幫助我們加強聽力喔！

● 與錢有關

a. Tighten your belt 勒緊褲帶

　　如果你需要 tighten your belt，表示你必須開始小心你的開銷了。是不是聽起來很熟悉呢？其實中文裏也有這個說法，形容經濟拮据，手頭不寬裕，需要節衣縮食度日。請看下例：

Woman: Do you think you can pay this bill sometime this week?

　　　　你想你這週可以繳這個帳單的錢嗎？

Man: Another bill? I'll have to tighten my belt this month!

　　　　又有帳單了嗎？我這個月得勒緊褲帶了！

b. Get money to burn 錢太多了

　　如果有人可以把錢拿來燒，表示這個人錢多到可以花在休閒娛樂上了，跟中國人說「燒錢」的意思可是差了十萬八千里喔！請看下例：

Man: How would you like to go to Paris with me?

　　　　要不要跟我一起去巴黎啊？

Woman: Where did you get money to burn?

　　　　你哪裡來的閒錢？

c. Cost an arm and a leg 花了我非常多錢

如果我們形容某事 costs an arm and a leg，意思就是說這個東西非常昂貴。說 cost me a fortune 也是一樣的意思。請看下例：

This house cost us an arm and a leg, but we have no regrets.

這棟房子花了我們很多錢，但是我們並不後悔。

Katie cost me a fortune!

凱蒂花了我很多錢。

（可能是他的女友或老婆很愛花他的錢買昂貴的東西）。

● 與人有關

a. The apple of your eye 最珍貴的人

如果你說某人是 the apple of your eye，表示你這個人是你最關心、喜歡的人。有一首歌就是這麼唱的："You're the apple of my eye. That's why I'll always be with you." 請看下例：

My granddaughter is the apple of my eye.

我孫女是我最珍愛的人。

b. Be not cut out for something 不是那個料

如果你是 not cut out for something, 表示你不是那樣的人或你不適合做那樣的事。你也可以說：not cut out to be...。請看下例：

I started studying finance but I quickly realized I wasn't cut out for it.

我開始讀財經，但我馬上就領悟到我不適合走那條路。

He is not cut out to be President.

他不是當總統的料。

c. To each his own 人各有所好

To each his own. 指的是每個人的品味、喜好皆不同。請看下例：

Woman: This place is great. I love the noise and activity in here.
You don't like it?

這地方太棒了。我愛死了這裡的熱鬧和進行的活動。

你不喜歡嗎?

Man: Not really. To each his own though.

不太喜歡,不過個人喜好不同囉。

● 與工作有關

a. burning the candle at both ends 一根蠟燭兩頭燒

説某人burning the candle at both ends 表示這個人太忙了,簡直裡外煎熬。請看下例:

W: John stays out all night at bars and then goes to work at 6 a.m.

John整夜都待在酒吧,到早上六點就直接去上班。

M: He's really burning the candle at both ends.

他真是一根蠟燭兩頭燒。

b. A blank check 空白支票;充分授權

如果你給某人 a blank check,就是説你給他一張空白支票,他想寫多少金額,就寫多少金額,意思就是你充分授權他以他認為最好、最恰當的方式處理問題。

2008 年九月歐巴馬在競選美國總統時恰巧遇到美國金融風暴的問題和金融業7000億疏困案的爭議,他就説了:"No 'blank check' for Wall Street." 意思是説布希的7000億紓困案不該是讓華爾街用在任何他們想用的地方,而應該保障一般美國人也能得到幫助。

請再看下例:

DAY 1
DAY 2
DAY 3
DAY 4
DAY 5
DAY 6
DAY 7
DAY 8
DAY 9
DAY 10
DAY 11
DAY 12
DAY 13
DAY 14

We are not giving the redevelopment project a blank check. The organizers will be working within a strictly limited budget.

我們並不是給這個改造計劃一張空白支票。這些組織機關都會在嚴格把關的預算下進行這個計劃。

c. A done deal 定案了

A done deal. 是用來表示已經達成一項協議或一個決定。我們通常會說：It's a done deal.或 It's not a done deal. 請看下例：

We've already hired someone for the position, so this is a done deal.

這個職位我們已經雇用了一個人，所以定案了。

We told them we needed more time to think about it, so it's not a done deal.

我們告訴他們我們還需要點時間考慮，所以這件事尚未定案。

● 有問題的時候

a. Get the roundabout 被對方迂迴地拒絕

roundabout 是馬路上的圓環、迴轉區。這裡的意思，就是迂迴、不直接爽快的回應。所以 got the roundabout 意思就是對方很間接迂迴地拒絕。請看下例：

Man: I got the roundabout when I asked my mother for a new car.

我問我媽媽能不能買一台新車時，她跟我打迷糊仗。

Woman: I know what you mean. That's happened to me.

我懂你的意思。我也有過一樣的經驗。

b. We're in the same boat. 我們在同一條船上。

We're in the same boat. 指我們處境相同，也就是都必須做類似的事情。請看下例：

W: I have to go to school, and then go to work everyday this week.

這個星期我必須上學,放學後再去上班。

M: We're in the same boat.

我們處境相同。

c. Take a crack at it 試試看

take a crack at it 就是指嘗試看看做某件事情。注意聽,在說話的時候,這幾個字都會連音喔。請看下例:

Woman: I just can't uncork the bottle. 我打不開這個瓶子。

Man: Can I take a crack at it? 我可以試試看嗎?

● 與天氣/氣氛有關

a. Once in a blue moon 非常少見

once in a blue moon 這個跟天氣有關的成語可以用來形容某事非常少見。說 blue moon 是因為老外覺得有時候因天氣的狀況,月亮看起來有可能感覺藍藍的呢。請見下例:

We only see our daughter once in a blue moon.

我們很少見到我們的女兒。

b. In the dark 一無所知;被瞞在鼓裏

如果某人在某個事情上 be kept in the dark,表示他沒有被告知跟此事相關的發展,因為 in the dark 就是黑漆漆、什麼都看不見的意思。相同的意思,你也可以說 be left in the dark。請看下例:

The personnel were kept in the dark about the merger until the last minute.

關於這個公司的合併案,人事部門一直到最後一刻都還被瞞在鼓裏。

c. It never rains but it pours 福無雙至、禍不單行

這個表達法是用來形容當壞事發生的時候，其他的壞事也會接踵而來。就是中文說的：「福無雙至、禍不單行」囉！請看下例：

First of all it was the car breaking down, then the fire in the kitchen and now Mike's accident. It never rains but it pours!

剛開始是車子拋錨，然後廚房著火，現在麥克又發生這個意外。真是禍不單行！

❯ 2. 動詞片語

英文常用的動詞片語同樣也是不勝枚舉，這裡我們只是列舉幾類常聽見的，幫助同學學習喔！

● 與計劃有關

a. Call off 取消

call off 就是 cancel，是取消的意思。仔細聽，call off 會連音。跟著說說看。請看下例：

W: What's going on? Why are you leaving already?

　發生什麼事？你為什麼已經要走了？

M: The bride called off the wedding, so I'll be going home, I guess.

　新娘取消婚禮了，所以我想我該回家了。

b. Carry out 執行、實行

Carry out 就是執行一項計劃或命令。去做一個測試或實驗也可以說 carry out。請看下例：

The plan was carried out to perfection.

這個計劃執行得很完美。

The government is carrying out tests on growing genetically modified crops.

政府正在執行基因改造農作物的測試。

c. Fall through 失敗、未發生

我們說一個計劃、案子等等 fall through，表示最後並沒有實現。請看下例：

The project fell through at the last minute because of a lack of funding.

因為缺乏財源，計劃在最後一刻告吹了。

d. Get on / get along 繼續、使有進展

Get on with 某事，就是繼續做某事，讓某事有進展的意思。也可以說 get long。請看下例：

Stop all the fuss and get on with your work!
別再小題大作地抱怨了，趕快回去工作吧！

How are you getting on with your new job?
你的新工作進展得如何啊？

How is he getting along with his studies?
他書讀得如何？ 他的研究進行得怎麼樣？

e. Go ahead 照常進行

我們說某事會 go ahead 就是說某事會發生、會照計劃進行。請看下例：

The conference will go ahead as scheduled.
會議會照原定計劃舉行。

DAY 1
DAY 2
DAY 3
DAY 4
DAY 5
DAY 6
DAY 7
DAY 8
DAY 9
DAY 10
DAY 11
DAY 12
DAY 13
DAY 14

f. Put off 延期、拖延

Put off 就是 delay，是延期、拖延的意思。我們會說 put off 某事，如果某 事用代名詞 it 代替時，就會說 put it off。注意，在說話時，put off 和 put it off 都會連音喔！ 請看下例：

Woman: Why are you going to the dentist today? I thought we
were going to SOGO.

你今天為什麼要去看牙醫？我以為我們今天要去SOGO？

Man: Well, I just can't put it off any longer.

我實在是不能再拖了。

● 開始與結束

a. Back down 讓步、放棄

在某事上 back down 就是因為別人對立的立場或其他阻礙而放棄、打退堂鼓了。請看下例：

He has backed down from the position he took last week.
他已經放棄了上星期的立場。

Local authorities backed down on their plans to demolish the building.
當地的政府當局已放棄他們拆除這棟建築的計劃。

b. Break out 爆發

Break out 就是很突然地開始，通常指疾病、戰爭、暴亂等等。請看下例：

He was twelve when the war broke out.
戰爭爆發時，他12歲。

Recently, a fatal disease broke out in China infecting thousands of children and causing the death of some of them.

補教名師王舒薇教你
1**4天聽懂**
老外說的英語

DAY 1
DAY 2
DAY 3
DAY 4
DAY 5
DAY 6
DAY 7
DAY 8
DAY 9
DAY 10
DAY 11
DAY 12
DAY 13
DAY 14

最近有一種致命的疾病在中國大陸擴散開來，數以千計的孩童受到感染有些並因此死亡。

c. Die down 逐漸減弱

Die down 就是平靜下來，或逐漸減弱的意思。請看下例：

The humid has gone and the wind has died down. It's actually a pretty nice day today.
潮溼已經遠離，風也漸漸減弱。今天天氣其實蠻不錯的。

When the applause died down, she started to sing.
當掌聲結束，她便開始唱歌。

d. Drop out 輟學

Drop out 指的是念書念到一半就離開學校，沒有完成學業。請看下例：

Dropping out of school has become more and more common at school.
學生輟學在學校越來越常見了。

Some students drop out of school because they suffer the setbacks at school.
有些學生輟學是因為在學校經歷成績倒退和挫折。

e. Move in/ move out 搬進去／搬出去

Move in 是搬進去，move out 就是搬出去。如果是搬進去跟某人住就是 move in with someone。請看下例：

We have just moved in.
我們剛搬進來。

Tom decided to move in with his girlfriend.
湯姆決定搬去跟他女朋友住。

Moving out is a great way to become independent.

搬出去自己住是訓練獨立很好的方法。

f. Opt out 選擇退出

Opt out 是選擇結束或退出某項已經在進行的服務或計劃等等，常用在市場行銷或組織的政策等等。請看下例：

You may click the "opt-out button" to notify the sender that you wish to receive no further e-mails.

你可以點「選擇退出方塊」來告知寄件者你以後不希望再收到郵件。

Are patients given the chance to opt out of having medical information stored on the database?

病人有被賦予選擇不希望醫療資料被存在資料庫上的機會嗎？

● 人的關係

a. Break up 分手

Break up 就是和男女朋友分手。當動詞用是 break up，兩個音節皆重；當名詞用是 breakup 重音變成在第一音節喔。請看下例：

My brother has just broken up with his girlfriend.

我哥哥才剛跟他女友分手。

Is it harder for the person who gets broken up with to get over the breakup?

被人分手的人是否比較不容易從分手的低潮中走出來呢？

He's still not over the breakup, but he's finally ready to move on.

他還沒完全走出分手的低潮，但總算是準備好要繼續過他的生活了。

b. Count on 依靠

Count on 是依靠、信賴的意思，可以 count on 人、也可以 count on 某件事會發生。我們也常說 Don't count on it. 表示不要相信這件

補教名師王舒葳教你
1**4天聽懂**
老外說的英語

DAY
1

DAY
2

DAY
3

DAY
4

DAY
5

DAY
6

DAY
7

DAY
8

DAY
9

**DAY
10**

DAY
11

DAY
12

DAY
13

DAY
14

事、不要對這件事太有信心。

You can count on me.

你可以信賴我。

A: Are you coming to our party this weekend?

你週末會來我們的派對嗎？

B: You can count on it.

一定去！

Don't count on lower fuel prices lasting very long.

不要期待低油價會持續多久。

c. Get on / get along 相處

我們上面有學過，get on with something 是繼續進行某事的意思。如果我們説 get on with someone 就是和某人的相處情形了。get on well 就是相處融洽，你也可以説 get along well。請看下例：

I've always got on well with Henry.

我和亨利一向相處融洽。

The two boys get on well most of the time.

這兩個男孩通常都相處融洽。

My sister and I don't get along.

我跟我姊姊處不來。

d. Get together 聚在一起

When can we get together again?

我們何時才能再相聚？

We get together once in a while.

我們每過一陣子會聚一次。

e. Hang out 和朋友一起消磨時光

Hang out 就是和朋友一起度過休閒的時間，如聊天、吃喝、逛街、玩樂等等。 你可以說 hang out at/in...，表示沒事常在那裡度過休閒時光。你也可以說 hang out with someone，表示你常和誰在一起。請看下例：

He hangs out in the pub down the street. He's there most nights.
他沒事都會去那間酒館。幾乎每晚都在那裡。

That new café in the city centre is a nice place to hang out with friends.
市中心的那間新咖啡店是和朋友一塊兒聊天社交的好地方。

I work long hours and don't want to hang out with people from work.
我工作時數很長，所以不想下班還和同事一起消磨時間。

f. Look down on　鄙視、看輕

Look down on someone 就是看不起、鄙視某人的意思。請看下例：

He looks down on his colleagues because he thinks he's better than they are.
他瞧不起他的同事，因為他自覺高人一等。

A lot of people look down on her because of her family background.
很多人因為她的家庭背景而鄙視她。

❯ 舒葳老師小叮嚀

英文中的成語、慣用語和片語是阻礙同學理解的一大因素。不熟悉這些成語、慣用語和片語，就算是背了再多的單字，往往也是有聽沒有懂。尤其是口語英文和閱讀英文有一定的差距，最大的差別之一，便是這些口語表達法的使用。我們在這裡介紹的只是部份的成語、慣用語和片語，同學一旦有了概念，以後便要多學習這些

口語常用的表達法，才能聽得輕鬆順暢喔！下面我們就來做更多的
練習吧！

Lesson 3 ▶ 再聽聽看

A .

　　請聽MP3，並填寫空格中的成語、慣用語及片語。並想想這些
成語、慣用語各代表什麼意思。

1.

W: Wow, you ate that ice cream fast.

M: Yeah, _____. It was so good.

2.

M: Well, I am sorry for what I did. Thank you for telling me about it.

W: It is OK. I just had to _____.

3.

W: It's _____ out there!

M: I know. We won't be going shopping today!

4.

W: So, how does the story end?

M: Well, _____, the titanic sinks and the girl lives.

5.

M: I don't think our classmates should confront Professor

DAY
1

DAY
2

DAY
3

DAY
4

DAY
5

DAY
6

DAY
7

DAY
8

DAY
9

**DAY
10**

DAY
11

DAY
12

DAY
13

DAY
14

Simms with these issues.

W: I know- I'm going to try to _____.

6.

She may not like the coffee cake, but _____

_____.

7.

James _____ while we painted the

entire house.

8.

Allen was _____ thinking about how to please his

parents with good grades.

B.

請聽MP3，並填寫空格中的片語。並想想這些片語各代表什麼
意思。

1.

He's impossible! How do you _____ him?

2.

I will have to _____ on the workers to make this deadline.

3.

Please _____ and let me out of the car. I need to get out

of here.

4.

Wow, you really _____. Why were you so _____

_____ him?

5.

Could you _____ for Chris while he is _____?

6.

M: I don't go to the bars like I did as a young man.

W: Actually, I've noticed that you' ve really _____

your drinking altogether.

7.

W: Why do you get so upset when Ralph tells his stories?

M: think he feels the need to _____ his life stories in an

attempt to make his life feel more grand and fulfilling. I wish

he would simply tell the truth.

8.

W: I don't understand what you are _____. What are

you trying to say about my dress? Do you or don't you like it?

M: Well, to be completely honest, I was trying to _____

_____, but I really don't like it.

DAY 1
DAY 2
DAY 3
DAY 4
DAY 5
DAY 6
DAY 7
DAY 8
DAY 9
DAY 10
DAY 11
DAY 12
DAY 13
DAY 14

● Answers

A.
1. I couldn't help it
2. get it off my chest.
3. raining cats and dogs
4. in a nutshell
5. talk them out of it
6. I'll cross that bridge when I come to it
7. didn't lift a finger
8. beside himself

B.
1. put up with
2. crack down
3. pull over
4. told him off   mad at
5. fill in   on vacation
6. cut down on
7. play up
8. getting at   spare your feelings

> 詳細解說 10-5

A.

1. W: Wow, you ate that ice cream fast.
    哇，你冰淇淋吃得真快。

M: Yeah, I couldn't help it. It was so good.
    是啊，我無法自制。實在是太好吃了。

> I couldn't help it. 就是「我沒辦法控制自己」、「沒辦法改變」。常用在找藉口，或合理化自己的行動的時候。

▶ 老外時常這麼說

I've tried to stop smoking, but I can't. I must smoke! I can't help it!
我嘗試戒煙，但失敗了。我得抽煙，我沒辦法不抽！

I should control my temper better, but I can't help getting angry.
我應該要控制自己的脾氣，但我就是不由自主地生氣。

A: Why do you spend so much time on the Internet?
　你為什麼花這麼多時間上網？

B: I can't help it. Maybe I'm addicted.
　我也沒辦法。也許我是上癮了。

2. M: Well, I am sorry for what I did. Thank you for telling me
　　about it.
　　嗯，我為我的行為感到抱歉。謝謝你告訴我。

W: It is ok. I just had to get it off my chest.
　沒關係，我只是需要一吐為快。

> 　　Get it out of my chest 從字面上理解就是「從胸中丟出來」，
> 也就是「一吐為快」的意思，表示「說出來就沒事了」。

3. W: It's raining cats and dogs out there!
　　外面正傾盆大雨！

M: I know. We won't be going shopping today!
　是啊。我們今天不會去購物了！

> 　　Raining cats and dogs ，雨大得貓和狗都從屋頂上被沖下來

DAY
1

DAY
2

DAY
3

DAY
4

DAY
5

DAY
6

DAY
7

DAY
8

DAY
9

**DAY
10**

DAY
11

DAY
12

DAY
13

DAY
14

了，就是「傾盆大雨」的意思。我們也可以用下面的說法來表示「傾盆大雨」：

❯ 老外時常這麼說

It's pouring. 雨下得很大；正傾盆大雨。

It's pouring down rain. 雨下得很大；正傾盆大雨。

I was caught in a downpour. 我被困在一場傾盆大雨中。

4. W: So, how does the story end?

   所以，故事最後怎麼了？

   M: Well, in a nutshell, the titanic sinks and the girl lives.

   這個嘛，長話短說，鐵達尼號沉了，女孩活下來了。

In a nut shell，照字面上理解是「在堅果殼裡」。堅果的殼很小，不能裝很多東西，因此「在堅果殼裡」就是「簡單地說」、「一言以蔽之」的意思。你也可以說：to put it in a nutshell 或 putting it in a nutshell。

❯ 老外時常這麼說

Just give me the facts in a nutshell.

簡單告訴我實際情況就好了。

I've got bills to pay, I've got to have my car repaired and I've just lost my job - putting it in a nutshell I'm fed up!

我有帳單要付，我有車要修，而且我剛失業——總之，我真是受夠了！

5. M: I don't think our classmates should confront Professor

Simms with these issues.

我認為我們的同學不應該在這些問題上和Simms 教授正面起衝突。

W: I know - I'm going to try to talk them out of it.

我知道，我會試著說服他們不要這麼做。

Talk someone out of something 就是「說服某人不要做某事」。如果是要「說服某人要去做某事」就要說 talk someone into something。

You've got to talk him into exercising.

你得說服他開始運動。

I don't know why I let you talk me into going.

我不知道我為什麼會讓你說服我去

（說話者去了，但後悔這麼做）。

Please talk me out of buying this bag!

拜託你說服我不要買這個袋子！

---

6. She may not like the coffee cake, but I'll cross that bridge when I come to it.

有可能不喜歡這個咖啡蛋糕，但真的發生再說吧。

I'll cross that bridge when I come to it. 照字面上理解是「等到我看到橋再過吧」。看到了橋再過橋，都還沒看到橋當然也就不需要想過橋的事，其實就是中文說的「船到橋頭自然直」，碰到問題再解決吧。

▶ 老外時常這麼說

DAY 1　DAY 2　DAY 3　DAY 4　DAY 5　DAY 6　DAY 7　DAY 8　DAY 9　DAY 10　DAY 11　DAY 12　DAY 13　DAY 14

A: What if Mom says no? 如果媽不答應怎麼辦？

B: I'll cross that bridge when I come to it. 到時候再說囉。

7. James didn't lift a finger while we painted the entire house.
我們在漆這整間房子的油漆時，James一點忙都沒幫。

> Didn't lift a finger 照字面上理解是「一根手指頭都沒舉起來」。如果別人在做事，他卻一根手指頭都沒舉起來，就表示「他一點忙都沒幫」囉。通常用來形容懶惰不幫忙的人。

▶ 老外時常這麼說

He spends all day stretched out on the sofa and never lifts a finger to help.
他整天躺在沙發上，從來不幫一點忙。

8. Allen was beside himself thinking about how to please his parents with good grades.
艾倫為了想如何能以好成績取悅他父母感到很焦慮。

> Beside oneself 照字面上理解是「在他自己旁邊」。這是什麼意思呢？這個意思是說某人的情緒已經到了很極端、不像自己的程度，很像靈魂已經出竅，在旁邊看著自己一樣。

▶ 老外時常這麼說

He was beside himself with anger.
他快氣瘋了。

She is beside herself with excitement because her holiday is approaching.

她因為假期的即將到來而欣喜若狂。

B.

1. He's impossible! How do you put up with him?

   他簡直是不可理喻！你是如何能忍受他的？

> Put up with 就是「忍受」的意思。

▶ 老外時常這麼說

I can't put up with this weather for much longer.

我沒辦法再忍受這個天氣多久了。

I can't put up with this shit anymore.

我再也無法忍受這些垃圾事了。

2. I will have to crack down on the workers to make this deadline.

   我得好好地逼一下這些工人，才有辦法在限期內趕工完成。

> Crack down 就是「嚴厲地要求」的意思，在這裡表示強加要求及催趕員工的作業。

▶ 老外時常這麼說

The presidential candidate promised to crack down on corruption.

總統候選人承諾要嚴懲貪污。

DAY 1
DAY 2
DAY 3
DAY 4
DAY 5
DAY 6
DAY 7
DAY 8
DAY 9
DAY 10
DAY 11
DAY 12
DAY 13
DAY 14

3. Please pull over and let me out of the car. I need to get out
of here.
請靠邊停車讓我下車。我需要離開這裡。

> Pull over 就是「靠邊停車」的意思，也可以用在「警察叫車子
靠邊停」。

▶ | 老外時常這麼說

James pulled the car over to the side of the road and stopped.
James把車子靠邊並停了下來。

The police pulled the car over and tested the driver for alcohol.
警察叫車子靠邊停，然後測駕駛的酒精濃度。

The police pull the speeding motorist over.
警察叫超速的架駛靠邊停。

4. Wow, you really told him off. Why were you so mad at him?
哇，你真的狠狠地罵了他一頓耶。你為什麼這麼氣他？

> Tell off 就是「責怪、責罵」的意思。Mad at someone 就是
「對某人非常生氣」的意思。

▶ | 老外時常這麼說

His girlfriend told him off for arriving nearly half an hour late.
他的女朋友因為他遲到了將近半小時而責罵他。

5. Could you fill in for Chris while he is on vacation?

補教名師王舒藏教你
1 4天聽懂
老外說的英語

DAY
1

DAY
2

DAY
3

DAY
4

DAY
5

DAY
6

DAY
7

DAY
8

DAY
9

DAY
10

DAY
11

DAY
12

DAY
13

DAY
14

克里斯放假的時候，你可以替他代班嗎？

Fill in 有兩個意思，在這裡是「替某人代班」的意思；另外也可以當「填表格」的意思。

▶ 老外時常這麼說

She has to take care of her mother in the hospital, so we have hired a temp to fill in for her.

她必須去醫院照顧她媽媽，所以我們已經請了一個臨時的工讀生來代她的班。

Please could you fill in the application form and send it back to us.

請你把申請表填妥，並寄回來給我們。

6. M: I don't go to the bars like I did as a young man.

我現在不像以前年輕的時候那樣常去酒吧了。

W: Actually, I've noticed that you've really cut down on your drinking altogether.

事實上，我注意到你連酒都不怎麼喝了。

Cut down on something 就是「減少某物的量」。

▶ 老外時常這麼說

The doctor told me to cut down on the fat in my diet.

醫生叫我減少飲食中的油脂。

In order to cut down on mailing expenses, we have asked members to send us their e-mail addresses for future correspondence.

為了減低郵資的開銷，我們已請會員寄他們的電子郵件信箱做為以後郵寄之用。

7. W: Why do you get so upset when Ralph tells his stories?

  Ralph 在説他的故事時，你為什麼那麼不高興？

 M: I think he feels the need to play up his life stories in an attempt to make his life feel more grand and fulfilling. I wish he would simply tell the truth.

  我覺得他需要藉著誇大他的人生故事，來讓他的人生顯得比較偉大、有成就。我真希望他能實話實説就好。

> play up something 就是「誇大某事的重要性」的意思。相反就是 play down，表示「輕描淡寫或貶低了某事的重要性」。

❯ 老外時常這麼說

The ad plays up the benefits of the product but doesn't say anything about the side effects.

那則廣告過份強調產品優點，但絲毫沒提及周邊影響。

He tried to play down my part in the work and play up his own.

他嘗試要貶低我在這個工作中的重要性，而誇大他自己的。

8. W: I don't understand what you are getting at. What are you trying to say about my dress? Do you or don't you like it?

  我不懂你是什麼意思。你對我的洋裝有什麼意見？

  你到底是喜歡還是不喜歡？

 M: Well, to be completely honest, I was trying to spare your feelings, but I really don't like it.

這個嘛，老實説，我剛才只是不想傷你的心，我實在不喜歡。

get at something 就是「暗示」，是「意有所指」的意思，也可以當「批評」用。

▶ 老外時常這麼說

What do you think she is getting at? I don't have a clue what she wants.

你覺得她意有所指的到底是在指什麼？我完全不知道她到底要什麼。

Her boss is always getting at her for being late.

她老闆老是在唸她遲到的事情。

▶ 聽力小秘訣

☺ 聽力對大多數同學來説會困難的原因之一，在於老外在説話時用的是「口語英文 (spoken English)」，包含了大量的成語、慣用語及片語。從小習慣學校所教的「讀寫英文 (written English)」的同學，一下子要聽英文的時候，自然會聽不懂。

☺ 大量學習英文中的成語、慣用語及片語必定能為你迅速提升英文聽力的理解程度。

☺ 平時在聽英文的時候，如果有遇到聽不懂的地方，先不要慌，聽關鍵字、靠前後文抓大意。等聽完後如果有錄音稿可看，再把聽不懂也看不懂的地方抓出來。

☺ 通常每個字都認識，卻怎麼也覺得文意不通的時候，都是因為你碰到了成語、慣用語及片語喔！ 強行用字面的意義解釋，當然怎麼説都

DAY
1

DAY
2

DAY
3

DAY
4

DAY
5

DAY
6

DAY
7

DAY
8

DAY
9

**DAY
10**

DAY
11

DAY
12

DAY
13

DAY
14

說不通了！

☺ 查「成語慣用語字典」或「片語字典」或問老師，學習你不會的成語、慣用語及片語。

☺ 當你的成語、慣用語及片語功力大增時，不僅你的聽力會變強，你的口語能力必定也是更上一層樓喔！

MEMO

DAY 11

聽力實戰練習1

常見**表達用語**及**對話模式**
Conversational Exchange

11-1~11-4

> 學習重點

　　前面我們學習了十個聽力重點訣竅，教你如何「有效率」地聽。沒有方法的聽，得花上很長的一段時間才能看到些許的進步；一旦掌握了「聽的方法」，聽力的練習便是有技巧、有方向的；才能在最短的時間掌握要領、有效地聽喔！

　　而學會了方法後，更要充分地練習，才能將這些「技巧」變成自己在聽的時候的「本能」。接下來的Day 11～Day 14，我們便要練習把理論應用出來。也就是說，同學在聽的時候，務必記得運用之前學到的方法，把專注力放在聽關鍵字，聽不懂的地方也要注意是否是連音、弱化，或是你自己發音的問題喔！

Lesson 1 ❯ 必備日常用語

> ❯ 舒葳老師說　MP3 11-1

請聽 MP3，並寫下你所聽到的。你知道這些用語各是什麼意思嗎？

1. _____

2. _____

3. _____

4. _____

5. _____

6. _____

7. _____

8. _____

9. _____

10. _____

11. _____

12. _____

DAY 1
DAY 2
DAY 3
DAY 4
DAY 5
DAY 6
DAY 7
DAY 8
DAY 9
DAY 10
DAY 11
DAY 12
DAY 13
DAY 14

● Answers

12. Shouldn't I tell him about that?   11. He won't go. Will he?

10. It's great. Isn't it?   9. How about that!

8. It's about time!   7. Come on!

6. Who's here?   5. Hurry up!

4. Watch out!   3. Look out!

2. Wha's up?   1. How's it going?

> **詳細解說** 11-2

請注意連音與消音，聽MP3，並跟著說說看。

1. How's it going? 最近如何？

2. What's up? 怎麼樣？

3. Look out! 注意！

4. Watch out! 注意！小心！

5. Hurry up! 快點！

6. Who's (h)ere? 是誰啊？

7. Com(e) on! 別這樣嘛！

8. It's about time! 是時候了！

9. How about that! 這樣如何！

10. It's great. Isn('t) i(t)? 很棒，不是嗎？

11. He won't go. Will (h)e？ 他不會去，對吧？

12. Shouldn('t) I tell (h)im abou(t) tha(t)？
   我難道不該告訴他那件事嗎？

　　1～9 句都是日常生活中很常聽到的打招呼的方式或普通用語，第10、11、12 三句則是「附加問句」的例子。這些句子常聽到且用字簡單，如果是用讀的，我們一看就懂，但乍聽之下卻被一閃而過的聲音嚇到，不知道對方說了什麼。事實上，只要我們能抓住連音

及消音的特性，多聽幾次，自己也學著說說看，下次聽到老外這麼
說時，我們一定就都能聽懂了！

Lesson 2 ❯ 讚美與回應

❯ 舒葳老師說 (MP3) 11-3

想像老外對你說出下面的讚美，並寫出你會有的回應。

1. You're looking smart today!

_____

2. I like your jacket. It really suits you.

_____

3. This is really delicious. You're such a good cook.

_____

4. Wow! You look absolutely stunning!

_____

5. Your article is the best I've ever read on this topic.

_____

6. What lovely flowers!

_____

● Answers

1. Oh! I've got an interview.
2. Oh thanks. I've had it for years actually.
3. Do you really think I am?
4. Don't I always?
5. Thank you. I'm flattered.
6. Glad you like them.

DAY 1
DAY 2
DAY 3
DAY 4
DAY 5
DAY 6
DAY 7
DAY 8
DAY 9
DAY 10
DAY 11
DAY 12
DAY 13
DAY 14

> **詳細解說** 11-4

老外常讚美人，因此讚美的用語以及回應的方式我們都應該要熟悉。回應的方式有很多種，視當時情境及你與對方的關係交情而定。可以是正經八百地道謝 (如: Thank you. I'm flattered. 也可以是俏皮地開個玩笑 (如: Don't I always?)。請再聽一次並跟著說說看。

1. A: You're looking smart today!

   你今天打扮得很好看喔！

   B: Oh! I've got an interview.

   噢，我今天有面試。

> Smart在用來形容穿著時，就是看起來「整潔、好看、吸引人」的意思。

2. A: I like your shirt. It really suits you.

   我喜歡妳的上衣，很適合妳。

   B: Oh thanks. I've had it for years actually.

   噢，謝謝。其實這件衣服已經很多年了。

> It really suits you. 是常用的讚美人衣著的說法。注意 suits you 的連音，以及 I have had i(t) for years. 的連音。Blouse 是女生的短上衣。

> **老外時常這麼說**

The dress/color suits you. 這件洋裝／這個顏色很適合你。

You look good in that dress/color. 你穿這件洋裝／這個顏色很好看。

3. A: This is really delicious. You're such a good cook.

真好吃。你的手藝真好 (真是個好廚師)。

B: Do you really think I am？

你真的這麼覺得嗎？

這是很客氣的回應。Do you really think I am？就是 Do you really think I am a good cook？的簡單説法。

4. A: Wow! You look absolutely stunning!

哇，妳真是豔光四射！

B: Don't I always？

我不總是如此嗎？

這是較俏皮的回應方法，適合用在比較熟的朋友之間。Don't I always？就是 Don't I always look stunning？的簡單説法。Stunning 就是非常亮眼，豔光四射的意思。

5. A: Your article is the best I've ever read on this topic.

你的文章是我看過同一個主題的文章中寫得最好的。

B: Thank you. I'm flattered.

謝謝你。我感到受寵若驚。

I'm flattered. 是很受人誇獎時的好用回應方式，就是「你這麼説／這麼做，我感到很開心且受寵若驚。

當別人對你誇獎或奉承、令你感到高興的時候，除了説：I'm flattered. 外，你可表示感謝説：I appreciate that.（我很感謝你這麼説），Thank you for the compliment.（謝謝你的讚賞），That's nice of you to say.（你這麼説真好），或 You have made me blush.（你讓我臉紅了）。

❯ 老外時常這麼說

I'm flattered you like my design.

你喜歡我的設計讓我受寵若驚。

I'm flattered you read my blog.

你會讀我的部落格真讓我感到受寵若驚。

I was flattered by the invitation to her party.

我竟然會受邀去她的派對，真是讓我感到受寵若驚。

6. A: What lovely flowers!

這些花真美！

B: Glad you like them.

很高興你喜歡。

> What lovely...! 真是美麗的…！是常用讚美的句子。Glad you like it / them. 也是好用的回應。

❯ 老外時常這麼說

A: What a lovely evening! 今天真是美好的一晚！

B: Glad you enjoyed it. 很高興妳玩得愉快。

A: What beautiful eyes you have! 你的家真棒！

B: Thank you. It's very sweet of you. 謝謝。你嘴巴真甜。

A: What lovely weather! 天氣真好！

B: It is lovely, isn't it？真的是很好，不是嗎？

DAY 1
DAY 2
DAY 3
DAY 4
DAY 5
DAY 6
DAY 7
DAY 8
DAY 9
DAY 10
DAY 11
DAY 12
DAY 13
DAY 14

Lesson 3 ❯ 同意與反對

❯ 舒葳老師說　(MP3) 11-5

老外會常用特定的一些說法表達同意或反對對方的說法，所以熟悉這些用語很重要喔！

請聽下面用語，如果是同意請寫○，部份同意請寫△，完全不同意請寫✗。

1. _____　　9. _____

2. _____　　10. _____

3. _____　　11. _____

4. _____　　12. _____

5. _____　　13. _____

6. _____　　14. _____

7. _____　　15. _____

8. _____

● Answers

1. I would agree with that. ○
2. I disagree, I'm afraid. ✗
3. I take your point but... △
4. Well, it depends. △
5. You're absolutely right. ○
6. Come on! ✗
7. That's right. ○
8. I don't think that's true. ✗
9. I see what you mean, but... △
10. That's true in a way, but... △
11. Absolutely. ○
12. I don't know about that. ✗
13. To a certain extent, but... △
14. That's rubbish! ✗
15. Exactly. ○

❯ 詳細解說　(MP3) 11-6

請看下面各類別的表達用語。當老外不完全贊同對方意見時，

補教名師王舒嵐教你
14天聽懂
老外說的英語

DAY 1
DAY 2
DAY 3
DAY 4
DAY 5
DAY 6
DAY 7
DAY 8
DAY 9
DAY 10
DAY 11
DAY 12
DAY 13
DAY 14

會先禮貌地表示肯定，再繼續說他不同意的地方喔。

完全贊同

That's right. 沒錯。

I would agree with that. 我同意。

You're absolutely right. 你說得一點都沒錯。

Absolutely. 完全正確。

Exactly. 一點都沒錯。

部份同意，但有意見

I see what you mean, but...　我知道你的意思，但是…

I take your point but...　我知道你的意思，但是…

To a certain extent, but...　某個程度是沒錯，但是…

That's true in a way, but...　某個程度是沒錯，但是…

Well, it depends.　這個嘛，要看情形。

持反對意見

I don't know about that. 我可不確定那麼說對不對喔 (客氣地否定)。

I don't think that's true. 我想那麼說是不正確的。

Come on! 拜託！

I disagree, I'm afraid. 恐怕我不能同意。

That's rubbish! 簡直是胡說八道！

Lesson 4 ❯ 告知壞消息

❯ 舒葳老師說

　　當老外要告訴對方壞消息時，通常會先「警告」對方：「我有壞消息要告訴你…」。也就是說，當你聽到老外說類似下面的句子時，你就知道，大事不妙了！想想看，你是否能猜到他接下來要說什麼？

1. Could I ask you a big favor?

   我可以請你幫個大忙嗎？（一定是個「大」忙）

2. You know I said I could lend you my car this weekend?

   你知道我說我這個週末可以借你車嗎？（現在應該是沒辦法借了）

3. You know that book you lent me?

   你不是借給了我一本書嗎？（可能是丟了，或毀損了）

4. I've got a bit of a problem.

   我不是很高興／我有點問題。（對方應該是對你有所抱怨）

5. I don't quite know how to put this, but...

   我不知道該怎麼說，但是…（要說些難以啟齒的事了）

6. There's something I've been meaning to tell you.

   有件事我一直想告訴你。（應該是會讓你震驚的事吧）

7. I've a confession to make.

   我得承認一件事。（對方可能有什麼事是你可能不想知道的）

8. I'm afraid I've got an apology to make...

   恐怕我有件事得向你道歉…（對方一定是做了對不起你的事）

❯ 聽力小秘訣

補教名師王舒蔗教你
14天聽懂
老外說的英語

DAY
1

DAY
2

DAY
3

DAY
4

DAY
5

DAY
6

DAY
7

DAY
8

DAY
9

DAY
10

DAY
11

DAY
12

DAY
13

DAY
14

☺ 同學應熟悉日常生活常用句型以及生活一般情境中慣用的應對用語，並在練習聽這些短句及常用表達法的同時，複習前面學過聽重音、消音及連音的技巧。

☺ 所有本課的句子，同學皆應反覆聽 MP3 並開口跟著說。讓自己的耳朵及說出來的英文皆與老外的聲音融為一體。

☺ 最後不要打開書，試試看自己是否也可以說出這些句子。

☺ 當你熟悉老外的說話模式時，聽力也會變得輕鬆自然！

MEMO

MEMO

DAY **12** 聽力實戰練習2
生活會話
Daily Conversations

12-1~12-4

> **學習重點**

　　聽完了常見句型與慣用的對話模式後，我們這課要練習的是短篇及長篇的對話。

　　對話是日常生活中及各類英檢中最常見的聽力活動之一，聽力重點在於聽關鍵字，抓到每個對話的重點即可。當然，片語及慣用語的熟悉也是很重要的喔！ 讓我們來小試身手吧！

Lesson 1 ❯ 短篇對話

 ❯ 舒葳老師說 🅜🅟🅣 12-1

請聽對話，並選出適當的答案。

1. What is the man meaning to say?
   A. The boss called and said he isn't coming.
   B. The project was been cancelled.

2. What is the man meaning to say?
   A. The audience was too quite.
   B. The audience was too noisy.

3. What is the woman meaning to say?
   A. She loves the place.
   B. She loves to work with tools.

4. What is the man meaning to imply?
   A. She helped him some time ago.
   B. He owes her money.

5. What is the woman meaning to say?
   A. She doesnt like either black or white.
   B. There's no one correct answer.

6. What is the man meaning to say?

DAY 1
DAY 2
DAY 3
DAY 4
DAY 5
DAY 6
DAY 7
DAY 8
DAY 9
DAY 10
DAY 11
DAY 12
DAY 13
DAY 14

A. He can meet anytime she wants.

B. He wants to meet at the convenience store.

7. How does the woman feel about the project length?

A. She found it agreeable.

B. She didn't do the project at all.

8. What is the woman saying about the driver's license?

A. Her license has expired.

B. Her friend has her license on a date.

9. How do they both feel about the job?

A. They work so hard that they feel ill.

B. They are unhappy with the job.

10. What is the woman meaning to say?

A. The movie is almost over.

B. Their dinner is ready.

● Answers

1.B 2.B 3.A 4.A 5.B 6.A 7.A 8.A 9.B 10.A

> 詳細解說 12-2

1.W: Jim, I thought you had a big project due tomorrow.

How can you be taking such a long lunch break?

M: The project has been called off. I have plenty of time to get the

rest of my work done now.

女：Jim, 我還以為你明天有案子要交呢。你怎麼能午休這麼久？

男：這個案子被取消了。我現在有充裕的時間完成我的工作了。

A. The boss called and said he isn't coming.

老闆打電話來説他不來了。

B. The project was been cancelled.

這個案子被取消了。（正確答案）

　　女方説 I thought you had a big project due tomorrow. 重音在 due，因此這句的意思是「我以為是這樣，但看起來卻好像不是如此」，表示疑問和驚訝。call off 是片語，就是 cancel（取消）的意思。因此答案是 B。

2. W: Did you enjoy the movie?

M: Yes, but I wish the crowd would've been more quiet during the show.

女：妳喜歡這部電影嗎？

男：喜歡，但如果觀眾能安靜點就更好了。

A. The audience was too quite. 觀眾太安靜了。
B. The audience was too noisy. 觀眾太吵了。（正確答案）

　　Would've 是 would have 在口語中的「縮音」説法。男方説 I wish...would've 就是他這麼希望，但事實上卻不是如此。

▶ 老外時常這麼說

I wish I'd've enjoyed movie more.

我希望我能更喜歡這部電影（但我不是太喜歡）。

3. W: I thought you'd enjoy dinner here.

M: You hit the nail on the head. I wish I'd've found it sooner.

男：我就知道妳會喜歡這裡的晚餐。

女：你説得一點都沒錯。我真希望我早點發現這個地方。

A. She loves the place. 她愛死這裡了。（正確答案）

B. She loves to work with tools. 她找不到這個地方。

　　男方說 I thought you'd enjoy dinner here. 重音在 thought，表示他早就料到，並且成真了。從重音的位置我們便可以判斷男生想的沒錯，女方是喜歡這裡的。

　　女方說 You hit the nail on the head. 「正打中釘子的頭」，是常用成語，表示「一針見血」、「完全正確」。

　　I wish I'd've found it sooner. 就是 I wish I would have found it sooner. 的口語說法。表示她希望能早點發現，但事實上她現在才發現。

> 老外時常這麼說

Her comment about the situation was so exact. It hit the nail on the head.

她對這個情形的評論完全正確。

4. W: Wow, thank you so much. You fixed that leak fast. How much do I owe you?

M: You're welcome, and don't worry about it. It's free of charge. I owed you a favor anyway, right?

女：哇，真謝謝你。你一下子就把漏水修好了。我應該給你多少錢？

男：不用客氣。這是免費的。反正我也欠你一份人情，不是嗎？

A. She helped him some time ago.
女方以前幫過他的忙。（正確答案）

DAY 1
DAY 2
DAY 3
DAY 4
DAY 5
DAY 6
DAY 7
DAY 8
DAY 9
DAY 10
DAY 11
DAY 12
DAY 13
DAY 14

B. He owes her money. 男方欠女方錢。

free of charge 是「免費」，注意重音在 free 和 charge。of 的 "o" 弱化。Owe 是「欠錢」；I owed you a favor. 是「我欠你一份情」的意思。

▶ 老外時常這麼說

I owe you. 謝謝，我欠你一次。（在口語中就是「謝謝你的幫忙」的意思。）I owe you one. 謝謝，我欠你一次。

5. W: The answers to many questions aren't always black and white.

M: I know, that's what makes working in this industry so hard.

女：很多問題的答案不總是非黑即白的。

男：我知道，那也是為什麼在這行工作這麼困難的原因。

A. She doesn't like either black or white.

她不喜歡黑色或白色。

B. There's no one correct answer.

沒有一個正確的答案。（正確答案）

black and white 是「黑白分明，善惡分明」。注意重音在 black 和 white。and 弱化了，並且 d 和 t 消音: black an(d) whi(te)

▶ 老外時常這麼說

It's not a simple black-and-white issue. This is often called a grey area in the decision making process.

這不是個黑白對錯分明的問題。在決策的過程中這就叫做灰色地帶。

（grey area 就是灰色地帶, 指不容易回答或難以界定的部分。）

6. W: When can we meet to discuss the project and transfer the data?

   M : At your convenience.

   女：我們什麼時候可以見面討論這個案子並轉交資料？

   男：看妳什麼時候方便都可以。

A. He can meet anytime she wants.
   女方要什麼時候見面他都可以配合。（正確答案）

B. He wants to meet at the convenience store.
   他要約在便利商店見面。

　　At your convenience. 是「看你方便」。正式的場合會聽到這樣的說法，就是「你決定，我都可以」的意思。這裡要注意的是 at your 中 t 和 y 的連音。

▶ 老外時常這麼說

Please call me back at your earliest convenience.

請儘快在你方便的時候回電。

7. M: Didn't you find that the project took forever to finish?

   W: Not at all. I was prepared for everything.

   男：妳不覺得這個案子好像永遠沒有做完的一天嗎？

   女：不會啊。我準備得很完備。

A. She found it agreeable. 她可以接受。（正確答案）

B. She didn't do the project at all. 她完全沒有做。

　　took forever 是「好像永遠都不會結束」，是表示很久的誇大說法。Not at all. 是「一點也不」。注意連音：Not at all. 並且 t 在這裡都發「彈舌音」。

DAY 1
DAY 2
DAY 3
DAY 4
DAY 5
DAY 6
DAY 7
DAY 8
DAY 9
DAY 10
DAY 11
DAY 12
DAY 13
DAY 14

▶ 老外時常這麼說

It took forever to download the files from the Internet.

從網路下載這些檔案花了好長的時間。

8. M: Why aren't you driving anymore?

W: My license is out of date.

男：妳為什麼都不開車了。

女：我的駕照過期了。

A. Her license has expired. 她的駕照過期了。（正確答案）

B. Her friend has her license on a date. 她的朋友借去約會了。

男方說 aren't... anymore. 就是「再也不…了」。be out of date 是片語，是「過時了」的意思。注意這裡的連音及消音，同時 of 弱化：out of da(t)e。另外 out of 的 t 發「彈舌音」。

▶ 老外時常這麼說

Their technology is pretty out-of-date.

他的的技術還蠻老舊的。

The information on this website is out of date.

這個網站的資訊是舊的。

The information on this website is updated once a week.

這個網站的資訊每週會更新一次。

9. W: This place just feels so unwelcoming now. I'm sick of it.

I think I'll start looking for a new job.

M: I know what you mean, I'm sick of this place, too.

女：這個地方現在真令人覺得冷漠。我受夠了。

我想我會開始找新的工作。

補教名師王舒葳教你
14天聽懂
老外說的英語

DAY 1
DAY 2
DAY 3
DAY 4
DAY 5
DAY 6
DAY 7
DAY 8
DAY 9
DAY 10
DAY 11
DAY 12
DAY 13
DAY 14

男：我懂妳的意思。我也受夠了。

A. They work so hard that they feel ill.
他們工作得太辛苦以致於都生病了。

B. They are unhappy with the job.
他們對於這個公司感到不愉快。（正確答案）

　　I'm sick of it. 就是對這件事感到生氣、不開心。注意這裡的連音：I'm sick of i(t). of 弱化，t 消音。另外，要注意的是，在 I'm sick of it. 中，f 介在兩個母音 o 和 i 中間，聽起來會像是發有聲音 / v /。

🔰 老外時常這麼說

I am tired of listening to your complaints.
我受不了聽妳抱怨了.

The way he treats his wife just makes me sick.
他對待老婆的方式令我生氣。

You make me sick! You're so lucky!
妳真讓我忌妒！妳真是太幸運了！

（口語中 you make me sick 也有「妳讓我忌妒」的意思。）

10. M: Boy, this movie is lasting forever and I'm starving.

W: It'll be over in an hour. We'll get something to eat, then.

男：天哪，這個電影真長。我餓死了。

女：再一個小時就結束了。我們那時候再吃。

A. The movie is almost over. 電影快結束了。（正確答案）

B. Their dinner is ready. 他們的晚餐好了。

　　...is lasting forever. 「…永遠持續著」，就是「真長，怎麼沒完沒了」的意思。所以我們知道他在抱怨這部電影太長了。 女方説 it'll be over in an hour 就是「再一小時就結束了」。注意It'll 的發音及連音be over in an (h)our.

▶ | 老外時常這麼說

Don't worry. The situation won't last.

別擔心。這個狀況不會持續太久。

Lesson 2 ▶ | 長篇對話

▶ 舒葳老師說 12-3

請聽MP3，選出適當的答案。

1. What is the man meaning to say about the game?

 A. It was an excellent game.

 B. The referees didn't do a fair job.

 C. It was a dull game.

2. What does the woman feel about all employees taking English classes?

 A. It's useful for everyone.

 B. It's a waste of time.

 C. It's costly.

3. What are they going to do next?

 A. To get some instant coffee at 7-11.

 B. To ask people at the 7-11 where the coffee shop is.

 C. To have a cup of coffee in the coffee shop.

4. Where is this conversation taking place?

    A. A baseball court.

    B. A furniture shop.

    C. A restaurant.

5. What are they going to do?

    A. To eat in a pricey restaurant.

    B. To share the bill between two of them.

    C. To find a less expensive restaurant.

6. How did the man break his thumb?

    A. Playing basketball.

    B. Working out in the gym.

    C. Falling down the steps.

7. What are they doing?

    A. Discussing their annual report.

    B. Talking about the boss's bad temper.

    C. Explaining why they are angry towards the boss.

8. What is the man going to buy?

    A. Food and flowers.

    B. Flowers and alcoholic drinks.

    C. Flowers and juice.

● Answers

1.B 2.C 3.B 4.B 5.A 6.C 7.B 8.B

 12-4

1. M: What did you think of the game last night?

DAY 1
DAY 2
DAY 3
DAY 4
DAY 5
DAY 6
DAY 7
DAY 8
DAY 9
DAY 10
DAY 11
DAY 12
DAY 13
DAY 14

W: Wow, what a finish. I couldn't've asked to see a better game.

M: It was good, but I thought the referees really made some big mistakes. It wouldn't've been that close had they called the game correctly.

男：妳覺得昨晚的比賽如何？

女：哇，太棒的結局了。我沒辦法要求更精采的比賽了。

男：是很精采，但我覺得裁判犯了些很大的錯誤。如果裁判判得正確，比數不會那麼接近。

A. It was an excellent game. 是一場精采的比賽。

B. The referees didn't do a fair job. 裁判判得不好。（正確答案）

C. It was a dull game. 比賽不精采。

What did you think of...? 問對方的意見。注意 did you 和 think of 的連音。I couldn't've 就是 I couldn't have 的縮音；It wouldn't've 就是 it wouldn't have 的縮音。

男方最後說 It was good, but...重音強調的是 was，其實就很像我們中文說的:「是很好啦，但是…」暗示了我們事實上雖然他也同意比賽精采，卻也有他覺得不滿的地方。在這裡，如果說話者只是要單純地同意比賽精采，沒有其他訊息想要強調，則重音會在 good: It was good. 喔！

另外，最後一句的 had they called the game correctly 是倒裝句，也就是 if they had called the game correctly. 的意思。男方在表達他有意見後，提到了裁判的判決不正確，表示正確答案就是 B. The referees didn't do a fair job. 了。

請再聽一次，並實際體會運用我們上面提到的技巧。

DAY 1
DAY 2
DAY 3
DAY 4
DAY 5
DAY 6
DAY 7
DAY 8
DAY 9
DAY 10
DAY 11
DAY 12
DAY 13
DAY 14

> **句型整理**

What did you think of...？你覺得…如何？

I couldn't've... 我沒辦法…了。

It was good, but I thought... 是很精采，但我覺得…

It would't've been... had they... 如果他們…就會…了。

2. M: I think we all should take these English courses. I can already tell that my job performance is improving and the boss seems to notice that I'm more confident with clients now.

W: Well, to be honest, I think they would be useful for everybody, but some of us don't really work closely with many foreigners. It's not that I think it's a waste of time, but it costs the company a lot of money to send you to the classes.

男：我覺得我們都應該上英文課。我真的可以感覺得到我工作表現進步，而且老闆似乎也注意到我現在面對客戶比較有信心。

女：這個嘛，老實說，我覺得英文課是會對每個人都有用。但是有些人其實不怎麼需要跟老外一起工作。我不是覺得浪費時間，只是送大家去上英文課會花公司很多錢。

A. It's useful for everyone. 對每個人都很有用。

B. It's a waste of time. 浪費時間。

C. It's costly. 花費太大。（正確答案）

在男生說 I think we all should take English course. 並表達對英文課的肯定之後，女方說 Well, to be honest,... 就表示她採取的是相反的意見。聽到 Well 和 to be honest, 都表示否定的態度喔！

不只如此，女方說 it would be useful, but... 重音在 would，也表示她雖然同意「是會有用啦，但是…」，但有其他的看法，表示她並不贊同每個人上英文課的這個想法。

It's not that... 就是「我不是覺得…」的意思,表示她並不是覺得浪費時間。既然她不贊同,又不覺得是浪費時間,那麼答案就應該是 C. It's costly. 囉!請再聽一次,並實際體會運用我們上面提到的技巧。

▶ 句型整理

Well, to be honest, ... 這個嘛,老實說…

I think they would be useful for everybody, but... 我覺得是會對每個人都有用啦,但是…

It's not that I think it's..., but ... 不是我覺得…,而是…

3. W: That's funny. I'm sure there was a coffee shop around here.

M: Hmmm, I don't know. Maybe the 7-11 manager will know if there is one close to here. W: Alright, let's go in. Maybe they'll know.

女:真奇怪。我確定以前這裡有一間咖啡廳的。

男:嗯,我不確定。也許7-11店長會知道這附近是不是有咖啡廳。

女:好吧,我們進去吧。也許他們會知道。

A. To get some instant coffee at 7-11. 去7-11買即溶咖啡.

B. To ask people at the 7-11 where the coffee shop is.
問7-11的人咖啡廳在哪裡。（正確答案）

C. To have a cup of coffee in the coffee shop. 去咖啡廳喝咖啡。

That's funny. 有兩個意思:「很奇怪」或「真好笑」。女方說 That's funny. 我們從她的語氣知道她的意思是「真奇怪!」。接著我們聽關鍵字,知道她說 I'm sure... coffee shop around here. 表示她覺得奇怪是因為她找不到 coffee shop。其實到這裡,我們就知道主題是要找咖啡店在哪裡了。

接著男方指出 maybe the 7-11 manager will know... 女方又說

DAY 1
DAY 2
DAY 3
DAY 4
DAY 5
DAY 6
DAY 7
DAY 8
DAY 9
DAY 10
DAY 11
DAY 12
DAY 13
DAY 14

let's go in. 並接著說 Maybe they'll know. 表示她同意男方的建議，決定進去問。因此答案是 B. To ask people at the 7-11 where the coffee shop is.

請再聽一次，並實際體會運用我們上面提到的技巧。

▶ 句型整理

That's funny. 真奇怪／真好笑。

I'm sure... 我確定⋯

Let's go in. 我們進去吧

4. W: Can I help you, Miss?

M: Yes, is this couch marked down ? It has a scratch here.

W: Yes, this is one of the clearance items. I believe it is ten percent off the original price marked. I'll check to make sure.

M: Thank you.

男：我可以為你服務嗎？

女：是的，這個躺椅有打折嗎？這裡有刮痕。

男：有的，這是我們清倉貨之一。我記得是原標價的九折。

我查一下，以確定折扣。

女：謝謝。

A. A baseball court. 棒球場

B. A furniture shop. 家具行（正確答案）

C. A restaurant. 餐廳

題目問這段對話發生的場合，如果能串聯內容中的關鍵字，我們就不難聽出說話者在哪裡。男方開頭說 Can I help you?，表示他一定是在某種商店，服務客人。女方問 Is the couch marked down?，couch 是「長沙發、躺椅」的意思，mark down 就是「打

折」。接著男方的回答中 clearance items 是「清倉貨」，又説是 ten percent off the original price marked。綜合這些關鍵字，我們就可以聽出他們是在家具行了。因此答案是 B. A furniture shop.

請再聽一次，並實際體會運用我們上面提到的技巧。

❯ 句型整理

Can I help you？我可以為你服務嗎？

Is the... marked down？這個…有打折嗎？

I believe... 我相信…；我想…

It is ten percent off the original price marked. 這是原標價的九折。

（marked price 就是 tagged price，也就是「標價」、「訂價」。）

I'll check to make sure. 我查一下以確定。

❯ 老外時常這麼說

We are offering a 10% markdown on children's shoes.

所有童鞋九折。

There's 10% off this week on all children's shoes.

所有童鞋九折。

All children's shoes are subject to a 10% discount.

所有童鞋九折。

All children's shoes are now reduced to $20 a pair.

所有童鞋減價至20元一雙。

5. M: What do you think of Le Petite?

W: The food is fantastic, but its kind of small and a bit overpriced.

M: That's OK. I really want a good meal tonight. Do you want to go? I'll get the bill.

W: Sure, I really do like the food.

男：你覺得 Le Petite 如何？

女：食物很棒，但份量有點少，而且也有點貴。

男：沒關係，我今晚真的想吃點好的。妳要去嗎？我請客。

女：好啊，我是真的喜歡那裡的食物。

A. To eat in a pricey restaurant. 去昂貴的餐廳吃飯。（正確答案）

B. To share the bill between two of them. 分攤晚餐的花費。

C. To find a less expensive restaurant. 找一間不那麼貴的餐廳。

　　題目問說話者接下去要做什麼，如果能串聯內容中的關鍵字，我們應該不難聽出答案了。 男方先說 What do you think of... 是問女方的意見。然後我們注意聽重音，便可以聽到女方的回應，強調的訊息在 food... fantastic... small... overpriced；而當女方提到 overpriced 表示這間餐廳有點貴，但男方說 That's OK. 表示不介意，並強調 really... good meal... 又說 I'll get the bill，表示他要請客付帳。女方最後說 sure... like... food。串聯重音字，我們可知他們在討論去昂貴的餐廳吃飯。因此答案就是 A. To eat in a pricey restaurant. 了。

　　在聲音方面我們要注意的是 kind of的連音和弱化：kind of small，重音在 small。a bit overpriced 中 t 消音: a bi(t) overpriced，overpriced 是複合形容詞。kind of 和 a bit 都是有一點的意思，在口語中常常聽到。

　　請再聽一次，並實際體會運用我們上面提到的技巧。

句型整理

It's kind of small. 有點小。

It's a bit overpriced. 有點貴。

I'll get the bill. 我請客。

▶ 老外時常這麼說

It's on me. 我請客。

It's my treat. 我請客。

A: Thanks for lunch. It was delicious. Next time lunch is on me.
謝謝你請的午餐。很好吃。下次午餐我請客。
B: Don't be silly. 不用這麼客氣啦。

A: I'm serious. 我是説真的。
B: Alright. Next time you'll treat. 好吧，下次你請。

6. W: Don't tell me you broke your thumb playing basketball. You
always get injured playing ball.
M: Actually, I tripped on the steps just outside the gym and never
got to play last night. (laughing)
W: Wow, you really need to stop going anywhere near the gym.
女：不要告訴我你打棒球弄斷大姆指。你老是因為玩球受傷。
男：事實上，我在健身房外的階梯上絆倒，昨晚根本沒去打球。
女：天哪，你真的應該停止去任何靠近健身房的地方。

A. Playing basketball. 打棒球。
B. Working out in the gym. 健身房。
C. Falling down the steps. 在階梯上絆倒。（正確答案）

女方説 Don't tell me...「不要告訴我…」，就表示她並不知道
對方受傷原因，只是猜測。而當男方説 Actually...時，我們就知道女
方的猜測: playing basketball 是錯誤的了。注意，聽到 Actually，就
表示説話者有「否定對方意見」的意思喔。男方繼續説 I tripped on

the steps... 表示「他在階梯上絆倒」，trip 當動詞是「絆倒」的意思，當名詞才是「旅行」。所以答案是 C. Falling down the steps

請再聽一次，並實際體會運用我們上面提到的技巧。

▶ 句型整理

Don't tell me...　不要告訴我…

Actually...　事實上…

I never got to...　我根本沒能…

7. M1: The boss seems so mad these days. We really should've finished the annual reports on time.

W : Yeah, his attitude has changed so much lately. I can feel it. His mood has worsened to the point that I can't even talk to him without making him mad about something.

M2: Yep, he has become a crotchety old man these days. You guys are so right. I feel like I'm walking on eggshells around here.

男一：老闆最近好像很生氣。我們那時真的應該要準時交年度報告的。

女　：是啊，他的態度最近變化好大。我感覺得出來。

他的情緒已經差到我每次跟他說話，都會感覺到我又因為什麼事情惹他生氣了。

男二：他最近已經變成了一個壞脾氣的糟老頭了。你們說得一點都沒錯。我覺得我在這裡好像走在蛋殼上。

A. Discussing their annual report.

討論他們的年度報告。

B. Talking about the boss's bad temper.

談論老闆的壞情緒。（正確答案）

DAY
1

DAY
2

DAY
3

DAY
4

DAY
5

DAY
6

DAY
7

DAY
8

DAY
9

DAY
10

DAY
11

DAY
12

DAY
13

DAY
14

C. Explaining why they are angry towards the boss.

解釋為何他們生老闆的氣。

題目問說話者在做什麼。當一群人在討論某事時，第一句話就是開場白，會帶入主題。因此聽懂第一句，就可以先預測這段對話大概是什麼主題了。這裡的第一句話是 The boss seems so mad these days. 因此我們知道主題是「老闆的壞情緒」。

後面我們繼續聽關鍵字、聽重音。這段對話中特別強調的是: attitude... much... feel... mood... worsened... point... mad... crotchety old man. 從關鍵字我們也可以得知他們討論的內容主題是什麼。因此答案是 B. Talking about the boss's bad temper.

請再聽一次，並實際體會運用我們上面提到的技巧。

❯ 句型整理

We should've... 我們那時應該⋯（但事實上並沒有）

I can feel it. 我感覺得出來。

to the point that... 已經到⋯的程度

I can't even...without... 我每次⋯都會⋯

You guys are so right. 你們說得一點都沒錯。

walking on eggshells 走在蛋殼上，比喻很危險、戰戰兢兢。

8. M : If you think about it, could you bring home some flowers for the dinner table tonight?

W: Sure, with the boss and his wife coming to dinner, it will be a nice touch.

M: Yeah. Oh, now that I think about it, we could also use some fine brandy for after dinner drinks. Could you pick some up?

W: Yeah, good idea. The boss loves a good drink after dinner.

補教名師王舒葳教你
14天聽懂
老外說的英語

DAY
1

DAY
2

DAY
3

DAY
4

DAY
5

DAY
6

DAY
7

DAY
8

DAY
9

DAY
10

DAY
11

**DAY
12**

DAY
13

DAY
14

男：想想看，你可以買一些花回來嗎？今晚晚餐可以放在餐桌上。

女：沒問題，今晚老闆夫婦來吃飯，放些花感覺會變好的。

男：是啊。喔，我現在想一想，我們餐後可以來點高級的白蘭地。
可以買回來嗎？

女：可以，好主意。老闆可喜歡餐後小酌了。

A. Food and flowers. 食物和花。

B. Flowers and alcoholic drinks. 花和酒。（正確答案）

C. Flowers and juice. 花和果汁。

　　題目問男生要買什麼，是細節，因此要仔細聽女方的要求和男方的回應。女方問：Could you bring home some flowers for the dinner table tonight？重音是 flowers 和 dinner table，可推測要買花裝飾餐桌。

　　後來男方又說 Now that I think about it,... 表示他有新點子，因此接著說的也可能是重點：we could also use some fine brandy... Could you pick some up? 重音在 brandy，pick up 是片語，是口語中「買」的意思，表示要買 brandy。We could use... 是「我們需要…」，也是口語中常用的表達法。因此答案應該是 B. Flowers and alcoholic drinks.

　　請再聽一次，並實際體會運用我們上面提到的技巧。

▶ 句型整理

If you think about it, ... 想想看，…

It will be a nice touch. 感覺會變好的。

Now that I think about it,... 我現在想一想…

We could use... 我們需要…

Could you pick some up？你可以去買嗎？

❯ 聽力小秘訣

☺ 當我們需要聽一段長篇的對話時，因為內容較多較細，很容易抓不住重點導致聽不懂。以下幾個步驟可以幫忙我們聽得更有效率：

☺ 釐清目的：在日常生活中當需要聽老外說話時，都會有一個特定目的，也就是說，雖然對方傳達的訊息可能很多，卻有一些訊息卻才是我們聽的真正目的，如: 開會的時間、約會的地點。另外有些時候，我們卻只需知道對方談論的主題、大意即可，如朋友間閒聊。如果能把注意力集中在聽到我們需要聽的重點，而非企圖聽懂每個字，就能既聽得懂又聽得輕鬆喔！

☺ 抓住重音：說話者永遠會把重要的訊息加強、變慢、且咬字更清楚。因此，我們往往只要聽到重音字、串聯起來，便可以猜到七、八成的內容了。

☺ 瞭解語氣詞及轉承語：英文的語氣詞或轉承語往往傳達了說話者的態度，如：well, actually, to be frank, to tell you the truth 等，都有反面的意思。抓到這些語句傳達的態度，我們其實就掌握了主要的訊息。同時，因為我們可以預期對方說話的方向，也更容易聽得懂囉。

☺ 熟悉句型：英文的句型也傳達意義。我們聽不懂，也常常是因為「沒聽過這種說法」。 一旦熟悉了常用句型，再聽到就不會慌，也就是比較容易體會對方要傳達的意思了。

DAY 13

聽力實戰練習3
廣播與廣告
Announcement and TV / Radio Commercials

13-1~13-4

> 學習重點

　　除了日常生活的對話外，另一個我們常會需要聽的，就是公共場合的廣播及電視和電台的廣告了！因為長度較長，又通常是一個人從頭說到尾，對於聽的人來說比較沒有喘息的空間，一般的英文學習者都會覺得這類的聽力很具挑戰性。因此，在聽這種長篇「獨白」的時候，運用我們之前教過的「語調」及「語意單位」等技巧就變得很重要喔！

　　現在讓我們來試試看吧！不要忘記運用聲調的提高降落及語句的停頓，來判斷說話者想表達的意義是已經告一段落，還是正要開始新概念。嘗試跟上說話者的節奏，掌握對方要說的重點吧！

加油！

Lesson 1 ❯ 公共場合的廣播

請聽MP3，並選擇適當的答案。每一段廣播有兩至三道題目。

A.

1. What is the purpose of the talk?

    A. To tell people what to see on the lake.

    B. To warn people against the unsafe condition.

    C. To advise people to stay inside for the bad weather.

2. What should people do?

    A. Take a closer look at the west end of the lake.

    B. Eat ice near the river.

    C. Not to go beyond the orange safety markers.

B.

1. What is the purpose of the talk?

    A. To announce a fire in the building.

    B. To explain the location of a department store.

    C. To instruct how to use elevators.

2. What should people do now?

    A. Call the fire department.

B. Move out of the building.

C. Collect their own stuff.

3. What should people use when moving out?

A. Stairs.

B. Elevators.

C. Escalators.

C.

1. Where is this announcement being made?

A. A department store.

B. An airport.

C. At school.

2. How should people be using escalators?

A. Stand to the right.

B. Stand to the left.

C. Move quickly.

D.

1. What is the reason for the delay?

A. Bad weather.

B. Mechanical problems.

C. Meals preparation.

2. When should passengers arrive at the gate by?

A. 8:30.

B. 8:00.

DAY
1

DAY
2

DAY
3

DAY
4

DAY
5

DAY
6

DAY
7

DAY
8

DAY
9

DAY
10

DAY
11

DAY
12

DAY
13

DAY
14

C. 10:00.

E.

1. Who is listening to the announcement?

    A. Hotel guests.

    B. Company staff.

    C. University students.

2. What is the party for?

    A. To welcome new staff.

    B. To celebrate a national holiday.

    C. To welcome hotel guests.

F.

1. What can people get at the repair shop?

    A. Well prepared skies.

    B. Free grooming package.

    C. Spare room keys.

2. What must people do to get assistance?

    A. Pay a minimum charge.

    B. Present your room key to the staff.

    C. See the manager.

● Answers

D: 1. A   2. B   E: 1. A   2. C   F: 1. B   2. B

A: 1. B   2. C   B: 1. A   2. B   3. A   C: 1. B   2. A

詳細解說　13-2

A.

Hello skaters. Please note that the west end of the lake is closed due to unsafe conditions. The ice is very thin near the River George's mouth, so please stay inside the orange safety markers you see on the lake. Have a great time on the lake.

各位溜冰者，你們好。請注意湖的西邊因為安全理由關閉。喬治河口的冰層非常薄，所以請留在你在湖上看到的橘紅色的安全標示內。祝你們在湖上玩得愉快。

1. What is the purpose of the talk?　此篇廣播目的為何？

　　A. To tell people what to see on the lake.

　　　　告訴人們湖上有什麼值得觀賞。

　　B. To warn people against the unsafe condition.

　　　　警告人們小心不安全的狀況。（正確答案）

　　C. To advise people to stay inside for the bad weather.

　　　　建議人們因惡劣天氣而留在室內。

2. What should people do? 人們應該怎麼做？

　　A. Take a closer look at the west end of the lake.

　　　　近距離觀賞湖的西岸。

　　B. Eat ice near the river.

　　　　在河附近吃冰。

　　C. Not to go beyond the orange safety markers.

　　　　不越過橘紅色的安全標示。（正確答案）

利用「語意單位」，也就是語氣的停頓和聲調，可以幫助我們

DAY 1
DAY 2
DAY 3
DAY 4
DAY 5
DAY 6
DAY 7
DAY 8
DAY 9
DAY 10
DAY 11
DAY 12
DAY 13
DAY 14

理解並跟上説話者的節奏。聲調提高表示是一個新概念的開始。以下「//」符號表示較長停頓，也就是語句結束；「/」則表示短暫停頓，表示同一個句子內一個較小的「語意單位」的完成。

Hello skaters.// Please note/ that the west end of the lake is closed/ due to unsafe conditions.// The ice is very thin near the River Gorge's mouth,/ so please stay inside the orange safety markers you see on the lake.// Have a great time on the lake.//

一開頭的 Hello skaters 告訴我們廣播的對象正在溜冰。而當我們聽到 Please note that... 就知道這個廣播在請溜冰的人注意某件事情，也就是這段廣播的目的囉。繼續由重音抓關鍵字：west... closed... unsafe... conditions... ice... thin 亦可以幫助我們知道主題跟安全有關。因此第一題的答案是 B. To warn people against the unsafe condition.

第二題問 What should people do?，因此當我們聽到説話者説：Please... 我們就應該特別留意。Please... 就是請聽者做或不做某事，不但正是題目想問的重點，我們一般在聽廣播時當對方講到 Please... 或 Please don't 也應該特別留意。結果我們聽到他説的是：Please stay inside the orange safety makers... 因此答案是 C. Not to go beyond the orange safety markers. 這裡的重點是抓句型。

請再聽一次，並實際體會運用我們上面提到的技巧。

❯ 句型單字整理

Please note that... 請注意⋯

Please stay inside... 請不要踏出⋯的範圍。

DAY
1

DAY
2

DAY
3

DAY
4

DAY
5

DAY
6

DAY
7

DAY
8

DAY
9

DAY
10

DAY
11

DAY
12

DAY
13

DAY
14

unsafe 不安全的 adj.

conditions 情況 n.

marker 游標 n.

B.

May I have your attention, please. A fire has been reported in the top floor of the building. Do not panic. The fire department is on the way. Please exit the building now. Move quickly and do not stop for personal belongings. Exit using the stairways. Do not use the elevators.

請注意。頂樓據報有火災。不要驚慌，救火隊已經在趕來的路上。現在請離開這棟大樓。快速行動並且不要停留下來拿私人物品。使用樓梯。不要使用電梯。

1. What is the purpose of the talk? 此篇廣播目的為何？

A. To announce a fire in the building.

宣佈大樓裏的火警。（正確答案）

B. To explain the location of a department store.

解釋一間百貨公司的地點。

C. To instruct how to use elevators.

說明如何使用電梯。

2. What should people do now? 人們現在應該怎麼做？

A. Call the fire department. 打電話給消防隊。

B. Move out of the building. 往大樓外移動。（正確答案）

C. Collect their own stuff. 拿自己的物品。

3. What should people use when moving out?

人們離開時應使用什麼？

A. Stairs. 樓梯。（正確答案）

B. Elevators. 電梯。

C. Escalators. 手扶梯。

利用「語意單位」，也就是語氣的停頓和聲調，可以幫助我們理解並跟上說話者的節奏。聲調提高表示是一個新概念的開始。以下「//」符號表示較長停頓，也就是語句結束；「/」則表示短暫停頓，表示同一個句子內一個較小的「語意單位」的完成。

May I have your attention,/ please.// A fire has been reported in the top floor of the building.// Do not panic.// the fire department is on the way./ Please exit the building now.// Move quickly/ and do not stop for personal belongings.// Exit using the stairways.// Do not use the elevators.//

廣播的主題都會在前一到兩句出現。我們聽到 A fire has been reported... 即知這是火警的廣播。答案是 A. To announce a fire in the building.

第二題他問：What should people do now? 因此當他說 Please... 時，就應該特別注意，因為他正要告訴聽者應該做什麼。而且 Please...的後面出現的通常也都會是重點。這裡重音有 exit... building... now。因此我們知道現在要離開這棟大樓。答案是 B. Move out of the building.

補教名師王舒藴教你
14天聽懂
老外說的英語

DAY
1

DAY
2

DAY
3

DAY
4

DAY
5

DAY
6

DAY
7

DAY
8

DAY
9

DAY
10

DAY
11

DAY
12

DAY
13

DAY
14

最後一題問：What should people use when moving out? 因此當我們聽到 Exit using... 時就要特別注意聽，因為 exit 就是題目中 "move out" 的意思。結果他說的是：Exit using the stairways. Do not use the elevators. 我們聽到重音有 exit... stairways... do not... elevators。我們知道要「使用樓梯，不要使用電梯」。因此第三題答案是 A. Stairs.

▶ 句型單字整理

...has been reported 據報有…

Do not panic. 不要驚慌…

is on the way …在路上

panic 驚慌失措 v.

fire department 救火隊

personal belongings 私人物品

stairways 樓梯 n.

C.

Please be courteous and stand to the right while on the escalator. The left side is reserved for those preferring to walk more quickly in order to make their flight. Please be courteous and everyone will make their gate in time for their departure.

當使用電扶梯時，請很有禮貌地靠右側站。左側是留給需要走快一點以趕飛機的人使用的。請各位注重禮儀，那麼每個人都能夠趕上飛機。

1. Where is this announcement being made?

這個廣播在哪裡進行？

A. A department store. 百貨公司。

B. An airport. 機場。（正確答案）

C. At school 學校。

2. How should people be using escalators?

人們應該如何使用電扶梯？

A. Stand to the right. 靠右側。（正確答案）

B. Stand to the left. 靠左側。

C. Move quickly. 快速移動。

　　利用「語意單位」，也就是語氣的停頓和聲調，可以幫助我們理解並跟上說話者的節奏。聲調提高表示是一個新概念的開始。以下「//」符號表示較長停頓，也就是語句結束；「/」則表示短暫停頓，表示同一個句子內一個較小的「語意單位」的完成。

Please be courteous/ and stand to the right/ while on the escalator.// The left side/ is reserved for those preferring to walk more quickly/ in order to make their flight.// Please be courteous/ and everyone will make their gate/ in time/ for their departure.//

　　廣播的第一話即說明廣播目的，也必定會是廣播的重點：stand to the right while on the escalator 也就是「使用電扶梯時請靠右側站」。因此第二題的答案是： A. Stand to the right.

　　我們再串聯關鍵字 make flight、gate、departure，便知道這是機場的廣播。第一題的答案是：B. An airport.

▶ 句型單字整理

s.t. is reserved for those ... （某物）是為了⋯的人保留的

make one's flight 趕上飛機

courteous 有禮貌的 adj.

escalator 電扶梯 n.

reserved 保留的 adj.

D.

This is to announce a new departure time for Flight 856 to Los Angeles. Severe thunderstorms delayed the connecting flight from Tokyo. The plane is now on the ground and is being serviced. The new departure time is scheduled for 8:30.

Due to the delay, meal vouchers will be available for passengers scheduled on this flight. Passengers are asked to please ready for boarding at gate 10 by 8:00. Thank you for your understanding.

我現在要宣佈前往洛杉磯856班次新的起飛時間。來自東京的轉機班機由於劇烈暴風雨延遲抵達。飛機現在已落地並在檢查中。新的起飛時間預計為八點半。由於時間的耽誤，我們將會提供餐券給預定要搭乘這班航班的旅客。旅客請於八點前到達十號登機門準備登機。謝謝各位的諒解。

1. What is the reason for the delay? 延遲的理由為何？

   A. Bad weather. 天候不佳。（正確答案）

   B. Mechanical problems. 機械問題。

   C. Meals preparation. 餐點準備。

2. When should passengers arrive at the gate by?

   旅客應在幾點前到達登機門？

A. 8:30. 八點半。

B. 8:00. 八點。（正確答案）

C. 10:00. 十點。

　　利用「語意單位」，也就是語氣的停頓和聲調，可以幫助我們理解並跟上說話者的節奏。聲調提高表示是一個新概念的開始。以下「//」符號表示較長停頓，也就是語句結束；「/」則表示短暫停頓，表示同一個句子內一個較小的「語意單位」的完成。

This is to announce a new departure time for Flight 856/ to Los Angeles.// Severe thunderstorms have delayed the connecting flight from Tokyo.// The plane is now on the ground/ and is being serviced.// The new departure time is scheduled for 8:30.// Due to the delay/ meal vouchers will be available for passengers/ scheduled on this flight.// Passengers are asked/ to please be ready for boarding at gate 10/ by 8:00.// Thank you/ for your understanding.//

　　第一句話即聽到主題：This is to announce a new departure time... 所以我們知道這是機場的廣播，告知乘客起飛時間的改變。第一題問：What is the reason for the delay? 因此接下來應該就會說原因，果然他說：Severe thunderstorms delayed... 現在我們知道是thunderstorms，也就是天氣的影響。第一題的答案是：A. Bad weather.

　　第二題問的是：When should passengers arrive at the gate by? 所以我們知道接下來我們應該注意的是到達 gate 的時間。然

DAY
1

DAY
2

DAY
3

DAY
4

DAY
5

DAY
6

DAY
7

DAY
8

DAY
9

DAY
10

DAY
11

DAY
12

DAY
13

DAY
14

後我們聽到他說：The new departure time is 8:30，但還不是我們要的訊息。後面他又說 Passengers are asked to please ready for boarding at gate 10 by 8:00. 在 8:00 前就要到登機門。因此第二題的答案是：B. 8:00.

　　事實上，當說話者提高語調，並說 Passengers are asked to please…時，我們就應該知道後面可能就是重點了喔！因為當語調提高表示新訊息要出現，而 Passengers are asked to please... 表示下面是乘客必須注意的訊息，一定是很重要的囉！

▶ 句型單字整理

This is to announce...　我現在要宣佈…

s.t. is scheduled for...　（某物）預計為（某時間）

s.t. will be available for s.b.　我們將會提供（某物）給（某人）

Due to...　由於…

severe　嚴厲的 adj.

thunderstorm　暴風雨 n.

connecting flight　轉機班機 n.

service　服務 n./v.

voucher　抵用券 n.

E.

Thank you for choosing the Grand Hyatt for your holiday stay. We will be having a welcoming party this evening for those of you that wish to attend. The party commences at 8:00 pm. Please attend and greet your fellow guests this evening. Thank you for your patronage and we hope you have a wonderful stay.

謝謝您選擇君悅大飯店度過您的假期。今晚我們將會為想要參加的人舉辦一個歡迎晚會。晚會將在晚上八點鐘開始。敬請光臨，認識其他在此住宿的朋友們。感謝各位對我們的支持，預祝您有一個美好的假期。

1. Who is listening to the announcement? 廣播的對象是誰？

    A. Hotel guests. 飯店顧客。（正確答案）

    B. Company staff. 公司員工。

    C. University students. 大學學生。

2. What is the party for? 晚會的目的為何？

    A. To welcome new staff. 歡迎新員工。

    B. To celebrate a national holiday. 慶祝國定假日。

    C. To welcome hotel guests. 歡迎飯店顧客。（正確答案）

利用「語意單位」，也就是語氣的停頓和聲調，可以幫助我們理解並跟上說話者的節奏。聲調提高表示是一個新概念的開始。以下「//」符號表示較長停頓，也就是語句結束；「/」則表示短暫停頓，表示同一個句子內一個較小的「語意單位」的完成。

Thank you for choosing the Grand Hyatt/ for your holiday stay.// We will be having a welcoming party/ this evening.// The party commences at 8:00 pm/ for those of you that wish to attend.// Please attend/ and greet your fellow guests this evening.// Thank you for your patronage/ and we hope you will have a wonderful stay.//

補教名師王舒葳教你
14天聽懂
老外說的英語

DAY 1
DAY 2
DAY 3
DAY 4
DAY 5
DAY 6
DAY 7
DAY 8
DAY 9
DAY 10
DAY 11
DAY 12
DAY 13
DAY 14

第一題問的是：Who is listening to the announcement? 廣播的聽眾是誰，也就是説，如果我們知道這段廣播的主題或目的，就會知道聽眾是誰了。而廣播的第一句話即是主題 Thank you for choosing the Grand Hyatt...，表示這是在飯店內，對住宿顧客所做的廣播。答案是：A. Hotel guests.

第二題問：What is the party for? 表示接下應該會聽到關於 party 的訊息，我們要知道的是 party 是為誰舉辦的。下面的關鍵字我們聽到：We... having... welcoming party... you... attend. 表示 party 是為聽者舉辦的，之後的 Please attend... greet... fellow guests... 更説明 party 對象便是聽者，而目的為歡迎新顧客。因此答案是：C. To welcome hotel guests.

句型單字整理

attend 出席 v.

commence 開始 v.

greet 打招呼 v.

stay 住宿 n.

patronage 光臨、照顧（通常在旅館業、餐廳會聽到） n.

F.

Hello skiers. Please note that skiing with unprepared skis can be very dangerous. We offer a free grooming package here at Sunnyvale in order to make your experience here as safe as possible. Please see the repair shop and show them your room key. They will be happy to help you. Thank you and have a wonderful time on our mountain.

各位滑雪者，大家好。請注意，未準備完善的雪橇是非常危險的。我們陽光

谷提供免費的滑雪道清理器具，讓您在此的體驗盡可能安全無慮。請到修理室，並出示您的房間鑰匙，他們會熱心地協助您。謝謝，並預祝您在我們的山上度過愉快的時光。

1. What can people get at the repair shop?

　　人們可以在修理室得到什麼？

　　A. Well prepared skies. 準備好的雪橇。

　　B. Free grooming package. 滑雪道清理器具。（正確答案）

　　C. Spare room keys. 備用的房間鑰匙。

2. What must people do to get assistance?

　　人們要怎麼做才能得到協助？

　　A. Pay a minimum charge 付最低消費。

　　B. Present your room key to the staff. 出示房間鑰匙。（正確答案）

　　C. See the manager. 見經理。

　　利用「語意單位」，也就是語氣的停頓和聲調，可以幫助我們理解並跟上說話者的節奏。聲調提高表示是一個新概念的開始。以下「//」符號表示較長停頓，也就是語句結束；「/」則表示短暫停頓，表示同一個句子內一個較小的「語意單位」的完成。

Hello skiers.// Please be aware/ that skiing with unprepared skis/ can be very dangerous.// We offer a free grooming package/ here at Sunnyvale/ in order to make your experience here/ as safe as possible.// Please see the repair shop/ and show them your room key.// They will be happy to help you.// Thank you/ and have a

DAY 1
DAY 2
DAY 3
DAY 4
DAY 5
DAY 6
DAY 7
DAY 8
DAY 9
DAY 10
DAY 11
DAY 12
DAY 13
DAY 14

wonderful time on our mountain.//

　　第一句話即聽到主題，知道這是對滑雪者發佈的廣播。並且聽到 Please be aware... dangerous. 就知道目的在請聽者注意某件事情的安全。第一題問的是：What can people get at the repair shop? 表示我們在廣播中會聽到 repair shop ，並且要注意的是在 repair shop 能拿到什麼。所以當他說：We offer... 時就要特別注意，因為 We offer... 和 What can people get 是一樣的意思。他可能會說：We offer... at the repair shop.

　　果然他先說了：We offer... free grooming package... Please see the repair shop... 表示提供的是 grooming package「滑雪道清理器具」，而需要的話就 see the repair shop「找 repair shop」。因此這題的答案是：B. Free grooming package.

第二題問的是：What must people do to get assistance? 要怎麼做，repair shop 的人才會幫你？他說的是：Please see the repair shop and show them your room key. 也就是要給他看你的房間鑰匙。答案是：B. Present your room key to the staff.

句型單字整理

Please be aware... 請注意…

...can be very dangerous ⋯是非常危險的

Please see the repair shop. 請到修理室。

skis 雪橇 n.

grooming 清理用的 adj.

repair 修理 v.

Lesson 2 ❯ 電視及廣播的廣告

❯ 舒葳老師說 13-3

請聽MP3，並選擇適當的答案。每一則廣告有兩道題目。

A.

1. Who would be interested in this ad?

   A. Couples who want to buy a new house.

   B. People who are going to get married.

   C. Students who have a big exam coming.

2. What should one do if he/she is interested?

   A. Take part in a draw.

   B. Call the number.

   C. Visit the shops.

B.

1. Who would be most interested in the product advertised?

   A. People who play computer games at Internet Cafes.

   B. People who want their house to be neat and clean.

   C. People who make frequent international calls.

2. How is the central wireless network connected to your computer, telephone, cable TV and etc.?

   A. By cable.

   B. By wire.

   C. By radio signals

C.

1. Who would most likely to be interested in this advertisement?

    A. People who are considering getting a pet.

    B. People whose pets need heath check or treatment.

    C. People who are looking for a new home for their pets.

2. What is TAPP?

    A. A pet store.

    B. A pet hotel.

    C. A pet hospital.

D.

1. What's the prize of this week's competition?

    A. Two concert tickets.

    B. Classical CDs.

    C. Music magazines.

2. What does a listener need to do to win the prize?

    A. Be the first to say what the piece is.

    B. Be the first to say the name of the composer.

    C. Be the first to say what period this piece was written.

E.

1. Who would be most interested in this advertisement?

    A. Children.

    B. Computer programmers.

    C. Tourists.

2. How can one get a free tickets to Bonnie's Fun Fair?

    A.To spend a particular amount of money on some product.

    B.To send personal information and take part in a draw.

DAY 1
DAY 2
DAY 3
DAY 4
DAY 5
DAY 6
DAY 7
DAY 8
DAY 9
DAY 10
DAY 11
DAY 12
DAY 13
DAY 14

C. To call and answer questions correctly.

F.

1. Who is the most possible target group of the advertisement?

   A. People who seek to look prettier.

   B. People who seek to be healthier.

   C. People who want to lose weight.

2. How often should a person use this product?

   A. Before each meal.

   B. Twice a day.

   C. Every other day.

● Answers

D:1.C 2.A   E:1.A 2.A   F:1.A 2.B

A:1.B 2.B   B:1.B 2.C   C:1.B 2.C

> **詳細解說** 13-4

A.

When the time has come for you to pop the question, will you be nervous or will you be confident in your decision? A purchase at Shay Company Diamonds will allow you to rest assured in your diamond decision. When the big day comes, you can be confident that she will love your selection, because the Shay Company has the very best diamonds in Chicago. She will fall in love with you all over again. You know that special moment deserves a special diamond for that special someone, so buy the perfect diamond. You can only find it at the Shay Company... Call 1-800-DIAMOND today.

當該你提問的重要時刻到來，你會緊張還是會對你的決定充滿信心？在Shay Company 採購鑽石會讓你很安心地選定你的鑽石。當大喜的那一天到來時，

你可以確信她會愛死了你的選擇，因為Shay Company擁有芝加哥最好的鑽石。她會再度與你墜入情網。你知道，特別的一刻，值得一顆特別的鑽石，給特別的那個人，所以，買最完美的鑽石。你只能在Shay Company找到。今天就打電話到1-800-DIMOND.

1. Who would be interested in this ad?

　　誰會對這個廣告有興趣？

　　A. Couples who want to buy a new house.

　　　　想買新房子的夫妻。

　　B. People who are going to get married.

　　　　將要結婚的男女朋友。（正確答案）

　　C. Students who have a big exam coming.

　　　　有大考來臨的學生。

2. What should one do if he/she is interested?

　　有興趣的人應該怎麼做？

　　A. Take part in a draw. 參加抽獎。

　　B. Call the number. 打電話到那個號碼。（正確答案）

　　C. Visit the shops. 到店裏去。

　　我們應該善用「語意單位」、語氣停頓和語調來幫助理解。以下「//」符號表示較長停頓，也就是語句結束；「/」則表示短暫停頓，表示同一個句子內一個較小的「語意單位」的完成。

When the time has come/ for you to pop the question,/ will you be nervous/ or will you be confident/ in your decision?//　A purchase

DAY 1
DAY 2
DAY 3
DAY 4
DAY 5
DAY 6
DAY 7
DAY 8
DAY 9
DAY 10
DAY 11
DAY 12
DAY 13
DAY 14

at Shay Company Diamonds will allow you to rest assured/ in your diamond decision.// When the big day comes,/ you can be confident/ that she will love your selection,/ because the Shay Company/ has the very best diamonds/ in Chicago.// She will fall in love with you/ all over again.// You know that special moment/ deserves a special diamond/ for that special someone,/ so buy the perfect diamond.// You can only find it at/ the Shay Company//Call 1-800-/DIAMOND/ today.//

第一句話 When the time has come for you to pop the question, will you be nervous or will you be confident in your decision? 就點出了這段話的主題，因此我們知道廣告產品跟結婚有關。在英文裡，ask the question 就有求婚的意思。

果然：A purchase at Shay Company Diamonds will allow you...，這裡廣告的是 Shay Company Diamonds。同時，廣告中被廣告的商品一定會不斷出現。這裡我們一直聽到 Shay Company Diamonds, diamond, 所以我們更確定這個廣告在賣的是鑽石。再加上其他的關鍵字：make the right decision、she will love your decision、she will fall in love with you again, special moment... 也確定廣告的對象是要結婚買鑽戒的人。

廣告的尾端通常是要你付諸行動。這裡他說 Call...，所以是打電話。在美國為了讓大家好記，商家的電話號碼常常變成英文字（像手機一樣，一個數字會和數個字母共用一個輸入按鍵）。

❯ 句型單字整理

DAY
1

DAY
2

DAY
3

DAY
4

DAY
5

DAY
6

DAY
7

DAY
8

DAY
9

DAY
10

DAY
11

DAY
12

DAY
13

DAY
14

ask the question 問這個重要的問題，在這裡是「求婚」的意思

purchase 購買 v.

rest assured 放心

the big day 大囍之日

deserve 應得、值得 v.

B.

Do you have cable, and telephone cords cluttering up your house? We have all had the trouble of sorting out computer, cable TV and telephone cords. But now we, here at Clean House, are pleased to present the solution to this unsightly mess. With our new universal wireless network you can plug your cable TV, your DSL lines and your telephone lines into one central wireless network. Store it in your closet, in the attic, wherever, just get that unsightly mess out of the living room. Each set comes with a central hub and five satellite receivers capable of handling a 200,000 ping area. We are offering this today for the low, low price of only $79.95. Get it today.

你家有纏成一堆的電線和電話線嗎？我們都有試著把家中的電腦、數據機、有線電視和電話的電線整理出頭緒來的慘痛經驗。但是現在，清潔屋推出了能夠對付這有礙觀瞻的髒亂的解決方案。有了我們新出品的世界無線系統，你可以把你的有線電視電線、有線數據機電線或撥接數據機電線和電話線都插到一個中央無線系統。把它放置在你的衣櫃、放在閣樓，或任何地方，隨你高興，就能把這個有礙觀瞻的髒亂趕出客廳。每一組都附有一個中央分享器以及五個衛星接收器，可用於二十萬坪的面積。以79.95的低價就可以買到。今天就買吧。

1. Who would be most interested in the product advertised?

   誰會對此廣告產品最有興趣？

A. People who play computer games at Internet Cafes.

在網路咖啡店玩電腦遊戲的人。

B. People who want their house to be neat and clean.

希望家裡整齊乾淨的人。（正確答案）

C. People who make frequent international calls.

常常打國際電話的人。

2. How is the central wireless network connected to your computer, telephone, cable TV and etc.?

電腦、電話等等如何連接到這個中央無線系統？

A. By cable. 電纜。

B. By wire. 電線。

C. By radio signals. 電波訊號。（正確答案）

我們應該善用「語意單位」、語氣停頓和語調來幫助理解。以下「//」符號表示較長停頓，也就是語句結束；「/」則表示短暫停頓，表示同一個句子內一個較小的「語意單位」的完成。

Do you have cable,/ and telephone cords cluttering up/ your house?// We have all had the trouble of sorting out computer,/ cable TV/ and telephone cords.// But now/ we,/ here at Clean House,/ are pleased to present the solution to this unsightly mess.// With our new universal wireless network/ you can plug your cable TV,/ your DSL line/ and your telephone lines/ into one central wireless network.// Store it in your closet,/ in the attic,/ wherever,/ just get that unsightly mess/ out of the living room.// Each set comes with a central hub/ and five satellite receivers/

DAY
1

DAY
2

DAY
3

DAY
4

DAY
5

DAY
6

DAY
7

DAY
8

DAY
9

DAY
10

DAY
11

DAY
12

**DAY
13**

DAY
14

capable of handling a 200,000 ping area.// We are offering this today for the low/ low/ price of only/ \$79.95.// Get it today.//

第一句話Do you have cable, and telephone cords cluttering up your house? 便會點出主題，因此我們知道這個廣告產品希望解決的是家裡cable、telephone cords cluttering up的問題。接下去敘述處理電線的痛苦後，果然we, at Clean House, are pleased to present the solution to this unsightly mess. 要提供你解決方案。

當我們聽到With our new universal wireless network... 就知道他會說明新產品的好處。每一個稍長的停頓都表示一個好處可能已經講完。停頓後語調上揚，表示要開始說另一個好處。我們聽重音，三個好處如下：

1) plug... cable TV... cable modem... DSL lines... telephone lines... one central wireless network....

也就是「通通插入一個中央無線系統」

2) Store... closet... attic... get... mess out... living room.

也就是「把…放置某處，把髒亂趕出客廳」

3) Each... central hub... five satellite receivers... 200,000 ping

「每一組都附有一個中央分享器以及五個衛星接收器，可用於二十萬坪的面積。」既然是無線的，就靠衛星接收器接收電波訊號即可。

廣告的最後自然會強調價錢有多麼划算囉！

> 句型單字整理

cable 電線 n.

cord 電線 n.

clutter up 擠成一堆、纏成一堆

misfortune 不幸 n.

sort out 整理出頭緒

unsightly mess 有礙觀瞻的髒亂

wireless 無線的 adj.

hub 活動中心、中樞 n.

satellite receiver 衛星訊號接受器

capable of... 有能力⋯的

C.

Your pet deserves the best and only the good health and grooming experts at Taiwan Advanced Pet Professionals can make sure your pet gets the best. Whether your dog has fleas, your cat has hairballs or a urinary tract infection, the professionals at TAPP can help. We can and do take care of the minor problems as well as the serious injuries. We, at TAPP, can be trusted to help your pets heal from a broken leg or a cancerous lesion. You can trust us. You can trust Taiwan Advanced Pet Professionals. At TAPP, we provide the most caring environments, the most up to date medical techniques, and the best veterinary science around. Let TAPP care for your pets like they deserve. They deserve the best, and TAPP provides it.

你的寵物值得你給牠最好的，而只有在擁有健康和清潔專家的「台灣卓越寵物專家」能確保你的寵物得到最好的照顧。無論是你的狗可能有跳蚤，你的貓的毛起了毛球或是尿道感染，「台灣卓越寵物專家」都能提供協助。我們能照顧小問題，也能解決嚴重的受傷。在TAPP，我們能幫助你的寵物從摔斷的腳，甚至是癌症的傷害復原過來。你可以信任我們，你可以信任「台灣卓越寵物專家」在TAPP，我們提供最溫暖的環境、最新的醫療技術，和最優質

的獸醫服務。讓TAPP給你的寵物牠們應得的照顧。讓「台灣卓越寵物專家」提供你的寵物值得的照顧。他們值得最好的，TAPP提供最好的。

1. Who would most likely to be interested in this advertisement?

誰最可能對這個廣告有興趣？

A. People who are considering getting a pet.

正考慮要養寵物的人。

B. People whose pets need heath check or treatment.

有寵物需要健康檢查或醫療的人。（正確答案）

C. People who are looking for a new home for their pets.

在尋找自己外出渡假時寵物可寄居之處的人。

2. What is TAPP? TAPP 是什麼？

A. A pet store. 寵物店。

B. A pet hotel. 寵物旅館。

C. A pet hospital. 寵物醫院。（正確答案）

我們應該善用「語意單位」、語氣停頓和語調來幫助理解。以下「//」符號表示較長停頓，也就是語句結束；「/」則表示短暫停頓，表示同一個句子內一個較小的「語意單位」的完成。

Your pet deserves the best/ and only the good health and grooming experts/ at Taiwan Advanced Pet Professionals/ can make sure your pet/ gets the best.// Whether your dog has fleas,/ your cat has hairballs or a urinary tract infection,/ the professionals at TAPP can help.// We can/ and do/ take care of the minor problems/ as

DAY 1
DAY 2
DAY 3
DAY 4
DAY 5
DAY 6
DAY 7
DAY 8
DAY 9
DAY 10
DAY 11
DAY 12
DAY 13
DAY 14

well as serious injuries.// We,/ at TAPP,/ can be trusted to help your pets heal/ from a broken leg/ or a cancerous lesion.// You can trust us.// You can trust/ Taiwan Advanced Pet Professionals.// At TAPP,/ we provide the most caring environments,/ the most up to date medical techniques,/ and the best veterinary science around.// Let TAPP care for your pets/ like they deserve.// They deserve the best,/ and TAPP provides it.//

第一句話 Your pet deserves the best 帶入主題，我們就知道這個廣告產品跟寵物有關，果然他説 and only the good... experts at... make sure... pet gets... best。

既然是廣告，接下去必定是説明這家廠商的幾點優勢，聽重音：

1) dog... fleas... cat...hairballs... infection... professionals... TAPP... help

2) We... can... minor problems... serious injuries

3) We... TAPP... trusted... help... pets... heal... broken leg... cancerous lesion.

把所有關鍵字串聯起來，我們知道這是一個獸醫的服務，照顧寵物清潔和醫療的問題。

較長的停頓後，聽到You can trust us. 就知道服務項目已經説完了，接著是另一個主題，強調為什麼可以信任他們。聽重音：most caring environments... most up to date medical techniques... best veterinary service... Let TAPP... pets... deserve. 這些是他們的優勢。

▶ 句型單字整理

deserve 值得；應得 v.

grooming 清理 n.

advanced 高級的 adj.

professional 專家 adj.

fleas 跳蚤 n.

urinary tract 尿道 n.

infection 感染 n.

minor 小的、次要的、輕微的 adj.

injury 受傷 n.

heal 治癒 v.

caring 仁慈的，提供情感支柱的 adj.

up to date 最新的 adj.

medical techniques 醫療技術 n.

veterinary 獸醫的 adj.

D.

Now, finally it's time for the highlight of the week - our weekly competition! Last week's prize of two National Theater tickets was won by Barry Jones. Congratulations, Barry. I hope you and your friend enjoyed the concert! This week we're offering a year's subscription to The World of Classical CDs to the first listener who can name this famous piece of music. I'm going to play the piece in a minute, but before I do, I'll give you some help, which should make your job a little easier. Are you ready? Right, now, listen carefully...

現在，終於到了一星期的高潮了─我們一週一度的競賽。上星期的獎品是兩張國家戲劇院的入場票，由Barry Jones贏得。Barry，恭喜了！希望你和你的

DAY 1
DAY 2
DAY 3
DAY 4
DAY 5
DAY 6
DAY 7
DAY 8
DAY 9
DAY 10
DAY 11
DAY 12
DAY 13
DAY 14

朋友喜歡那場音樂會！這個星期，我們提供的獎項是一年期的「古典音樂世界雜誌」。要得到這個大獎，你必須能夠說出我放的這首曲子的名稱。我馬上就會開始放這首曲子，但是在那個之前，我會先給各位一點協助，好讓各位能更輕鬆地說出答案。準備好了嗎？好，現在，注意聽⋯

1. What's the prize of this wee's competition?

   本週比賽的獎品為何？

   A. Two concert tickets. 兩張音樂會門票。

   B. Classical CDs. 古典音樂CD。

   C. Music magazines. 音樂雜誌。（正確答案）

2. What does a listener need to do to win the prize?

   想贏得獎品聽眾需要怎麼做？

   A. Be the first to say what the piece is.

      說出這首曲子為何。（正確答案）

   B. Be the first to say the name of the composer.

      說出作曲家的名字。

   C. Be the first to say what period this piece was written.

      說出這首曲子寫於哪一個時期。

我們應該善用「語意單位」、語氣停頓和語調來幫助理解。以下「//」符號表示較長停頓，也就是語句結束；「/」則表示短暫停頓，表示同一個句子內一個較小的「語意單位」的完成。

Now,// finally/ it's time/ for the highlight of the week// - our weekly competition.// Last week's prize of two National Theater tickets/

DAY
1

DAY
2

DAY
3

DAY
4

DAY
5

DAY
6

DAY
7

DAY
8

DAY
9

DAY
10

DAY
11

DAY
12

DAY
13

DAY
14

was won by Barry Jones.// Congratulations,/ Barry.// I hope you/ and your friend/ enjoyed the concert.// This week/ we're offering a year's subscription to/ The World of Classical CDs/ to the first listener/ who can name this famous piece of music.// I'm going to play the piece in a minute/ but before I do,/ I'll give you some help,/ which should make your job a little easier.// Are you ready?// Right,// now,/ listen carefully... //

　　第一句話 Now, finally it's time for the highlight of the week 帶入主題，我們就知道這是一個節目的一部份，是什麼節目呢？our weekly competition 一週一度的競賽。

　　我們聽到 Last week's prize... 就知道主持人先談談上週的狀況：two National Theater tickets was won by Bryan Jones...。停頓後，我們聽到 This week... 就知道今天的主題要開始了，他說 we're offering a year's subscription to The World of Classical CDs，給誰呢？聽重音：...first listener... name... famous music. 第一個說出名曲的名稱的人。

　　接著比賽就要開始了：I'm going to play ... but before I do... 聽到 but，表示還沒有真正要開始，不開始要做什麼呢？I'll give you some help. 也就是說主持人會先提供練習和幫助喔。

▶ 句型單字整理

the highlight of the week　一星期的高潮。

competition　比賽　n.

offer　提供 v.

subscription 訂閱 v.

name 說出…的名稱 v.

piece 曲子的單位 n.

I'll... but before I do... 我要…但是在那之前…

E.

Tired of the daily grind? Ready for a day of excitement at Bonnie's Fun Fair? You can receive a free ticket to Bonnie's Fun Fair, by simply purchasing NT 1000 worth of any Robinson Bothers games and puzzles. Send in the original dated receipt with the prices of the items circled and a completed redemption form to Galaxy Toy Offer, P.O. BOX 5112, Taipei, Taiwan. The redemption form must include your name, address, daytime phone and age and be postmarked no later than June 20th 2004. For detailed information, call 886-2-23975599.

厭倦日常生活中的瑣事嗎？準備好要參加小白兔遊樂園一日遊了嗎？只要你購買價值新台幣1000元的Robinson Brothers遊戲和拼圖，就可以得到一張小白兔遊樂園的免費入場券。把寫有日期的收據上的價格圈起來，並填寫申請表格，一起寄到台北郵政5112信箱，銀河玩具公司。表格上必須填上你的姓名、地址、日間聯絡電話和你的年齡，郵戳日期必須在2004年6月20日前！詳細活動辦法請洽：886-2-23975599。

1. Who would be most interested in this advertisement?

   誰是此廣告的最可能對象？

   A. Children. 兒童。（正確答案）

   B. Computer programmers. 軟體工程師。

   C. Tourists. 觀光客。

2. How can one get a free tickets to Bonnie's Fun Fair?

要如何才能得到免費入場券？

A. To spend a particular amount of money on some product.

花一定的金額買遊戲和拼圖。（正確答案）

B. To send personal information and take part in a draw.

郵寄個人資料參加抽獎。

C. To call and answer questions correctly.

打電話參加益智問答並回答正確。

我們應該善用「語意單位」、語氣停頓和語調來幫助理解。以下「//」符號表示較長停頓，也就是語句結束；「/」則表示短暫停頓，表示同一個句子內一個較小的「語意單位」的完成。

Tired of the daily grind?// Ready for a day of excitement at Bonnie's Fun Fair?// You can receive a free ticket to Bonnie's Fun Fair,/ by simply purchasing NT.1000 worth of any Robinson Bothers games and puzzles.// Send in the original dated receipt/ with the prices of the items circled/ and a completed redemption form to Galaxy Toy Offer/ P.O. BOX 5112,/ Taipei,/ Taiwan.// The redemption form must include your name,/ address,/ daytime phone/ and age/ and be postmarked/ no later than June 20th/ 2004.// For detailed information,/ call 886-2-23975599.

第一句話 Tired of the daily grind? Ready for a day of excitement at Bonnie's Fun Fair? 告訴我們廣告主題是 a day at Bonnies Fun Fair。接下來一聽到 You can receive a free ticket... 我們就可以預期他會說 by... 經由什麼樣的方法。果然他說：by simply

---

DAY 1
DAY 2
DAY 3
DAY 4
DAY 5
DAY 6
DAY 7
DAY 8
DAY 9
DAY 10
DAY 11
DAY 12
DAY 13
DAY 14

purchasing NT.1000 worth of... 購買價值1000元的東西即可。

　　接著，我們應可預期廣告會詳細敘述活動辦法。聽重音：1) Send... receipt... prices... circled... and... completed... form... Galaxy Toy Offer, P.O. BOX 5112, Taipei, Taiwan. 聽到 and，知道是兩個步驟。2) ... form must include... name, address, daytime phone... age... 3) It must be postmarked no later than June 20th 2004. 聽到 must 通常都是重點。

▶ 句型單字整理

grind　繁複、困難但無聊的活動 n.

day tour　一日遊

fun fair　遊樂場

purchase　購買 v.

worth　價值 n.

receipt　收據 n.

redemption form　申請表格

send A along with B　把A和B一起寄

personal information　個人資料

postmark　郵戳 n.

F.

Sylvia Internal Skin Care is a vital part of the way to take care of your skin. You'll see the improvement not only on your face, but all over your body. Your skin becomes smoother, softer, and more radiant. It's an all-over body approach, not the same old facial and skin cream. Sylvia Internal Skin Care has been scientifically tested for efficacy.

It has the clinically proven ability to improve the skin's density and appearance. Simply take two tablets of Sylvia Internal Skin Care each day – one in the morning and one at night, and you may notice a firmer, smoother, more radiant look in less than three months. And of course, a good moisturizer is still recommended for additional protection. Find Sylvia Care products at your local pharmacy. Your best skin is yet to come.

使用西微雅內服護膚產品，是妳呵護自己皮膚的必須步驟。這個改變不只臉部的，而是全身的。妳的肌膚會變得更滑、更順、更有光澤。這是一個全身性的方案，而非只是一般老式的面霜或乳液。西微雅內服護膚產品的效果經過科學測試，並經過臨床證明能改變皮膚的緊實度和外觀。每天只要服用兩顆西微雅內服護膚產品—— 早上一顆晚上一顆，妳就可以在大約三個月後到更緊實、更滑順、更有光澤的外觀。當然，我們建議妳仍需使用保濕乳液，以達到更多的保護。西微雅護膚產品在妳家附近的藥房有售。妳最佳的肌膚狀況即將來臨了。

1. Who is the most possible target group of the advertisement?

誰對這個廣告的產品會最有興趣？

A. People who seek to look prettier.

想看起來更美的人。（正確答案）

B. People who seek to be healthier.

想更健康的人。

C. People who want to lose weight. 想減重的人。

2. How often should a person use this product? 此產品如何使用？

A. Before each meal. 三餐前。

B. Twice a day. 每天兩次。（正確答案）

C. Every other day. 每兩天一次。

我們應該善用「語意單位」、語氣停頓和語調來幫助理解。以下「//」符號表示較長停頓，也就是語句結束；「/」則表示短暫停頓，表示同一個句子內一個較小的「語意單位」的完成。

Sylvia Internal Skin Care/ is a vital part of the way/ you/ take care of your skin.// You'll see the improvement/ not only on your face,/ but all over your body.// Your skin becomes smoother,/ softer,/ and more radiant.// It's an all-over body approach,/ not the same/ old facial and skin cream.// Sylvia Internal Skin Care/ has been scientifically tested for efficacy.// It has the/ clinically proven/ ability to improve the skin's density/ and appearance.// Simply take two tablets/ of Sylvia Internal Skin Care/ each day// – one in the morning/ and one at night,/ and you may notice/ a firmer,/ smoother,/ more radiant look/ in less than three months.// And of course,/ a good moisturizer/ is still recommended/ for additional protection.// Find Sylvia Care products/ at your local pharmacy.// Your best skin/ is yet to come.//

第一句話 ...Skin Care... vital part... take care of your skin. 即帶入主題，我們知道這個廣告產品是跟護膚有關。

接著敘述產品的功效。聽重音：

1) .... improvement not only... face... all over your body

2) ... skin becomes smoother, softer,... more radiant

3) ... all-over body approach, not ... same old ⋯

接著是不同層面的優勢：...Skin Care... scientifically tested... efficacy.... clinically proven... improve... density... appearance

當我們聽到 Simply...「只要…」，就知道接下去是要告訴你怎麼做。果然他說：take two tablets... each day? One... morning and one... night。聽到And of course... 知道要開始另一個主題：a good moisturizer is still recommended。當廣告告訴你 ...is recommended.「我們建議你…」通常這個建議都是重點訊息喔！

廣告的最後常是購買方式和最後促銷：Find... products at your local pharmacy. Your best skin is yet to come.

▶ 句型單字整理

vital 重要的；必須的 adj.

radiant 有光澤的 adj.

approach 方式 n.

scientifically tested 經過科學測試的

efficacy 效果 n.

clinically proven ability 經過臨床證明的能力

density 密度；緊實度 n.

appearance 外觀 n.

tablets（藥丸）顆粒 n.

moisturizer 保濕乳液 n.

recommend 建議 v.

additional 額外的 adj.

available 可以得到的 adj.

DAY 1
DAY 2
DAY 3
DAY 4
DAY 5
DAY 6
DAY 7
DAY 8
DAY 9
DAY 10
DAY 11
DAY 12
DAY 13
DAY 14

local 當地的 adj.

be yet to come 就是會來但尚未來臨

not the same old... 不是老是那一套…

Simply... 只要…即可

▶ 聽力小秘訣

☺ 廣播與廣告都有一定的習慣與模式。習慣這樣的模式有助於聽力的理解。

☺ 廣播與廣告一開始都會先說明主題與目的，因此聽清楚開頭很重要。知道了這篇廣播／廣告主題為何，便對接下來會聽到的東西有了心理準備，就會比較容易聽懂。

☺ 廣播與廣告中一直重覆的關鍵字，也能幫助我們抓到主題、目的、對象和場合。

☺ 聽長篇聽力時，若能辨別哪一類的語句後面會接重要訊息，便能讓你在訊息出來前事先預備以集中你的注意力。譬如說，以下的這些句型都是在提示我們說話者馬上要進入重點，聽到這些，就表示你得特別注意聽了：

You must...
Remember to...
Don't forget...
Simply...
It's recommended...
It's important...

☺ 另外，一般的祈使句也常會接重點。例如：

Send...

Complete...

Find...

Call...

Listen carefully...

既然說話者在請你做某些事情，這些事情就有可能是重點。

MEMO

DAY
1

DAY
2

DAY
3

DAY
4

DAY
5

DAY
6

DAY
7

DAY
8

DAY
9

DAY
10

DAY
11

DAY
12

DAY
13

DAY
14

MEMO

DAY

聽力實戰練習4
新聞與氣象報告
News and Weather Reports

14-1~14-2

　　最後,我們要來練習聽新聞與氣象報告。這也是我們在生活中常需接觸到的聽力類型。因為同樣也是長篇獨白,因此除了一般的發音、重音及連音等技巧外,使用「語調」及「語意單位」來幫助聽力仍然是本課的重點。

　　另一個重點則是熟悉老外在報新聞及氣象時的習慣模式。聽多了,熟悉了一貫的模式,也會幫助你越聽越懂喔。

DAY 14 聽力實戰練習4
新聞與氣象報告
News and Weather Reports

MP3 14-1~14-2

Lesson 1 ▶ 新聞與氣象報告

▶ 舒葳老師說 14-1

請聽MP3，並選擇適當的答案，每段文章有兩道題目。

A.

1. What is the speaker's purpose?

　　A. To state the latest findings on Mars.

　　B. To describe a space adventure.

　　C. To compare life on Earth and that on Mars.

2. What did the speaker say about Mars?

　　A. There was water on Mars.

　　B. There wasn't water on Mars ever.

　　C. There was life on Mars.

B.

1. What's the point the speaker is trying to make?

　　A. The important of creativity at work.

　　B. Relation between creativity and the atmosphere of the
　　　 workplace.

　　C. Pressure at work brings effectiveness.

2. A playful atmosphere in the work place is particularly important
　 for which type of company?

　　A. An advertising company.

　　B. A shoe-making factory.

DAY
1

DAY
2

DAY
3

DAY
4

DAY
5

DAY
6

DAY
7

DAY
8

DAY
9

DAY
10

DAY
11

DAY
12

DAY
13

**DAY
14**

C. Real estate brokers.

C.

1. What isn't true about the robber?

    A. He is often in black.

    B. He rides a black motorbike.

    C. He has broken into more than ten houses.

2. Why is he considered dangerous?

    A. People have been reported injured.

    B. He carries weapons with him.

    C. He has previous criminal record.

D.

1. What's the purpose of the news?

    A. To tell an upsetting news about boy from a poor family.

    B. To explain how one can improve his English ability.

    C. To report the story about a boy who has won a competition.

2. What is NOT true about the boy?

    A. He has just started going to English classes.

    B. He is self-motivated and diligent.

    C. He won the first prize of the context.

E.

1. What is Saturday evening's weather forecast?

    A. Hot and humid all over the island.

    B. Heavy rain over the entire island.

    C. Light showers over the northern part.

2. Some people are planning for a picnic on Sunday. When should

they go?

A. After around 10:00 AM.

B. After around 3:00 PM.

C. After around 6:00 PM.

F.

1. What is the main problem with the typhoon?

   A. Heavy rain.

   B. Strong wind.

   C. Both.

2. What is said about people who work for private companies?

   A. They can have a day off tomorrow.

   B. They should ask their boss if they need to work tomorrow.

   C. They should wait for farther information to be announced.

● Answers

B .2   A .1 :F   B .2   C .1 :E   A .2   C .1 :D

B .2   C .1 :C   A .2   B .1 :B   A .2   A .1 :A

▶ 詳細解說   14-2

A.

After months and even years waiting for an answer, we at the 6pm evening news have finally brought you the answer. The American and European space agencies' rocket to Mars has successfully touched down on the northern surface of Mars. We have been receiving radio signals from the landing craft and are now awaiting a basic response to our first processing request sent from earth this morning. The most momentous news so far, is that the Martian Lander has confirmed reports indicating the presence of water on the surface of Mars.

DAY 1
DAY 2
DAY 3
DAY 4
DAY 5
DAY 6
DAY 7
DAY 8
DAY 9
DAY 10
DAY 11
DAY 12
DAY 13
DAY 14

Now, we wait for the answer to the biggest question of all, is there any evidence of life on the surface of Mars? Tune in tomorrow for continuing reports on the space expedition.

在長久的等待之後，我們在六點鐘晚間新聞為大家帶來一個您期待已久的問題的解答。美國和歐洲太空總署前往火星的火箭已經成功地在火星北邊的表面著陸了。我們已經陸續收到從著陸的火箭上傳來的信號，現在在等待的是，他們對我們今天早上傳過去的初步問題做回應。目前對歷史最有決定性意義的發現，是火星登陸號已經證實火星表面有水存在過的跡象。現在我們只需要等待我們最重要的問題的解答：火星表面有沒有生命的跡象？明天轉到這個頻道，我們將有火星探險的後續報導。

1. What is the speaker's purpose?

這段話的目的、主旨為何？

A. To state the latest findings on Mars.

陳述火星上的最新的發現。(正確答案)

B. To describe a space adventure.

形容一太空探險的經過。

C. To compare life on Earth and that on Mars.

比較地球和火星上生命的不同。

2. What did the speaker say about Mars? 説話者如何敘述火星？

A. There was water on Mars. 火星上曾經有水。(正確答案)

B. There wasn't water on Mars ever. 火星上從來沒有水過。

C. There was life on Mars. 火星上曾經有生命。

善用「語意單位」及語氣停頓和語調來幫助理解。以下「 // 」符號表示較長停頓，也就是語句結束；「 / 」則表示短暫停頓，表示

281

同一個句子內一個較小的「語意單位」的完成。

After months/ and even years waiting for an answer,/ we/ at the 6pm evening news/ can finally bring you part of the answer.// The American and European space agencies? rocket to Mars/ has successfully touched down/ on the northern surface of Mars.// We have been receiving radio signals from the landing craft/ and are now awaiting a basic response/ to our first processing request/ sent from earth this morning.// The most momentous news so far,/ is that the Martian lander has confirmed reports/ indicating the presence of water on the surface of Mars.// Now,/ we wait for the answer to the biggest question of all,/ is there any evidence of life on the surface of Mars?// Tune in tomorrow/ for continuing reports on the space expedition.//

新聞一開始 After months and even years of waiting for an answer, we at the 6pm evening news have finally brought you an answer.

即說明這段新聞的主題：我們帶來一個大家期待的問題的解答。後來當我們聽到 The most momentous news so far is that... 就知道播報員要給我們一些重要的資訊，也就是題目要問的重點。他接著說：the... has confirmed reports... presence of water... Mars. 因此我們知道火星上有水。

最後一段他用疑問的句型說：Is there any evidence of life on the surface of Mars? 表示我們還不知道這個問題的答案，要 Tune in tomorrow for continuing reports... 看明天的報導了。

▶ 句型單字整理

surface 表面 n.

signal 信號 n.

landing craft 著陸的火箭

craft 座艙 n.

momentous 非常重要的；對歷史有決定性意義的 adj.

confirmed 確定的；證實了的 adj.

presence 存在 n.

evidence 證據 n.

expedition 探險 n.

Tune in tomorrow for... 明天請轉到這個頻道繼續收看⋯

DAY 1
DAY 2
DAY 3
DAY 4
DAY 5
DAY 6
DAY 7
DAY 8
DAY 9
DAY 10
DAY 11
DAY 12
DAY 13
DAY 14

B.

Good evening. CCB News. I'm Mark Kory. A recent Gallup poll comparing working environments suggests improving the atmosphere in the workplace can create higher creative output. Many businesses reported that employees that truly enjoy their workplace are more creative in their problem solving and that employees that find work miserable have trouble solving simple problems that arise each day. So if you find your workplace isn't providing you and your employees with an enjoyable experience, get up and bring some levity to the workplace. Your improved productivity and the employees'creativity may just surprise you.

晚安，CBB新聞。我是Mark Kory。最近一項蓋洛普比較工作環境的民意調查，發現改善工作場所的氣氛能提高工作的創意。很多公司表示，真正享受工作環境的員工在解決問題上有較多的創意；而覺得工作很痛苦的員工，則沒辦法解決每天工作上遇到的簡單問題。所以如果你覺得你的工作環境不能

給你和你的員工愉快的工作經驗，那麼你得想辦法為你的公司注入一點輕鬆的氣氛了。你工作效率的增加和你的員工的創意可能會給你意想不到的驚喜。

1. What's the point the speaker is trying to make?

本篇報導的重點為何？

A. The important of creativity at work. 創意在工作上是重要性。

B. Relation between creativity and the atmosphere of the workplace.

工作表現與工作氣氛有關。(正確答案)

C. Pressure at work brings effectiveness. 工作壓力帶來工作效率。

2. A playful atmosphere in the work place is particularly important for which type of company? 氣氛歡愉的工作場合對哪一種公司特別重要？

A. An advertising company. 廣告公司。(正確答案)

B. A shoe-making factory. 製鞋工廠。

C. Real estate brokers. 房地產經紀公司。

善用「語意單位」及語氣停頓和語調來幫助理解。以下「//」符號表示較長停頓，也就是語句結束；「/」則表示短暫停頓，表示同一個句子內一個較小的「語意單位」的完成。

Good evening.// CCB News.// I'm Mark Kory.// A recent Gallup poll comparing working environments/ suggests improving the atmosphere in the workplace/ can improve creative output// Many businesses reported that employees who truly enjoy their workplace/ are more creative in their problem solving/ and that employees that find work miserable/ have trouble solving simple

DAY 1
DAY 2
DAY 3
DAY 4
DAY 5
DAY 6
DAY 7
DAY 8
DAY 9
DAY 10
DAY 11
DAY 12
DAY 13
DAY 14

problems that arise each day.// So,/ if you find your workplace isn't providing you/ and your employees with an enjoyable experience,/ get up and bring some levity/ to the workplace.// Your improved productivity/ and the employees' creativity/ may just surprise you.//

談話開頭都會先說明主題：A recent Gallup poll comparing working environments suggests... atmosphere... workplace... improve... output 因此我們知道主題是工作環境並且與職場氣氛、工作表現有關。

整個新聞接下去就會談到此份調查的細節：Many businesses reported that...

1) employees... enjoy their workplace...creative ...

2) employees ... find ... miserable have trouble solving simple problems

上面兩句中間的and that 表示連接兩個完整的「語意單位」，也就是說有兩個重點。

最後他說 So,... 表示要做結論或建議。祈使句：get up and bring some levity to the workplace... improved productivity... creativity... surprise you. 如果 levity 這個字不會，應該也可以從前後文猜到與良好氣氛有關。關鍵字告訴我們會幫助創造力與創意。因此，以創意為導向的行業自然是最更需要輕鬆愉悅的工作環境的了。

> 句型單字整理

Gallup poll 蓋洛普民意調查

atmosphere 氣氛 n.

miserable 愁雲慘霧的 adj.

levity 輕鬆的氣氛 n.

productivity 生產力、創造力 n.

C.

In Sanchung recently there has been a series of amazing bank robberies. The suspected mastermind works alone, but those who have witnessed the crimes have dubbed him the Black Rider. This name comes from his tendency to wear all black leather riding gear as he zips away from the scene of the crime. His motorcycle is completely black also, and he often rides away without any safety lights or headlights after committing his armed robberies. The police consider him armed dangerous. Please use extreme caution if you see this man, anyone matching these characteristics or any odd behavior around any Sanchung area banks. Make your way to the nearest phone or use your mobile phone to inform the police immediately.

最近在三重發生了一連串的不可思議的銀行搶劫。這個智慧型嫌疑犯獨立犯下這些案件，但那些看過他的人稱之為黑騎士。這個名字的由來是因為他習慣穿一身黑色皮製騎士裝，從犯案現場蛇行離去。他的摩托車也是全黑，而且常在武裝犯下搶案後，不開安全燈或大燈就騎著他的黑色摩托車揚長而去。他因身帶武器而被警方視為危險人物。如果你看到這個人，請特別小心——任何符合以上特徵，或在三重地區銀行附近舉止怪異之人，請就近以打電話或打你的手機向警方報案。

1. What isn't true about the robber?

哪一個選項不符合對此搶劫者的敘述？

A. He is often in black. 他常穿一身黑衣。

B. He rides a black motorbike.

他騎黑色摩托車。

C. He has broken into more than ten houses.

他已闖入了十戶以上民宅。(正確答案)

2. Why is he considered dangerous? 他為什麼被視為危險人物？

A. People have been reported injured. 據報導有人受傷。

B. He carries weapons with him. 他身上攜帶武器。(正確答案)

C. He has previous criminal record. 他有犯案前科。

善用「語意單位」及語氣停頓和語調來幫助理解。以下「//」符號表示較長停頓，也就是語句結束；「/」則表示短暫停頓，表示同一個句子內一個較小的「語意單位」的完成。

In Sanchung recently/ there has been a series of amazing bank robberies.// The suspected mastermind works alone,/ but those who have witnessed the crimes/ have dubbed him/ the Black Rider.// This name/ comes from his tendency to wear all black leather riding gear/ as he zips away from the scene of the crimes.// His motorcycle is completely black,/ and he often rides away/ without any safety lights or headlights/ after committing his armed robberies.// The police consider him armed/ and dangerous.// Use extreme caution if you see this man,/ anyone matching these characteristics/ or if you witness any odd behavior around any/ Sanchung area banks.// Please,/ make your way to the nearest phone/ or use your mobile phone to inform the police/ immediately.//

DAY 1
DAY 2
DAY 3
DAY 4
DAY 5
DAY 6
DAY 7
DAY 8
DAY 9
DAY 10
DAY 11
DAY 12
DAY 13
DAY 14

新聞報導一開始即說明 In Sanchung recently... bank robberies. 我們知道這篇報導是關於「三重的銀行搶劫」。

接著 The suspected... , but those... the Black Rider. 我們知道接下去是關於嫌疑犯的資訊。從重音抓關鍵字，我們聽到 Black Rider... tendency... all black leather riding gear... motorcycle... black... rides away 等等，我們可以推測他身穿黑衣並騎摩托車。從 ...committing his armed robberies、... police... armed dangerous，關鍵字armed出現兩次，因此我們可以推知他有武裝。

▶ 句型單字整理

robbery 搶劫 n.

mastermind 有高度智慧的 adj.

suspect 嫌疑犯 n.

those who have witnessed the crimes 那些犯罪的目擊者

dub 稱某人為；為某人取綽號 v.

tendency 傾向 n.

riding gear 騎士裝

zips away 蛇行離開

the scene of the crime 犯罪現場

commit 犯案 v.

armed 武裝的 adj.

consider him ... 認為他⋯

characteristics 特徵 n.

DAY 1
DAY 2
DAY 3
DAY 4
DAY 5
DAY 6
DAY 7
DAY 8
DAY 9
DAY 10
DAY 11
DAY 12
DAY 13
DAY 14

D.

Although much of the news tends towards the negative these days, we are proud now to bring you this human-interest story. In the recent English Spelling Bee for high school children all over Taiwan, there was a young boy who consistently proved better than the rest. Not only was his incredible accuracy in spelling English words remarkable, but also his background. He never attended an English cram school. He does not come from a rich family and never had any tutoring. It was through his own interest and incredible work ethic that he managed to study the English language all by himself. He learned by reading the paper, listening to the radio, TV and books he bought for himself. Just to let you know how amazing this feat was, the winning word, that he alone spelled correctly, was Antidisestablishmentarianism, the longest word in most English language dictionaries. Tonight on SWW TV's evening news program, we will proudly recognize this boy's feat and award him the Spelling bee's million-dollar prize. Congratulations Mark, you make us all proud!

雖然最近的新聞都傾向負面的報導，但今天我們很高興為您帶來一則人文趣聞。在最近舉辦的全台高中英文拼字比賽，有一個男孩持續地表現出眾。令人讚賞的，不只是他在拼字上令人無法置信的正確度，還有他的背景。他從未上過英文補習班。他並非出生於富裕家庭，也沒請過家教。他憑著自己的興趣和異常的認真態度，自己苦讀英文。他從讀報紙、聽廣播、電視、和他自己買的書來自修。你知道他的成就有多麼讓人驚嘆嗎？讓他拿下冠軍的字，他也是唯一一個拼出這個字的參賽者，是「反對國家政府和教堂之間應該有官方正式關係的主張」(Antidisestablishmentarianism)。這是英文字典中最長的一個字。今晚，在SWW電視新聞中，我們將榮幸地肯定這個男孩的成就，並且頒發這個拼字比賽的百萬元獎金。恭喜你，Mark我們都很為你感到驕傲！

1. What's the purpose of the news? 新聞主旨為何？

   A. To tell an upsetting news about boy from a poor family.

     敘述一個來自貧苦家庭的男孩的令人難過的故事。

   B. To explain how one can improve his English ability.

     解釋如何能改進自己的英文能力。

   C. To report the story about a boy who has won a competition.

     報導一個贏得比賽的男孩的故事。(正確答案)

2. What is NOT true about the boy?

   關於這個男孩，以下的哪一個敘述不正確？

   A. He has just started going to English classes.

     他才剛開始去補習班上課。(正確答案)

   B. He is self-motivated and diligent.

     他自己有高度學習動機，並且很用功。

   C. He won the first prize of the context.

     他贏得比賽冠軍。

    善用「語意單位」及語氣停頓和語調來幫助理解。以下「//」符號表示較長停頓，也就是語句結束；「/」則表示短暫停頓，表示同一個句子內一個較小的「語意單位」的完成。

Although much of the news tends towards the negative these days,/ we are proud to bring you this/ human-interest story.// In the recent/ English Spelling Bee/ for high school children all over Taiwan,/ there was a young boy who consistently proved better than the rest.// Not only was his incredible accuracy/ in spelling

English words remarkable,/ but also his background.// He never attended an English cram school.// He does not come from a rich family/ and never had any tutoring.// It was through his own interest/ and incredible work ethic/ that he managed to study the English language/ all by himself.// Just to let you know how amazing this feat was,/ the winning word,/ that he alone/ spelled correctly,/ was Antidisestablishmentarianism,/ the longest word in most English language dictionaries.// Tonight/ on SWW TV's evening news program,/ we will proudly recognize this boy's feat/ and award him the Spelling bee's/ million-dollar prize.// Congratulations Mark,// you make us all proud!//

　　第一句話，當我們聽到 Although... news tends... negative, ...「雖然通常是負面的，…」，我們就知道接下去會聽到的，會是一個令人高興的新聞。因為 although 後面接的句子都會是跟前面的 idea 是相反的。也就是說 Although + A 子句, B 子句。A 子句和 B 子句會表達相反的意念。

　　當我們聽到 Not only was his incredible accuracy in spelling English words remarkable... 我們就知道除了比賽成績優異，還有其他故事，果然他說：but also his background. 他的背景也很值得一聽。所以我們也可以推知接下去應該會介紹他的背景。

　　接下去的幾個重點：1) He never attended an English cram school. 2) He does not... a rich family and never... tutoring. 3) It was... his own interest and incredible work ethic... study the English language all by himself. 4) He learned by reading the paper, listening to the radio, TV and books... 都是在介紹他的背景，之後的

DAY 1
DAY 2
DAY 3
DAY 4
DAY 5
DAY 6
DAY 7
DAY 8
DAY 9
DAY 10
DAY 11
DAY 12
DAY 13
DAY 14

> 較長的停頓告訴我們這個主題已經結束了。
>
> 　　當我們聽到語調提高 Just to let you know how amazing this feat was...，我們知道這又是一個新的 idea 的開始。詳細説明他的表現。停頓之後的 Tonight on SWW TV's evening news... 語調提高，又是一個新的 idea。最後的 million-dollar prize Congratulations, Mark... 重新強調他贏了大獎的這件事。

▶ 句型單字整理

English Spelling Bee 英文拼字比賽

negative 負面的 adj.

consistently 持續地，一再不斷地 adj.

proved 被證明 adj.

incredible 令人不可置信的 adj.

accuracy 正確度 n.

remarkable 非常優異的 adj.

attended 出席 adj.

feat 某人做的某件令人讚賞的事 n.

recognize 認可、肯定 v.

prize 獎金、獎品 n.

E.

For those of you planning outdoor activities this weekend, you can expect fair skies for most of the day Saturday with temperatures in the high 30's. However, things may change by Saturday evening with a storm front moving in. We can expect light, scattered showers over

DAY 1
DAY 2
DAY 3
DAY 4
DAY 5
DAY 6
DAY 7
DAY 8
DAY 9
DAY 10
DAY 11
DAY 12
DAY 13
DAY 14

the northern part of the island bringing slightly cooler temperatures in the 20's throughout Saturday evening. This rain should taper off by mid-Sunday morning. The partly cloudy skies will persist for the rest of the morning, and move out by mid-afternoon on Sunday, when things will improve dramatically. The sun will come out and the skies should be clear for the rest of the day on Sunday and through the night. And that's all for today's weekend weather report.

計劃這個週末要從事戶外活動的人，你可以預期星期六幾乎整天都是晴天，氣溫大約是37-39度。但是星期六晚上暴風雨鋒面接近，可能會變天。輕度陣雨會散佈整個本島北部，帶來星期六晚上微涼的二十幾度的氣溫。雨勢在星期天早上中間時段就會變少。幾乎整個早上都是部份多雲的天氣，但是在下午的中間時段以前雲量就會散去，天氣會立即轉好。天氣會放晴，並且一直持續到晚上。以上是今天的週末氣象預報。

1. What is Saturday evening's weather forecast?

   星期六晚上的氣象預告如何？

   A. Hot and humid all over the island. 全島炎熱潮濕。

   B. Heavy rain over the entire island.

   　　北部有豪雨。

   C. Light showers over the northern part.

   　　島上某些地方有些雨。（正確答案）

2. Some people are planning for a picnic on Sunday. When should they go?

   有一群人計劃星期天要野餐，他們應該什麼時候能去？

   A. After around 10:00 AM. 大約早上10:00以後。

B. After around 3:00 PM. 大約下午3:00以後。（正確答案）

C. After around 6:00 PM. 大約下午6:00以後。

善用「語意單位」及語氣停頓和語調來幫助理解。以下「//」符號表示較長停頓，也就是語句結束；「/」則表示短暫停頓，表示同一個句子內一個較小的「語意單位」的完成。

For those of you planning outdoor activities this weekend,/ you can expect fair skies/ for most of the day Saturday/ with temperatures in the high 30's.// However,/ things may change by Saturday evening/ with a storm front moving in.// We can expect light,/ scattered showers/ over the northern part of the island/ bringing slightly cooler temperatures/ in the 20's/ throughout Saturday evening.// This rain should taper off/ by mid-Sunday morning.// The partly cloudy skies will persist/ for the rest of the morning,/ and move out/ by mid-afternoon on Sunday,/ when things will improve dramatically.// The sun will come out/ and the skies should be clear/ for the rest of the day on Sunday/ and through the night.// And/ that's all for today's/ weekend weather report.//

開頭聽重音，我們聽到 weekend、fair skies、Saturday、temperatures、high 30's，告訴我們週六會有好天氣。但接下去當我們聽到 However...「但是…」，就知道應該要說壞消息了，果然他說：Saturday evening... a storm front，「週六晚會有冷鋒」。

接下來聽到We can expect... 就表示他要開始敘述接下來的天氣變化：

1) scattered showers、the northern part... island、cooler

補教名師王舒葳教你
14天聽懂
老外說的英語

DAY 1
DAY 2
DAY 3
DAY 4
DAY 5
DAY 6
DAY 7
DAY 8
DAY 9
DAY 10
DAY 11
DAY 12
DAY 13
DAY 14

temperatures … 20's，我們知道北部會有輕微的陣雨。

2) ...rain... taper off by mid-Sunday morning. 星期天早上雨量減少。

3) ...partly cloudy... persist... rest... morning, and move out...
mid-afternoon... Sunday,... improve dramatically.
幾乎整個早上都是部份多雲，雲量在下午的中間時段以前散去，天氣立即轉好。

4) ...sun... come out... skies... clear... rest of Sunday... through
the night. 天氣會放晴，並且一直持續到晚上。

▶ 句型單字整理

expect 預期 v.

fair skies 晴空

temperatures in the high 30's 近40度的氣溫，high 30's大約是37-39度

a storm front 暴風雨鋒面

scattered 散佈 adj.

taper off 變小、變少

persist 持續 v.

clear 放晴 v.

mid Sunday morning 星期天早上中間時段，約十點左右

mid afternoon 下午中間時段，約二、三點左右

F.

As of 8pm this evening, due to the continuing effects of the typhoon pummeling northern Taiwan with record rainfalls, we have to report the official closings of many schools and government offices for tomorrow. The flooding has so far caused an estimated 1 million in property damage and flooding over much of Taipei with more flooding expected tomorrow. The official list of closings consists of all elementary and secondary schools, Taipei University, Taiwan Normal University, and National Taiwan University. In addition, all government offices not directly involved with disaster prevention and recovery will also be closed. The decision to close individual businesses will be left up to the owners of each business, but we expect many stores and offices to be closed tomorrow. Please stay tuned for more information.

今晚八點鐘，由於颱風帶來的豪雨對北臺灣的持續影響，我們必須宣佈明天許多學校及公家機關停止上班上課。目前為止，豪雨所導致的淹水估計已經造成了一百萬的財物損失。台北市到處淹水，並且預期淹水區域明天會繼續擴大。已公佈停止上課的學校包括：所有中小學、台北大學、臺灣師大，和臺灣大學。 另外，所有不涉及災害防治及重建的公家機關也都停止上班一天。私人公司是否上班上課，將由公司自行決定，但我們可以預見許多商家及公司明天會停止營業。請不要離開，我們還會有陸續的報導。

1. What is the main problem with the typhoon?

   這個颱風最大的威脅為何？

   A. Heavy rain. 豪雨。(正確答案)

   B. Strong wind. 強風。

   C. Both. 兩者皆是。

2. What is said about people who work for private companies?

   報導怎麼說私人公司的員工？

   A. They can have a day off tomorrow. 他們明天放假一天。

   B. They should ask their boss if they need to work tomorrow.

   他們應該問老闆是否要上班。(正確答案)

C. They should wait for farther information to be announced.

他們應該等晚一點的宣佈。

善用「語意單位」及語氣停頓和語調來幫助理解。以下「//」符號表示較長停頓，也就是語句結束；「/」則表示短暫停頓，表示同一個句子內一個較小的「語意單位」的完成。

As of 8pm this evening,/ due to the continuing effects of the typhoon/ pummeling northern Taiwan with record rainfalls,/ we have to report the official closings of many schools/ and government offices for tomorrow.// The flooding has/ so far caused an estimated/ 1 million/ in property damage,/ and we expect the water to keep rising over much of Taipei/ throughout the day tomorrow.// The official list of closings consists of all elementary and secondary schools,/ Taipei University,/ Taiwan Normal University,/ and National Taiwan University.// In addition,/ all government offices/ not directly involved with disaster prevention and recovery/ will also be closed.// The decision to close individual businesses/ will be left up to the owners of each business,/ but we expect many stores/ and offices to be closed tomorrow.// Please stay tuned for more information.//

報導的一開始即說明主題，聽重音：...effects... typhoon... northern Taiwan... record rainfalls... official closings... schools... government offices 表示因颱風及豪雨之故，宣佈停止上班上課。

接著的 flooding...1 million in property damage... flooding... Taipei... more flooding expected... 我們知道大家深受淹水之苦。

DAY 1
DAY 2
DAY 3
DAY 4
DAY 5
DAY 6
DAY 7
DAY 8
DAY 9
DAY 10
DAY 11
DAY 12
DAY 13
DAY 14

當我們聽到 The official list of closings consists of... 表示要開始宣佈停止上班上課的學校機構：elementary and secondary schools, Taipei University, Taiwan Normal University, and National Taiwan University. 注意音調到全部說完時才下降，因此當他語調仍上揚時我們應該知道還要繼續注意聽。聽到 In addition..., 表示這個主題還沒結束：all government offices... not involve disaster prevention... also... closed. 說明公家機關的狀況。最後一個 item 則談到私人公司：The decision... individual businesses... left up... the owners... business，表示由老闆自行決定。

▶ 句型單字整理

as of 當

pummel 衝擊、造成災害 v.

rainfall 雨量 n.

flood 淹水、洪水 n.

estimate 估計

property 財物 n.

damage 傷害、損失 n.

involve 參與、有關的 v.

disaster 災害 n.

prevention 防治、避免發生 n.

recovery 復原、重建 n.

tune 轉到某電視台或廣播頻道 v.

Please stay tuned... 不要轉台，留在這個頻道上

▶ 聽力小秘訣

補教名師王舒薇教你
14天聽懂
老外說的英語

DAY
1
DAY
2
DAY
3
DAY
4
DAY
5
DAY
6
DAY
7
DAY
8
DAY
9
DAY
10
DAY
11
DAY
12
DAY
13
**DAY
14**

☺ 在新聞播報中，新聞主題通常在第一句話就會出現。有時候第一句話則是用來轉承及連接上一則新聞的開場白，即便如此，主題也一定在第二句話就出現。聽清楚主題句是聽力的第一步，如此才能幫助我們更聽懂細節。

☺ 新聞播報通常以主題句先概述重點，再開始敘述重點下的細節；氣象報導則會開宗明義地馬上進入正題，講天氣，並依氣候出現的時間順序播報。瞭解播報員說話的架構或順序，能幫助我們容易抓到重點。

☺ 聽長篇聽力時，熟悉特定轉承語的用法和語意，能幫助我們預測接下來的內容，讓你的聽力大大加分。以下是一些例子：

a. 表示接下去是相反或對比的語意： However,... 然而... On the other hand,... 另一方面，...Having said that,... 雖然這麼說，但是... Although + A 子句, B子句…雖然A 子句, B子句（A子句與B子句意義相反）

Despite + A 子句, B子句… 儘管A子句, B子句（A子句與B子句意義相反）

b. 表示接下去是相同概念的補充說明：In addition,... 除此之外…
On top of that,... 不僅如此… Besides,... 除此之外… Moreover, ... 還有… What is more,... 還有…

c. 表示要舉例說明：For instance,... 譬如說… To give you an example,... 譬如說… Take…as an example,... 譬如說…
Consider... 想想…

d. 表示原因或影響： Due to the... 由於… Owing to the... 由於…
Since... 既然… In consequence,... 因此… Hence,... 因此…
Therefore,... 因此…

☺最後，無論是句子還是對話，短篇或者長篇，一定要多聽。再重覆聽時便可以邊聽邊看錄音稿，用這本書學到的東西診斷自己聽不懂的原因，是單字不會嗎？是自己發音不正確嗎？是連音聽不懂嗎？是不瞭解慣用語的意思嗎？是語調會錯意嗎？找到原因後對症下藥，不會什麼就學什麼。學會了自己不懂的東西後，再持續多聽幾次，你的聽力一定大躍進！

MEMO

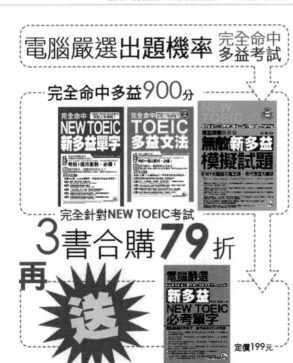

定價220元

定價220元

定價220元

定價220元

我識出版集團
I'm Publishing Group

全國各大書店熱烈搶購中！
大量訂購・另有折扣

劃撥帳號◆19793190　戶名◆我識出版社
服務專線◆（02）2578-8578・2577-7136

國家圖書館出版品預行編目資料

補教名師王舒葳教你14天聽懂老外說的英語 /
王舒葳著. - 初版. - 臺北市：我識, 2009.02
面 ； 公分

ISBN 978-986-6481-03-1 (平裝附光碟片)

1. 英語 2. 讀本

805.18   97025378

補教名師**王舒葳**教你
14天聽懂
老外說的英語

書名 / 補教名師王舒葳教你14天聽懂老外說的英語

作者 / 王舒葳

審訂 / Organis Rivers

發行人 / 蔣敬祖

主編 / 陳弘毅

執行主編 / 張愛玲

執行編輯 / 楊堡方・常祈天

美術編輯 / 彭君如

內文排版 / 楊鎖竹

法律顧問 / 北辰著作權事務所蕭雄淋律師

印製 / 凱立國際資訊股份有限公司

初版 / 2009年02月

出版 / 我識出版集團－我識出版社有限公司

電話 / （02）2578-8578

傳真 / （02）2578-8286

地址 / 台北市光復南路32巷16弄4號1樓

郵政劃撥 / 19793190

戶名 / 我識出版社

網路書店 / www.17buy.com.tw

網路客服Email / iam.group@17buy.com.tw

定價 / 新台幣349元 / 港幣116元

台灣總經銷 / 彩舍國際通路

地址 / 台北縣中和市中山路二段366巷10號3樓

港澳總經銷 / 和平圖書有限公司

地址 / 香港柴灣嘉業街12號百樂門大廈17樓

電話 / (852) 2804-6687   傳真 / (852) 2804-6409